I0667490

The Western Take

G.R. Williams

Gareth Williams

garethrichardwilliams2@outlook.com

**Grosvenor House
Publishing Limited**

All rights reserved
Copyright © G.R. Williams, 2024

The right of G.R. Williams to be identified as the author of this
work has been asserted in accordance with Section 78
of the Copyright, Designs and Patents Act 1988

The book cover is copyright to G.R. Williams
Book cover design by Brian Jones
Cover images copyright to mikkelwilliam and
lynnebeclu, courtesy of iStock

This book is published by
Grosvenor House Publishing Ltd
Link House
140 The Broadway, Tolworth, Surrey, KT6 7HT.
www.grosvenorhousepublishing.co.uk

This book is sold subject to the conditions that it shall not, by way of
trade or otherwise, be lent, resold, hired out or otherwise circulated
without the author's or publisher's prior consent in any form of
binding or cover other than that in which it is published and
without a similar condition including this condition being
imposed on the subsequent purchaser.

This book is a work of fiction. Any resemblance to
people or events, past or present, is purely coincidental.

A CIP record for this book
is available from the British Library

ISBN 978-1-83615-011-4
eBook ISBN 978-1-83615-012-1

Chapter One

The heavy rain had put off many of the regulars and the saloon was quiet. A few cards scattered over a large table, and an empty glass on top of a rickety old piano, provided the only indication of custom that day.

Approaching lights out, the only patron left in the bar was Braun. Drunk as usual, he was a little wobbly on top of his favourite stool. He'd been drinking for twelve hours straight, and Ed the bartender was growing impatient. "I want to finish up for the night, goddamnit. You've been sipping that drink for close to an hour now."

Braun slurred his response. "Thhiiss..., is my last drink."

Ed slapped his forehead in frustration. "I know it's your last drink. I told you I wouldn't serve you any more liquor after this one. But being the spiteful sonofabitch that you are, you're deliberately taking forever and a day to finish up." He sighed. "It's the same shit with you all the time, Braun."

Even in Cheston, a town of many boozers, Braun was considered the biggest pain in the ass drunk of them all. He'd been drinking from the minute he'd rolled out of bed, and he was down to his last few bucks. He'd been able to finance his drinking following a desperate sale of his only suit to a young stagecoach driver passing through town earlier that day. The suit was tatty by most people's standards, but to Braun it had acted as leisure wear, workwear, and his Sunday best. This explained why he was sitting in the bar wearing nothing but sweat and urine-stained Long Johns, a heavily frayed purple waistcoat, and a pair of mud-caked brown boots.

Ed's tired old drinking den didn't warrant strict dress codes, so providing you weren't naked, the only material that mattered was the leather of a wallet.

Braun pointed a crooked finger at the glass tumbler in front of him and hiccupped through his next sentence. "Look, Ed, I ain't go' shit apart from this—"

Ed rubbed his forehead in frustration and interrupted. "Let's not go through this again, damnit. I hear this crap from you every night, and I'm tired of it." He leant over the bar and edged a little closer to Braun. He was angry, but he didn't want to boil over. Keen to avoid shouting, he spoke through the corner of his mouth. "I spend more time listening to you than anyone else, the wife included. I used to have some good conversations in here. I'd put the world to rights with all kinds of people. Ain't like that now, though. No sonofabitch will come near me unless they want a drink, and all because you're sat right there in front of me all the goddamned time."

Braun carried on, oblivious to Ed's complaints, and hiccupped his way through a refrain that would be a common theme with the blues years later. "I got no woman, no work, no friends, *Hic*, even my dog ran away from me. *Hic,* and now..." He pulled at his Long Johns. "...I ain't got no clothes. Ha-*Hic*-ha-ha!!" He placed his head in his hands and shifted between laughter and hiccups.

Ed reached the end of his tether and pulled the drink from Braun. "Give me that! You may not have anything to get up for tomorrow, but I do, Braun, and I ain't got all night. I'm finished with this crap, okay?! I don't want to listen to your bitching and complaining for a minute longer."

Aware of how irritable Ed's manner was becoming, Braun's agitation grew, and he reached over the bar to wrestle the drink out of Ed's hand. "You give me that back now, Ed. I paid my money."

Ed sighed and stepped back out of Braun's reach. He tried a soft-soaping approach instead. "What if I keep hold of this shot of whiskey for you? It's three years old, and I'm sure it'll taste even better with an extra day to its age. Huh?" He patted Braun on the shoulder. "You've had a good ol' session today. Now, you go home, sleep it off. Plenty of rest is just what you need. You'll be nice and straight for tomorrow."

Braun looked despondent but begrudgingly accepted Ed's suggestion. "Alright, alright, I'll get on outta here, but don't you forget to keep that drink for me?"

Ed nodded. "Don't worry, buddy, I'm a man of my word and..." He lowered his voice to make his next offer sound more attractive as he humoured Braun. "...I might even put an extra slug in it. On the house, but..." He raised a finger. "...only if you leave here quietly, and don't go making all hell's worth of noise on your way out."

Braun had a habit of shouting as he left the saloon and would often yell up to the windows to get some attention from Ed's wife, who lived upstairs with her husband. This tendency backfired on him one very drunken evening a few months prior. His exit that night consisted of a quarter hour of stumbling and falling in his attempts to cross the twenty metres it took to get from the barstool to the doorway. All the while he was bellowing an old folk tune at the top of his voice.

This commotion drove Ed's wife so mad that she put aside the sewing kit she was using to mend a trouser zipper for her husband, and she waited by the window for Braun to get outside. Once she could see him on the saloon landing, she pulled the window open and poured the entire contents of a near full bedpan all over him, soaking him from head to toe.

Ed was furious and came close to barring Braun that night, but following his wife's actions he relented, because he did not approve of her behaviour, especially since he had to take a mop and bucket outside to clean it up before the desert sun dried it into the wood.

Braun amazingly didn't have any recollection of the incident when he turned up the following day. However, Ed and the rest of the bar's patrons had to put up with the terribly unpleasant smell of the contents of his wife's bladder marinated on Braun for days afterwards.

Braun responded. "Don't you worry none about that, Ed, I'll tiptoe outta here all quiet, like a slippy, slidy snake."

Ed sighed at the stupid remark as Braun swung around on his stool ready to exit. Just as he was about to get to his feet, they heard a horse trotting and slowing down outside.

A man pulled up next to the saloon, and the horse whinnied quietly as the man tied it up to a post a few metres from the entrance.

Braun and Ed looked at each other, slightly confused. It was highly unusual for somebody who'd been riding horseback to show up so late at the saloon; most of the customers were local townspeople who'd arrive on foot, and with the weather so horrendous and with the clock close to midnight, this was a peculiar occurrence.

The man made his way slowly up three wooden steps onto the outside landing area of the saloon. He was soaking wet and agitated as he swung the doors wide open and stepped through.

Standing half a metre from the doorway for a few seconds, he wiped the rain off a heavily scuffed leather poncho, adding to the small puddle that formed around him as he tipped his Stetson hat forward and the rim-gathered rainwater emptied onto the wooden floor.

He was a monstrously built man, six foot four and broad shouldered, with an imposing demeanour. He stood with his legs wide apart, his arms hung clenched to his sides, with hairy, thick-fingered hands rolled into fists.

Ed waited until the stranger finished wringing himself out before addressing him.

"I can see that you could do with a drink, friend, but I'm afraid I'm unable to oblige. We're finished for the night. You're just—". He looked at his watch. "—a half hour too late."

The man stared at the floor; his head was lowered into a position where his hat covered the top half of his face, but the bottom half revealed a strong, stubbly, tanned jaw, propped up by a neck as thick and wide as his head.

The stranger responded as Braun glared at him open-mouthed. "I'm not here for a drink."

Ed blinked and kept his eyes closed for a couple of seconds. Anticipating trouble, he asked, "Then what can I do you for, friend?"

Ed waited for a response that didn't come, and before the length of the silence became too uncomfortable, he made a courteous offer. "If you need to dry off, I can provide you with fresh towels, and I'd sure be glad to fill up your flask with coffee."

The stranger growled, "I don't want no towel, and I don't want your coffee."

Braun joined in before Ed could respond. "Just what exactly do you want, huh, mister? My buddy here is just trying to help, ain't that right, Ed?"

Ed focused on the man and said, "Look, I'm trying to be hospitable here. I don't want any trouble, it's late and this man..." Ed put his hand on Braun's shoulder. "...and I are ready to call it a night."

The stranger scoffed "Call it a night huh? Now, I'm not sure what the deal is with you guys, but it looks like your buddy should be tucked up already in those filthy old bed clothes." Braun raised his voice and stuttered, "They ain't so dirty, I wash them a couple of times a month and the... the... these are my only clothes, you sonofabitch. I got nothing." He turned to his friend. "Ain't that right, Ed? Just the clothes on my back and this here drink."

He began fidgeting and Ed took over, first addressing Braun. "Let's settle down now. Ain't nothing for any of us to get upset about. We've established that we are closed for the night..." He looked to the stranger. "And our new friend don't want what's being offered, so I'm sure he's about to leave..." He paused and added, "Ain't that right, mister?"

Ed discreetly reached for a fully loaded handgun positioned accessibly on a small shelf just underneath the bar surface. It had been wedged there out of view for several years, and although he'd come close to grabbing it before, this was the first time Ed knew that he was going to need it.

The stranger's stare hadn't moved from the floor, but he somehow realised what Ed was up to. He pulled a gun quickly from a holster and said ominously, "I wouldn't do that if I were you, bartender."

Ed tipped his head concedingly, and the stranger continued with a threatening tone. "Now put your goddamn hands where I can see them, or I will shoot your face right offa that big head of yours."

Ed immediately abandoned any more thoughts of heroism and held his arms up. The stranger moved towards the bar slowly as Ed kept his arms hoisted. Braun was mumbling incoherently, his head slumped against the bar.

The stranger kept his gun focused on Ed as he spoke. "Now, turn around slowly and empty that money box for me."

Ed nodded, and with his arms still raised he moved around steadily towards the cash register. He opened it and began pulling out some wads of notes. There wasn't much cash inside, but he deliberately took his time as he started fingering another firearm, a small pistol that he kept inside the register.

The stranger quickly grew impatient. "Come on! Dammit. My trigger finger is getting itchy." Just as the stranger finished his sentence, Ed turned around and fired a hopeful shot at him. The shot startled the stranger, but unfortunately for Ed it flew way off target.

The stranger retaliated by pulling the trigger of his own firearm, shooting Ed through the right lens of his glasses. The bullet burrowed through his head, passed through the other side and into a full bottle of brandy shelved behind the bar. The bottle smashed and soaked Ed's newly lifeless body as it dropped to the floor.

The stranger didn't flinch and immediately made his way around the bar, ensuring that his eyes and gun were firmly focused on Braun. "Now, Mr Long Johns. You've just seen what happened to the bartender. So, you're going to need to take it easy, unless you wanna be swimming in that pool of liquor with your buddy."

Braun's head remained on the bar as he mumbled, "Wwwhhaat d'you do that ffoorr, huh? Ed was a good man; you shouldn't have done that."

The stranger retaliated, "Look, I'm sure he was a swell guy, real nice how he kept a bum like you topped up with the cheap stuff in this shit mark town. But he made a choice, a wrong fucking choice, by deciding to take a shot at me."

He shook his head in mock dismay and tutted a few times. "I didn't want to shoot the bastard, believe me, I really didn't. All I wanted was for this to be clean and fast. Complications I do not like. I get mad, and when I get mad, folks get hurt, and like your friend, some folks die. He was damn stupid, and he paid the price for it."

He carried on around the bar as Braun started crying as he slammed his clenched fist repeatedly against the bar surface.

The stranger snapped. "I've only just met you, Long Johns, but first impressions and all, I've gotta say that you don't look like you've got much to live for. But if you want," he made a sweeping gesture with his free hand, "what little you've got to continue. If you really want to keep marching on. If it somehow matters to you. Well, you'd better settle down now, okay?" Braun carried on whimpering as the stranger made his way around the bar to the cash register. He pulled a half full, strapped cotton bag out from underneath his poncho and began filling it with notes and coins. He grabbed a few of the expensive cigars that Ed kept for special occasions and flung them into the bag with the money. And with the gun pointed in Braun's direction, he skipped back around the bar.

A creaky noise emerged from what sounded like a set of stairs being trod on. The stranger realised that somebody had been alerted. "Shit."

He picked up the pace, backing up towards the saloon doors with the bag in one hand and the gun in the other, his eyes firmly fixed on Braun.

He was about to leave when a rotund, middle-aged lady in a pale pink dressing gown kicked a door open. She was armed with a double-barrelled shotgun, and she screamed tearily, "Arrggghh!"

She fired a shot at the stranger but proved to be just as lousy a shot as her husband. The intended target was handed a wide berth as she put a large hole in the backside of a framed painting of a buffalo.

The stranger responded immediately, demonstrating his composure and skill as a gunman by firing two rounds into Ed's wife's chest. Her eyes dilated as a pained primal guttural noise exited her mouth, and her overweight body crashed to the floor.

Braun, in the midst of shock trauma, temporarily lost his balance and fell from his stool. The stranger turned to him, but lightning quick he pulled a pistol from inside his waistcoat and fired, striking the stranger on the right side of his neck with a fluke, one-in-a-thousand hit that a sober Braun, reliant on mind rather than instinct, would never have been able to produce.

The stranger's priorities changed. He dropped the gun and bag and moved both hands to the wound.

Braun stayed sitting on the floor, watching as the man dropped to his knees, hopelessly trying to stem the flow of the oozing spring of blood chugging out of his neck. Within seconds the stranger's knees buckled, and he fell flat on his back. He quickly blinked several times and his arms dropped, through a combination of acceptance of the losing battle and through incapability, as all his bodily functions shut down rapidly.

Braun staggered to his feet and slowly advanced in the direction of the dying man. By the time he'd covered the six metres to reach him, the stranger had breathed his last.

Braun crouched and ran his hands through the inside of the stranger's poncho. Noticing another two bags strapped to the upper torso, he flipped up the poncho and attempted to untie the heavy-set knots that kept them from coming loose. In his inebriation, he struggled with this and soon gave up in favour of hacking through them with a blade.

Going back to the bar, he uncovered a half blunt but adequate chopping knife which he used to slash through the thick cotton fixed to the man. There wasn't much give between the chest and the material, so he cut into the man's skin, getting blood on his hands in the follow-through of the strap break. He wiped it on the floor and pulled off the remaining strands of cotton with his hands.

Unzipping the bags, he was astonished to find them crammed full of money, mostly of various denominations but predominantly higher marks.

Braun looked at the dead man and said, "All that money and you still wanted Ed's takings for the day?" He sighed and added, "Well, you paid the price for your rotten greed." He grabbed a one dollar note and placed it on the bar as he addressed Ed's corpse mournfully.

"I'll take that extra shot now, Ed."

He climbed over the bar to claim the drink promised to him and topped up his glass with a generous measure of whiskey. He threw it straight down his throat and strapped the bags to himself, creating a second tight knot. Unable to conceal them under his lightweight waistcoat, he pulled the leather poncho over the stranger's head and placed it over his own.

At this point paranoia kicked in, sobering him up a little as he picked up the other bag and scanned the room to survey the carnage.

He sighed as he homed in on Ed's wife's corpse laid out in an unflattering position, her legs wide apart and head drooped to one side. Her pale pink nightdress looked especially washed-out, with dollops of fresh moist blood splattered across. It was only when he focused on the colours that he noticed something else. Something that he initially put down to his imagination as it was only through heavy concentration that he could make it out.

A very light and thin, blue, gel-like substance trickled from her eyes, nose, and mouth. The colour was faint and as delicate as the blue against the sky from a rapidly disintegrating rainbow.

He spat on his hands and rubbed his eyes, trying to establish whether they were playing tricks on him or not. But this action did not alter what he could see. He had not been around the deceased at the moment of death before, and his initial thoughts considered that this was released from someone when their spirit left them.

But something else troubled him and he had an immediate attraction to it. His poorly exercised mind attempted to understand, as a medley of emotions shifted from one to another rapidly, like a high-speed computer jogging through all its components. This was quickly played out and a suitable match wasn't found.

This was novel, and after a brief ponderous period the mind temporarily switched off as something else took over. An undefinable push from within, an unexplainable longing guided and lured him trance-like to the lady's body.

He crouched down next to her head and put his ear close to her mouth, listening for breath, but nothing came out. He touched her neck for a pulse; no sign of life was realised. Curious, he reached down with three of his fingers and scooped up a strip of the faint blue gel secreted from her eyes. It was thinning out and losing moisture by the second. Once removed, it left no residue behind on the lady's face.

He smelt the goo and inhaled the scent as deeply as his flared nostrils would allow. The smell was unlike anything he'd experienced; the closest resemblance was apricots fresh from the tree mixed with burning wood, but that was just an initial note. The depth and complexity of the odour passed beyond what his scent glands could fathom. It was utterly intoxicating and left him ready for his next instinctive action.

He pushed his fingers into his mouth and rubbed the gel onto the flesh inside of his cheek, allowing the capillaries to absorb the substance quickly into the bloodstream. This produced the desired effect and instantly filled his entire being with euphoric energy. It was instantaneous and too much for his body to take, as his legs weakened and sent him to the ground momentarily. Thankfully, just as rapidly, he bounced back up.

Under a spell, Braun approached the other two corpses, delighting as he saw that they also had the substance leaking from their facial orifices, although the quality and potency of the matter had swiftly degraded in both cases.

What he pulled from the stranger's face was a reddish-brown colour and of a sea foam-like texture. He balanced this carefully on his fingers and placed it inside his mouth, rubbing it into his gums.

On Ed's face, the stuff was of a blue, similar to his wife's, but it had degenerated to the form of near dust. Despite his mild reverie and instant craving, his muscle memory guided him to the few times he'd inhaled snuff. It hadn't been a great experience for him initially, but after a further few dabbles with added sprinklings of jasmine and lavender, he'd quite enjoyed it. He decided to take this the same way and constructed a line of it onto the back of his right hand, pressing down his weaker left nostril to snort up the powder through three forceful inhalations.

Sitting on the floor, Braun waited momentarily for the substance to make an impact. His pupils dilated and filled the entire lens of his eyes, leaving them as black as the darkest corner of an unlit underground train station. This effect permeated for a few seconds, and with nowhere else to go it retracted, creating another anomaly as his pupils shrunk to the size of pin pricks before settling back to a regular size again.

He left the saloon, and amidst the fresh air his mind became the dominant lead again, returning him to the state of shock prior to his feeding. He had no recollection of what had happened after strapping the money bags to himself. Despite this, he bizarrely didn't have a sense of time lost or disorientation. His physical and mental self shut down briefly as something else took over, an enigmatic instinct that pushed everything else back.

Despite his shock and distress, he felt a heightened sense of awareness, and his inebriation was no longer present. He was still uncertain on his feet, but he put this down to the high winds and torrential rain as he stretched his arms out to keep himself balanced against the gales.

He knew he had to flee the scene and cumbersomely stepped over to the horse. His survival sentience was fully intact, and any concerns of the cold night getting the better of him were quashed as he noted a thick woollen blanket strapped up to the rear of the horse. It was a full moon, a perfectly clear night, the stars at their brightest. Braun drew on a memory, an old cowboy assuring him that if such conditions were in place, any good horse should be able to see perfectly well through the darkness.

With a vague idea of what direction to head in, he untied the horse, flopped onto its saddle, and rode out of town.

Chapter Two

The horse halted suddenly as Braun hit the floor with a hard thud. The soft, sandy terrain broke the fall somewhat, but his back-led impact still knocked the wind out of him. He groaned and rubbed his face as the harsh desert sunlight penetrated his eyes. The daylight surprised him; his last memory recalled riding through the pitch black with nothing more than a hopeful sense of direction.

It was hot, exceedingly hot, and despite his whole life being basked in near extreme heat, he'd never fully accustomed to it and longed to feel something else. It would often get chilly in the night, but he craved to feel an icy cold, the sort of low temperatures that would leave him just as uncomfortable at the other extreme, to feel something new and different. His frustration grew as he cursed himself for being so restless. He knew he'd soon tire of any alternative, and countless other people from lands afar would swap ten days of their deep painful cold for one day of sun-soaked radiance.

Climbing to his feet carefully, he winced as he looked down at his Long Johns. A sticky, moistened clump of material had stuck to the hairs of his left inside leg and prompted him to moan, "I've damn pissed myself." He slapped the side of the horse. "Hope I didn't get any on you, big fella."

He took a substantial swig of warm water, courtesy of a flask hanging from the horse's saddle, and poured a few drops over his head. The sun had not long risen but the heat was already kicking in, serving to aggravate an already fierce hangover. In a bid to cool down, he removed his inherited leather poncho, folded it over and placed it into a bag hanging from the saddle, as he tried to gather his bearings. The horse had covered many miles throughout the night, and Braun intuitively surmised that they were on the track to another town and hopefully somewhere that he could get a drink.

He fed the horse some water and checked to see if anybody was around before pouring two of the bags of money onto the sand. Lacking in any sort of education, he didn't know how to count big numbers, but he could plainly see that he was in the possession of a vast amount of money. Making a couple of piles with the notes, he flicked through them a few times before bringing a wad up to his nose. The notes and coins smelt musty and unpleasant, but the scent pleased him all the same, with assurances that the situation was real and not imaginary.

After struggling a couple of times, he eventually managed to climb back on top of the horse and carried on heading in the same direction for a further five hours until reaching civilization.

He arrived just after midday at a small town just inside San Diego. The year was 1880, and the newly developed area was flourishing following the gold rush. Braun had heard mutterings of this, but it hadn't influenced his decision to head there. He'd conceded that his working days were behind him, due to poor health brought on by chronic alcoholism. He was in his early forties and young enough for employment, but he felt and looked a much grander age. His face was ashen-tired and craggy, with a scruffy unkempt beard. Matted shoulder-length hair retained a few blond strands of youth but was mostly overpowered by a heavy influx of grey.

He was a mess, and his body struggled as the remaining remnants of alcohol in his system dissolved. *Where can I get a drink?* was the first thought that crossed his mind as he passed into the town. Travelling in, he'd decided that he was going to get a nice suit fitted before anything else, but now the raging urge for alcohol overwhelmed the more sensible option. In typical fashion of most towns during the period, he didn't have to venture too far before finding a suitable watering hole, as he spotted a sign advertising liquor outside of a barn. Braun smacked the horse's side, rolled off, and pulled some rope from out of the saddle bag. He tied the animal to a post next to three more horses surrounding a rusty, weather-beaten drinking trough.

Once satisfied that the knot was strong enough to keep the horse from running off, he eagerly walked up to the barn and pulled open a heavy wooden door. It was an old working farm space that had been converted into a saloon, and although it retained a lot of its old features, this wasn't designed to give the place character. It was thrown together in a slapdash manner, due to lack of funds and desire to give the place a homely feel. Tightly compacted bales of hay scattered across the room were used as makeshift benches, and a rickety old ladder leading to the upper mow of the barn remained if people wanted to risk climbing up to the top with their drinks. The bar itself consisted of stacked boxes and shelving units for the spirits. Braun dusted himself down and flinched as he realised that he should have put the poncho back on to preserve a degree of modesty over his Long John-clad appearance.

This minor concern rapidly subsided as he looked up to see something that startled him to a point where he struggled to believe what was in front of him. The few patrons of the bar detected his obvious distress and looked over, prompting him to go back through the swing doors to get some much-needed fresh air.

Once outside, he staggered over to the horse's trough, ready to vomit, when an ageing, near jet-black stallion appeared to be aware that his water was about to be flavoured with barfed chunks of whiskey and bile.

Braun knelt and bowed his head ready for the inevitable. But the horse used his head to nudge him and released a sound steeped in frustration as it blew through thick, reverberating, rubbery lips. This knocked the weakened Braun to the floor, puking as he fell over.

He waited until he was sure all the vomit had pumped out of him, climbed to his feet, and scooped up some water from the trough, washing off the mess he'd made on himself until it was just another stain to join in with the dozens of others spread throughout his Long Johns. The reactionary reflex was unpleasant, but once released, part of his fear had passed, and he felt strangely compelled to re-enter the barn to face what had frightened him so much.

He stood outside the eight foot-high swing doors, taking several deep breaths, after which he slapped himself across the face several times – once or twice a little too hard. The rosy-cheeked burn proved a useful distraction as he pushed through the doors.

He squinted and held it for a second or two before slowly opening his eyes wider, adjusting them to the strange sight. This confirmed that what he'd prayed was a figment of his imagination, was not as such. What greeted him was the sight of a bartender and three men doing nothing particularly unusual, just the sort of laughing, brooding, and shit-talking that you'd expect in such an environment. But the difference lay in what Braun could see; something they all had in common. As clear as the tangible elements to the barn, across all the folk he could see smoky balls of colour living inside them, slightly across from the centre of their chests, and projecting through their flesh and clothing. The colours and sizes varied, but all were of a circular shape.

Braun sensed they were unaware of the strange phenomena that emanated from them, and he knew that addressing it could firstly draw attention to himself, and secondly create a scene, probably ending up with him labelled a nut and being forced to spend time in the local jail. For a split second, he considered the possibility that he had indeed lost his marbles, but this consideration quickly evaporated. His gut and intuitiveness told him this was not a trick of the mind.

As he stood in the doorway, a wrought sense from deep within was basking in its power, as though a longing was being nourished.

Within seconds of gazing at the mesmeric, strange, and beautiful impressions that fell before him, he realised that he was beginning to draw attention. So he dropped his head towards the sawdust-scattered wooden floor and slowly shuffled his way to the bar. Sweaty and shaky, he became acutely aware of all the eyes fixated on him.

A tiny, elderly bald man, with no more than six teeth in his mouth, was cleaning some glasses. Unimpressed as he glanced over at Braun, he rolled his yellowy eyes and started talking to three tough-looking men in their twenties propping up the bar.

Braun at this point saw something that frightened him. Standing behind the old barman was something of human size and shape but with a profile etched in a thin blue border. The form inside the border was of a similar colour but edged towards sky blue, just a shade or two lighter than the line of blue that framed the man.

The detail to it was fragile, like fog, but Braun could see through its shape and movement that it was an apparition of a man. His features and clothes could be made out, although any fleshy tones he may once have had were replaced by the misty texture swarming his entire presence. His clothes and bushy moustache were very much in the style of a citizen of the mid-to-late 1800s and typical of someone who had until recently been amongst the living. And just like seeing that first star in the night sky, it wasn't long before Braun started seeing more, and he watched as the ghost appeared to be playing out some bar duties. He served another of his kind, made from the same mysterious foggy apparition, but more sizeable in height and width. The phantom barman handed over a shape indicative of a small measure of drink.

Braun took a good look around, seeing several apparitions across the room with varying degrees of visibility. Some appeared to demonstrate behaviour based on a former human existence; others stood still and either stared upwards to the ceiling or with their heads hung low, tilted towards the floor.

In the farthest corner of the barn from the door, a cluster of ghosts huddled together loosely, heads faced into the angle of the corner. None of them appeared to be communicating with each other, at least not in a conventional sense.

Braun's fear was not recognised, and apart from a few inquisitive glances when he first arrived, his presence wasn't of great interest to the human guests of the establishment. Attempting to bring a modicum of normality to his situation, he addressed the barman's ignorance. "You servin', buddy?"

As the barman turned to him, Braun tried not to stare at the strange orangey glow pulsating between the man's chest and stomach. He was becoming increasingly aware of his own body's absorbent sensations, as a craving was quivering and pulling towards what appeared to be the man's energy spring.

The barman pointed to Braun's outfit and responded, "You just rolled outta bed or somethin'?"

Before Braun could answer, the barman added dismissively, "Come back when you've got some clothes on."

The three young men at the bar laughed, but Braun remained undeterred and answered, "I'm itching for a slug of whiskey, fella." He cleared his throat. "Just a little somethin' to throw down my neck before I head outta here."

"I'll be with you in a minute," said the barman, and he carried on laughing and joking with the other three customers for a couple of minutes.

During this period, Braun looked around at the ghosts, counting a dozen. Some were no more than oddly-shaped forms of mass, others resembled the phantom barman, with detail in their faces and clothes.

Four stood separately staring at the floor, and the other six remained huddled in the corner.

Their movements were few, managing only mild, slow shuffled, side-to-side motions. Braun's feelings towards them had quickly changed. No longer scared, his fear had transitioned into curiosity. They appeared sad and lonely, and he began to feel enormous pity towards them. Not wanting to dwell on this, he snapped out of it and concentrated on the human activity in the barn.

Frustration rattled him as he watched the barman topping his friends' drinks up.

He said, "Come on now, Mr Barman, I'm no trouble. All's I want is one little drink. That's it, nothing more. I don't want no chitter chatter, food, card games, whatever you've got going on here..." He wiped his nose on his sleeve. "I don't want any of it. Nothing. Just a drink, buddy, alright? It's damn hot out there today, and my throat is real fucking dry. Need to get me some of that whiskey buzz, too."

He looked at the barman's friends, faking a laugh as he tried to drum up some support. "You fellas know what I mean, don't ya, boys?"

This didn't produce a flicker of interest. The only reaction was the youngest of the party clearing his throat in an aggressive, grunting style, as all sets of unfriendly eyes locked into him.

Turning his back to the barman, he finished up his plea. "So, how about it, huh? Can you do that for me?"

The barman pulled his elbows off the bar slowly, as though it was a real chore for him. He sighed and pulled his back into the best posture his ageing hunched back allowed, then said to the three cowboys, "'Scuse me please, fellas."

The man's orangey glow ball darkened a few shades to marmalade as he puffed his chest out. He turned to

Braun. "I'm not serving you a damn drop. Okay?" He looked Braun up and down. "If you were any good, you'd have some proper clothes on. Those damn Long Johns just tell me that you're running away from somebody or something, and I don't want that here in my place, alright?" He prodded his finger in Braun's direction and added, "And to tell you straight, mister, even if you were wearing a nice, shiny confederate uniform, I still wouldn't hand you a glass of the dirtiest rainwater. Now get that damn straight, you wretched sonofabitch. I just don't like the look of you."

He turned his back to Braun and finished with, "I want you the hell outta here! That's all, and I will only ask you once before my young friends here get ready to clip your horns."

Braun relaxed his jaw and replied, "That how it is?"

The barman turned back around to face Braun. "That's right. Now, if you know what's good for you..." He tilted his head, gesturing towards the cowboys. "... you'll walk on out of here now."

Braun's desperation for alcohol got the better of him, and he reached into the inside pocket of his waistcoat, pulling out the small pistol. He shouted, "LOOK, MISTER, LAST NIGHT WAS A HELLUVA NIGHT. A HELLUVA FUCKING NIGHT AND FOR REASONS THAT I CANNOT BEGIN TO EXPLAIN, IT AIN'T LOOKING TOO SWELL FOR ME TODAY NEITHER."

His exasperation was obvious as he dragged out his next sentence. "NOW-I'M-DAMN-CLOSE-TO-LOSING-MY-MIND, OKAY! SO, FOR THE LOVE OF GOD, GIVE ME A DAMNNNEDDD DRINK! I DON'T CARE IF IT'S YOUR CHEAPEST

FIREWATER CRAP. IT DON'T MATTER IF IT'S BLENDED WITH INDIAN PISS. I'LL TAKE WHATEVER YOU'VE GOT, AS LONG AS IT'S WET AND ALCOHOLIC, OKAY, MISTER? NOW PLEASE JUST GET ME A FUCKING BOTTLE!"

The barman immediately grabbed a bottle of whiskey from the unit behind him and handed it over silently, as the other three customers glared menacingly at Braun. One of them, the smallest of the gang, spat tobacco on the floor in Braun's direction but not close enough to provoke a reaction.

Braun put the whiskey down and placed a couple of notes onto the bar. He addressed the room. "It's a shame that I have to wave this thing around..." He shook the pistol a little, prompting two of the men to put their hands in the air as he continued, "...to get anything done." He wiped his sweaty forehead and sighed. "C'mon now, boys. Life's tough around these parts for all of us. Why've we got to make it harder for each other?" He looked around and shouted, "HUH?"

One of the cowboys, the biggest of the three responded, "Take it easy, fella."

Braun answered, "I was taking it easy, you stupid asshole. It's your friend here who's being difficult."

Braun walked towards the men and waved his gun slowly across all four. He stopped short by about five yards. Not caring at this point, he spoke out. "Can you see that strange ball of light coming out of your chests?"

The tallest of the three patrons glanced down at his chest and answered, "What are you talkin' 'bout? Ball of light? Damn, son, are you crazy? The only thing coming out of my chest are a couple of hairy nipples. I don't see no..." He laughed. "...li'l ball of light!"

Undeterred, Braun carried on, "How 'bouts you other fellas, huh? Can you see it? Take a look at yourselves. How can you not see those big, bright, smoky balls all sticking out of you?"

The man to the right of the tall man answered, "As long as you're waving that gun around, I'll see whatever you want me to see. Ball of light? Yup, you got it. Suuuurrreee, I see it. Two buffalos around that table over there smoking cigars and playing cards? Yup, I see that as well."

Pissed off with the sarcasm, Braun lost his composure and fired a shot upwards into the ceiling. The desired dramatic effect wasn't made, as the bullet only produced a barely audible mild splutter through the hay and straw-thatched roof.

A thought dawned on him, his next sentence taking him by surprise. "That's the damn problem. Nobody can see what's really inside of them. Y'all carry on hating and judging, talking, and talking, hearing but not listening, thinking but not feeling. None of y'all want to reach inside and allow yourself to run on what God has given you." He moved closer to the tall man and stretched out his gun-free left hand.

The tall young man said, "What the fuck you doing?"

Braun's right hand pointed the gun to within inches of the man's mouth, and with his left he reached out, spreading his fingers into a clasped motion just outside of touching distance of the energy ball.

The man backed away and Braun snapped, "DON'T move or... believe me, I *will* shoot you."

The man stopped, as his two friends and the bartender exchanged nervous glances.

Braun concentrated hard, and through his fingers he began to pull some of the energy field away from the tall man. It scraped off him like an air-based, springy goo, and the life drained from the man's face. The lenses of his eyes were devoid of colour, leaving two pin-prick pupils and milky eyeballs staring back.

Braun pulled at the energy to a point where it appeared it might break off, but he lost control and it snapped back onto the body it was attached to. Before the man could regain his composure, Braun started again. The other three bar patrons stood watching open-mouthed and unwilling to react to the situation as Braun's gun focused on the tall man.

This time, Braun decided not to overthink it. Instead, he used the magnetic invisible force to reach out and attach itself to the light. Again, it was pulled from the man's chest, forming a beam that was stretched further and further from the man until it ran up Braun's forearm. The straight line finished at the elbow as it veered off and pressed against his own chest, setting up a bridge between the two men as absorption began.

Within seconds, the victim started rocking from side to side and foam bubbled through the corners of his mouth. The other three men shouted at Braun to stop, and the barman yelled, "Stop it. You're hurting him!"

Braun, in his trance-like state, consumed the energy garnered from the man. Yet he still had a scrap of focus in the perception of his other reality, enabling him to react to the other three men as they considered making moves to try to stop the situation. Only the apprehension of their friend's head being blown off left them cautious.

Braun, despite his trance, was aware of this and immediately re-directed his energy extraction pull, creating four prongs to split the beam between the men. The impact was fast, and within seconds they bridged together through their chests, with all four displaying the symptoms of the first victim. Dead-eyed, furious ragdoll shaking, and mouth foaming ran through them all. After ten seconds of this, Braun experienced an infiltration of energy consumption, powering each one of his senses. His smell, sight, and hearing peaked at ten times their regular magnitude. The blood in his veins had been infused with something that took him far beyond the realms of human capabilities, taking him to highly advanced extra-terrestrial levels of focus, power, and sensory sharpness. So acute was this that he was able to smell what the men had eaten for their breakfast through the spittoon twenty yards from him. He could clearly see thousands of fleas fidgeting throughout bales of hay on the other side of the barn. He could hear dogs barking from the far side of town.

The awesomeness of the experience hit him in unusual ways, as he produced his first erection in fifteen years. It throbbed with might and left his penis on the verge of explosion as the furious blood flow coursed through him. This naturally unsettled him, and although he found it extremely difficult to break it off, the obvious diminution of the victim's energy resources left the man on the brink of death.

Forced to focus on letting go, the separation of Braun's mind and spirit had to be brought together to stop it. The elderly barman's eyes had closed over and his body was limp. The other three seemed to be fading out fast, too. So Braun concentrated on his breathing, trying to create a visual of his mind being a store that had closed for lunch, with any thoughts being represented as the owners taking an afternoon nap. This, combined with the breathing exercises and an amplified concentration, enabled him to slowly release the men from incapacitation.

The energy beams that radiated from the men and into Braun rapidly faded in colour. Their bold and bright appearance diluted to stonewashed pastels, and the link weakened until it broke.

The men hit the ground and Braun stumbled back a few paces. Two of the younger men managed to remain on their feet, although their legs were very wobbly. The first man that Braun had reached into, and the ageing barman, were crumpled into strange shapes on the ground. Several of the ghosts looked expectantly at the floor dwellers, as though awaiting their arrival in the afterlife.

This shocked and shamed Braun as he snatched the bottle of whiskey and slowly backed out through the door, with his gun fixated on the two standing men. Just as he passed through the exit, the two men on the floor reached a semi-conscious state and their necks and shoulders began to wriggle.

Braun's thoughts became a little more hopeful. *God, please, please let them be alright.* Still, for his own safety, he was unwilling to stick around to find out.

Hasty footsteps from within could be heard as the door was shut and locked with a wooden bolt pulled from one side to the other. Three fifteen-gallon barrels, tightly packed together, stood upright to the left of the entrance.

The ghost of a curly-haired, straw hat-wearing young woman sat in the middle of the barrels. She was mostly light blue, with a slight tone of green. Her calf-length gingham dress swayed as her legs swung back and forth, her head tilted down to the floor, concealing her face.

Braun was alarmed to see that his visions weren't exclusive to the bar, but his fear remained focused on the men and doing what he needed to keep them off his tail. So he skipped over to the barrels with the intention of using them to his advantage.

Despite his panicked state and the questionable existence of the ghostly woman, he still maintained some decorum, and acknowledged her. "Sorry to interrupt you, ma'am, but I'm really going to need those barrels."

Instantly the ghost jumped off, and she looked up and stared at him. Only a few distinguishable features of the woman could be detected outside the faint impression of her clothes and curly hair. Two characterless circles represented eyes. They were of a darker green than the rest of her and appeared to protrude 3D like from her misty form. A similar effect was positioned where a mouth would be on her heart-shaped face. The circle moved and stretched in many directions, like a small elastic band, as though she was trying to communicate with Braun. He heard a peculiar, sad, distorted moan, like a pained seal honking through a feedback-laden microphone.

He said, "I'm sorry, but I can't understand what you're saying."

Undeterred, she carried on making strange ethereal noises, as her shape became more animated by the second.

Braun looked at her with pity and said, "I wish I could help you."

The woman didn't stop, and moved closer to Braun. He sidestepped and crouched next to one of the huge barrels. Amazingly, he wrapped his arms around it and picked it up with relative ease. He wobbled over to the door with the barrel, like a world's strongest man competitor, as the men inside tried to kick the door down.

An elderly lady passed by on the street. She stopped, scratched her head, and addressed the amazing feat of strength. "Just how can a scrawny old thing like you pick up that huge barrel?"

Braun reached the door and wedged the first barrel against it. He turned to the old lady. "Hey, I may be scrawny, but I ain't that old. Well, certainly not compared to you. And this barrel? Pffff, I could keep hold of this thing from one end of town to the other. Why that is..." He managed a slight shrug despite the weight. "...I have no idea. But I've learned very recently that once you get your foot into the door of the unknown, you can see and do things very differently."

She laughed and said, "Alright, maybe you aren't too long in the tooth. It must be all them greys in your beard. But I reckon my eyes could be lying to me. My husband was twice the size of you. He was never out of that place, and when the liquor was low, he'd be the first outside with at least two others." She scratched her head. "Hmmmm, they'd waddle one of those barrels in together. Always real awkward for them, and I just don't see how you're able to move that on your own."

Braun ran over to the other barrel. The ghost was still facing him, unleashing more odd, weird sounds. At this point Braun lost patience and took it out on the lady. "I'd love to stand around talking all day, but that hollering and cussing in there is the sound of a bunch of men who want to put a bullet in my head. So do forgive me if I seem a little distracted. But if you want to make yourself useful, you could move that last barrel for me."

The old woman waved her stick at Braun and replied, "I reckon you've got it coming. You just seem all sorts of wrong to me."

Braun noticed she was wearing a necklace with a crucifix pendant, and he answered back, "I seem wrong, huh? Are you saying God made a mistake with me?"

She muttered to herself and walked off, while Braun quickly moved a second and a third barrel to barricade the men inside. He suspected it wouldn't be long before they were able to break down the obstacle, so he quickly pocketed the pistol and untied the horse.

He simultaneously jumped onto the saddle and forcefully slapped the horse's side as the men pushed through the door and clambered over the barrels to the outside. They immediately began firing bullets as his horse stampeded through the town. Three bullets closely whizzed by and a fourth struck him on the shoulder. He screamed in pain and lay forward with his arms wrapped loosely around the horse's neck.

Another bullet flew through the bottle of whiskey. His disappointment left him as crushed as the remainder of the bottle, and his tight grip released the jagged top half of it. This briefly became his primary concern.

"Aw, come on! The shoulder I can live with, but not the damn bottle!"

Braun somehow managed to evade a barrage of bullets, leaving the town behind him, and after riding for a few hours, he found himself in the area of Ramon.

Throughout the journey, Braun had been thumbing around the wound on his shoulder. The bullet had passed right through, and he was satisfied that it was just a deep cut. It had burrowed to a depth that stripped the flesh to the dermis level of skin. Strangely, though, it appeared to be healing at an abnormal rate of time.

Braun's body was functioning at a faster, enhanced level, although the amplified sensory function was unwelcome as he rode through desert land. The smell of animal excrement and carcasses from long distances left him feeling sick, and the sun exposure through pin-sharp, highly defined sight only stung his eyes, making it difficult for him to see. Yet, despite the problematic elements of his new self, a euphoric energy coursed throughout his body, squashing the negative results of his new-found inner strength like an animal refusing to waste time dwelling on what evolution hadn't given them.

Braun regularly sipped water along the way, but frustratingly, despite the major improvements throughout his constitution, his thirst for alcohol continued to hanker.

Wanting to avoid a repeat of what had happened in the last town, he decided that before he did anything else, to avoid any more unwanted attention it would be wise to purchase a suit. He was extra keen to lose the Long Johns now that the murky white colour had been dyed with a smattering of blood around the left shoulder, to go alongside the yellow urine stain around the crotch area.

Ramon was bustling with people, both living and dead. Ghost men on ghost horses trotted alongside the living. Phantom figures appeared to be going about a daily routine just like their human counterparts.

The town was well equipped, and it wasn't long before Braun found a tailors to purchase a suit, along with a needle and thread for his wound. The suit he'd opted for had been intended for another customer, but with it being the only one small enough for his wiry frame, he offered the shop owner double the marked price. This was duly accepted, and after getting changed in the owner's private space at the back of the small shop, Braun walked out in a nice new outfit and a curve-rimmed, black top hat, wrapped with a dark brown ribbon around the base. The suit was loosely fitted and allowed him to discreetly continue with the money strapped around him.

The smart new clothing did wonders for his confidence, and respectability was now something he'd gain at first glance, instead of being something he'd have to work hard to earn.

The jet black, small-tailed suit was complimented with a silken black, gold-buttoned waistcoat, and the outfit was completed with a white frilly shirt and a dark cherry coloured puff tie. Happy with the look, but still wanting to add a little more prestige to his appearance, he visited a jewellery store directly opposite on the other side of the dusty road.

He purchased a handcrafted, gunmetal pocket watch, rounding off the ensemble as he passed the chain through one of the buttonholes, placing the watch into his inside jacket pocket.

Braun stood on the landing outside the jewellers and looked down. Running his hands across the soft fabric, he enjoyed the touch and smell of the new clothes.

He walked across to the unit next to the jewellers and looked at his reflection in the window. He had to straighten the tie a little and set the hat somewhat, but he was astonished by what he saw. He liked what stared back at him. *Goddamn it, Braun McCleary, you're actually looking decent for just about the first time in your life,* he thought.

He chuckled and shook his head in disbelief. He couldn't do anything about his lived-in, craggy face, but his beard and messy hair, coupled with the new outfit, gave him an eccentric dandy look that pleased him.

He continued looking and adjusting himself for a few moments before he heard soft giggling. He peered through the window to see several young ladies staring back at him as they awaited treatments in a hair salon. The initial embarrassment turned his face a deeper red than the broken-veined, ham hock hue that already seasoned it. However, he quickly embraced the moment and took a bow as he removed his hat in a sweeping, extravagant manner. This made them laugh even more, but they were not teasing him; their reaction was of a playful manner. This fun exchange lifted Braun's spirits higher, and he headed further into the half mile-long high street that made up two-thirds of the town. He walked with a loose-limbed purpose and doffed his hat to a few ladies as he passed them by. His external appearance granted him the confidence and rejuvenation that he had already received supernaturally on the inside.

The clothes took a little bite out of the money, but he knew it was well spent in his quest to be respectable. He recognised this importance, pending any short-term or long-term intentions to stick around and establish himself in Ramon.

A quick detour into a liquor store followed, where he picked up a few jars of the shopkeeper's highly potent, homemade moonshine, and as difficult as it was, he managed to resist the urge to open a jar on the street and ruin his new, refined image.

He figured there may have been places of accommodation further down the town or around the corner, but he liked the look of a nearby four-storey wooden corner building called The Redmond.

The place had recently benefitted from a fresh lick of red paint, which had proved effective in hiding some of the wear and tear of the sandblasted eighty-year-old hotel and saloon combo. Braun was immediately impressed as he walked in. The décor was of a far higher standard than he was used to. Wooden floors were heavily scratched in places, due to spur damage, but they had clearly been recently varnished and polished. The reception area's walls were constructed of tightly packed, thick logs, and it was more indicative of a North Dakotan cabin.

It looked beautiful, but it wasn't practical or climate suitable for Texas, with the logs removing much needed ventilation. Taxidermy adorned the walls, with framed deer and elk heads watching over the place.

Braun struggled to look at them. Anything dead now scared him, and although his own perception of reality wasn't a subject that he'd spent a lot of time brooding over throughout his slovenly life, his idea of it was now totally warped to the point of distressed confusion. This conflicted with the elated joy that accompanied the freakish physical and sensory prowess that rattled throughout his mind, body, and spirit. Not wanting to have his buzz tainted in any way, he tried to ignore the spooky happenings that surrounded him as he approached the desk. He was unable to tell whether his mind was playing tricks on him or not as he watched the heads of the elk and the deer moving violently, as though they had just woken to find that a huge wooden wall had been fitted around their necks. Braun imagined their bodies flailing desperately on the other side. They grunted faintly, and the noise slowly rippled through the air towards Braun.

He was determined to keep himself within the realms of the real, and walked to the service desk against the far wall. He stared straight ahead. *Don't look, you asshole, it's your mind fucking with you. IGNORE IT, FOR THE LOVE OF GOD, IGNORE IT. Just... hold steady, right, take it easy. Check in and take a couple of drinks - straighten your ass out.*

He was concerned that his stress levels would overwhelm him, but he knew that playing cool was the only option to keep them at bay. He rang a bell on the front desk and waited a few seconds before a portly, well-dressed man emerged from behind a curtain to host the front desk. His checked orange and green suit blended well with his mid-length, curly ginger hair. The bushy moustache was of the same colour but flecked with the odd grey hair. Rested on his chest was another orb-like ball of pulsating smoke, and the neon pink colour of it shone brightly in the mostly brown wooded room.

Braun now saw this effect on everyone, and he suddenly felt a thump beating from one side of his chest to the other with the force of a rapidly foot-pedalled kick drum. The salacious pull inside him urgently craved to suck it up as he practically drooled at the thought, knowing he could easily bring it through.

But he urged for the willpower he'd searched for all his life. His humanity needed to override this force, but it was getting stronger. His lips salivated with the anticipation of a long-term junkie about to shoot up with the purest heroin.

The yearning waned a little as the man greeted Braun, providing a much-needed distraction.

"What can I do you for?"

Braun was taken with the man's friendly demeanour and responded in kind. "Good afternoon, sir. I would like to book your very best room for the next week."

His thoughts threatened to overpower him. *And drink in whatever that beautiful thing is pushing out of you.*

The man responded, still with a jolly tone, but clearly on the hunt for information. "You here for business or pleasure?"

After the last couple of days, Braun was rife with paranoia, and answered the man, "Am I required to say, innkeeper?"

He hoped that by acknowledging the man's position, he could groom the ego and limit the probing.

"No, sir, of course you are not. Your business is exactly that. Please don't take it as snooping. It's just…" He leant a little closer to Braun and lowered his voice. "…I've had some trouble here in the past. Hell, just last week, two men, older guys, damn both in their fifties, you'd think they'd know better." He shook his head. "But they got into a fist fight over a game of chess. Always thought it was a peaceful game, but it sparked some serious aggression in those two clowns!

"It would have been all fuss and feathers, but several other fellas got caught up in it, and it meant six broken tables. I lost count of how many glasses got smashed, and I'm guessing a few broken noses. Theeennnn I had all kinds of hassle involving the Sheriff and a couple of Marshals. The bastards were trying to point the finger at me and my place as somewhere that attracts this kind of trouble." He cleared his throat. "Whole thing caused no end of bother. So, I do like to get a lowdown on folks before I welcome them into my place. It ain't personal, I'm just trying to run a respectable business here."

Braun's paranoia eased off a little, and he understood the man's hesitancy following the brief explanation. "Look, I won't fill your head full of crap and tell you that I'm a saint, 'cause, well, who is?

'But what you should know is that when it comes to brawling, I try and avoid any of that. I'm no tough guy. I couldn't put the squeeze on a grape in a food fight, and any of my threats to kick ass, more often than not end up with my own being kicked good and proper." Braun laughed. "Those old idiots behaving like that? Pfft! Brawling's a young man's game, and I don't find no fun in a game where I'm always the loser. I like to keep to myself, innkeeper, and I'll put plenty of money in your registers in exchange for whiskey. I'll be a good boy, and that's my word, honest to God."

He held his hands up, and the man nodded in modest recognition. "We've got a few rooms available, but as for the best one? Hmm, well to be frank with you, none of them are anything special really. People just use them for sleeping and fucking, if truth be told."

Braun was surprised by the man's blunt use of language, but it was offered in a pleasant way. "Okay. I sure hope to be doing at least a little of one and a lot of the other…"

Both men laughed. "So, I guess a bed is all I need. You got any rooms to the rear, facing the mountains?"

"Yep, we've got one on that side. It'll cost you a little more than our standard room, though."

Braun nodded. "I'd say it's worth a few extra bucks. It's got to beat looking over at the jailhouse on the other side of the road." He reached out and shook the man's hand. "The name's McCleary, and don't worry, my troublemaking days are long behind me."

The man smiled. "We'll see about that, McCleary. Ha-ha. Sure, glad to meet you, sir, the name's Dan."

"How much do I owe you, Dan?"

"Ten bucks will get you a week."

Braun threw a small pile of notes onto the desk and said, "Will this cover it?"

Dan answered honestly, "You've given me too much, buddy."

He slid a few notes back over to Braun and passed him a key. "It's room nine on the second floor."

Braun thanked the man and headed up a winding staircase, passing the ghosts of a young man and his lady holding hands. He didn't want to acknowledge them but also didn't want them to pass straight through him, as intuition told him the consequences of such could be harmful. His new state of being appeared to be constructed from auras and energy taken from the living or the recently deceased, and he didn't want to chance a collision with the dead.

He stepped to the side to allow them past, and they appeared to respond to the recognition of their presence with strange noises through pained seal-like patterns. The acoustics of the hotel influenced the sound and furthered Braun's anxiety, as the broken radio transmission effect bounced off the walls, briefly connecting the parallel dimensions.

Braun didn't look back as they passed him, and he tried to divert his thoughts by glancing down at the saloon as he reached the halfway point of the stairs. It was through an open doorway to the left of the reception area and was decorated in similar fashion to the hotel side of the business. The bar, eight metres long, dripped with green linoleum, with more taxidermized animal heads scattered over the walls. They had been obtained through hunts across the nearby Cuyamaca mountain range, and an ill-fitted nature meets domesticated human life theme was created.

Braun dropped off a few things in his room. It was basic but functional – just a bed, a couple of unexciting cheap oil paintings, and a well walked-over, braided rug. The room would probably qualify as a two star by modern standards, but the mountainous views were unquestionably worthy of the full five stars.

A basic wooden table and chair were set up in front of the window for any patrons of the room to enjoy the stunning landscape. Braun naturally veered over and took a seat. He stared out the window and sat down to take in the view. The mountains sat proudly and mystically underneath a perfect Californian blue sky.

Braun was staggered by how much green speckled over the surface, considering the dry heat. It was a welcome accessory to the beauty, and the different shades of greens and yellows from the trees and plantation, set against the pale pinks and greys of the rocks, created a beautiful tapestry with the lakes and streams sequinned as they shimmered under the glare of the sun.

In awestruck contentment, he shook his head and said aloud, "Well, ain't that something."

He opened a jar of moonshine, took a big swig, and gulped as he enjoyed the instant warm, fuzzy feeling of addiction-fuelled gratification. His head tilted back between sips, and he basked in relief for several minutes until he felt ready to tackle the gash on the ball of his left shoulder. It really wasn't bad at all and completely belied the state that it should have been in after a well sharpened bullet had opened him up.

However, with only a few feeds to his belt, the initial rapid recovery of this area had ground to a halt as he'd reached Ramon. He was now left with an ugly wound that needed some attention.

The moonshine served as a cleanser and an anaesthetic, as Braun poured it over the area prior to wonkily applying a needle and thread to stitch up the cut.

He looked at his handiwork. *The pattern? Not too impressive*. But he was satisfied that the stitches were locked in effectively. He wiped himself down, and, keeping hold of the needle, he crouched down beside the bed to pull the linen back, revealing the mattress. He made an incision into the side, just wide enough to pull the material apart to a length and width that enabled him to slide a few handfuls of the money inside. The white of the thread was a close match to the colour of the mattress, and he stitched the hole back up, a discreet hiding place successfully created.

Braun didn't stay in his room for long and decided to venture out for a wash. Neglecting the option to go to the downtown bath house, he pursued his preferred choice of outdoor cleansing.

After picking up a bar of soap from a convenience store, he took a ride on his adopted horse to a nearby stream at the foot of a mountain. It had been months since he'd last cleansed, and as he scrubbed himself, he felt and saw the layers of congealed grey and black grime as it peeled from his skin. The stale stench of unwashed flesh was more pungently noticeable to him as it wrestled with the perfumed scent of the soap. The smell was repellent but it provided a rush of excitement, as the release of the foul odour represented the relinquishment of a miserable past.

Chapter Three

The Redmond Hotel saloon was busy. Ten of the twelve tables were occupied, with limited standing room against the bar. People of all kinds of professions inhabited the place. If you wanted a drink in town, The Redmond was where you drank. Marshals, doctors, and the town mayor stood and sat alongside outlaws, prostitutes, and stagecoach drivers.

The odd skirmish aside, the crowd mostly got along or tolerated each other. People were free to speak their minds, but an unofficial house rule discouraged overtly antagonistic discussion. This was clear to the locals, and any foray into this type of conversation from strangers was normally apprehended, mostly successfully by the bartender Kieran. His harsh, intimidating, thick Irish accent and six-foot four bear-like frame put off many potential loose tongues.

This evening was as tame as Kieran could have wished for, and the most exciting event was a man having his mid-length beard shaved off in a well-lit rented space cornered in the room next to the front window.

Some atmosphere was created through a skinny bare-chested and bare-footed teenage boy sitting atop a stool in the opposite corner. Only a pair of dirty grey trousers preserved his modesty as he sang and strummed a guitar along gently to 'The Streets of Laredo'. A few patrons tapped their feet along to the pleasant rendition, but his youthful optimism didn't do justice to the mournful spirit of the song.

As Braun took a long drag on a cigar and slurped his way through his ninth drink of the day, he was grateful that he hadn't been met with the hostility that his mere existence seemed to bring out of people. The whiskey he'd been served up tasted no better than high-proof, liquidised horse shit. But it kept him topped up, and despite the lack of pleasantries in the taste department, the steak and beans that he'd chowed down on with his fourth drink helped to soak up the liquor.

He wasn't feeling too good, and as he stared into his glass, ignoring two flies nesting in his beard, he attempted to escape some extremely dark thoughts by directing some small talk to a couple of men sitting at a neighbouring table. They were preoccupied with a game of cards, and after noticing that their dungarees, boots, and exposed flesh were covered in dirt and soot, Braun surmised that they mined for a living. One of the two – a bald-headed, curly moustachioed man in his fifties – had been irritating Braun through frequent shrill howls of laughter at his own jokes, as though he were trying to influence his buddy to follow suit and find him as hilariously funny as he found himself. These bouts were followed by phlegmy coughing fits. Yet, despite this annoyance, Braun attempted to make conversation, addressing both gentlemen. "What you boys playing?"

Curly moustache responded, "We're having a friendly game of faro."

His smiling buddy joined in. "Ain't nothing friendly about it. Don't believe that. We got two bucks and a lot of bragging rights riding on this game."

Braun asked, "Who's winning?"

Both men pointed at each other at the same time, responding the same way. "He is."

All three laughed, and Braun said, "One of you guys must be bluffing."

The older of the two responded, "Why don't you put a few bucks down and find out which one of us is calling the bluff?"

The younger of the two was a weird looking guy – also bald, with a massive, almost rectangular sun- and booze-frazzled, pink head. His eyes, nose and mouth gathered compactly dead centre of the rectangle. His small features proved difficult to distinguish with such thick layers of soot covering them, and Braun found himself unreasonably put off by the man because of his peculiar looks.

The man said, "Pull up a stool."

Braun shook his head. "If it's all the same with you, fellas, I'll pass." He pointed to his drink. "I can't afford to take on any other vices."

Big head-small face tipped his hat respectfully and replied, "Got you, buddy. Have a few too many myself."

Braun attempted to make some further small talk with the men, but he was met with short and sharp answers. He realised that they were wrapped up in their game, and they weren't prepared to humour or engage him if he wasn't willing to throw some money down and join in with the cards.

The short exchange did nothing for him, and he was grateful that it had nosedived so shortly after it took off. The vigour and enlivenment that he had pulled into his body had slowly been wearing off throughout the day, and as his chit-chat efforts petered out, what little merriment he had left all but disappeared. He almost felt a thud inside as it hit the bottom, and his mood completely turned in an instant.

He was no longer seeing the ghosts, although this he wasn't too cut up about, but the depression and self-loathing that had plagued him all his life was back and extremely intense. The high reaches of jubilation that he'd experienced over the previous twenty-four hours had met their extreme opposite and left him sinking to Earth's core depths of desolation.

The magnificent colour pallet that oozed through everything living was gone, replaced by visions clad in grey and washed-out tones. His edge and buoyancy lost, and all his thoughts were related to frustration and confusion at the dramatic mood switch. The alcohol didn't provide its usual magic either; it numbed the nervous energy that usually accompanied such bouts of depression, but the obliteration of thought pattern that he'd hoped for had not worked. The depression held his mind hostage, with any attempt of negotiation going unheard. This gloom flowed through a weakened body and the stress pumped his cortisol release into unchartered territory.

He was grateful to be sitting on a comfortable seat. He sensed that if he stood, his legs probably would have buckled from underneath him, and the only action that the body seemed willing to produce was right-armed whiskey courier trips back and forth to his mouth.

Braun's instincts told him that the effects would be devastating if the mystery left him entirely. For the first time in many years, he had a will to keep going. All throughout adulthood, his sole objective had been to drink himself stupid, and he was quite content to speed up his expiration.

Despite his lack of religious beliefs, he'd always hoped for an afterlife, another side that would offer something that life hadn't. Many of his sober periods had been racked with existential questions, thoughts that had haunted billions before him and would trouble billions after he was long gone. Most of his demons were self-created, but he would still ponder whether he'd been dealt a bad hand in the personality stakes. Was he just naturally lazy, weak, and worthless? Or was he a pre-determined statistic of order? The failure needed for somebody else's success to be measured against. Would this change for him if the great beyond existed? And if so, would that require his character to be compromised? Would he even be the same person? Did he want to be the same person? But if he wasn't, how would he know who he used to be?

The drink suppressed most of these thoughts, and even if nothing followed, the sweet release of death was something that he'd always looked forward to. However, the situation had Changed; the ecstasy he'd experienced served as a catalyst for him to want to continue. He'd tasted something that he suspected could give him the kind of strength and power in this life that he'd always fantasised of owning in a paradisiacal afterlife.

Braun was aware of two burning sensations within. One was the obvious whiskey buzz, but there was another, and this one was different. It was mild, but it bubbled enough for him to know it was there. And although the depression had almost consumed him entirely, every now and again, if he was able to meditate, shut his thoughts out, and focus fully on the weak but gently apparent numinous emanation, he could detect a smidgeon of the glow that had fizzed throughout him earlier on.

This created conflicted desires. He knew that if he was able to feed again, the power could be re-ignited, but a struggle lay within his reluctance to potentially harm somebody in the process. Even throughout his depressive state, the urge to feed was overbearing, and he knew that if he didn't act quickly, what little was left inside of him would burn out and could mean permanent loss of the phenomenon. It had a mysterious staying power like a flamed candle in a church that remained alight after all the wax had long melted. But Braun knew that it would fade sooner rather than later, and he needed to act quickly to prevent this.

The option to carry it out in the saloon was quickly dismissed, and in his search for inspiration he knew that the best way was to acquire the services of a prostitute. He really didn't want to go down this route, as he had always sympathised with those of that profession. He could relate to them; he had been considered a lower class of citizen back in Cheston. Town drunk, village idiot, and local punching bag all rolled into one. Some of the sassier whores he'd met could handle themselves and set their own rules, but he'd seen too many quiet girls who'd clearly been pushed or felt they had no choice but to enter that line of work.

He had paid for sex at times in his life, during his younger days, and on each occasion he had been left with deep-set guilt and shame afterwards. His life had been spent abusing his own body, so the thought of using somebody else's for his own gratification left him thoroughly miserable.

He looked over at the gaggle of ladies gathered at one end of the bar. Several appeared to be in the middle of phony flirtatious routines as they laughed along with ugly, drunken idiots, most of them old enough to be their fathers. A well-dressed, cruel-faced woman in her thirties sat on a nearby table on her own, watching as the potential hook-ups were negotiated through staged mating rituals. No-one was bothering her, and Braun guessed that she was the Madam. He made a note to himself that he'd need to keep a close eye on her as he mulled over his next move. The obvious appeal in using a prostitute was driven by the ease in which he could take one up to his room and avoid a public scene.

He noticed two dead flies bobbing up and down in the last dregs of his whiskey, but he drank it up anyway as he anxiously took to his wobbly legs. He made his way over to the bar, wanting to get a closer look at the ladies, like a customer in a fancy restaurant picking out a lobster from a tank. He was a little unsteady on his feet and drew a few chuckles as he stumbled a couple of times en-route.

The bar area was still busy, but he managed to sandwich himself between two lone-drinking old cowboys. The saloon beverage selection lacked in variety and didn't stretch beyond cheap red-eye whiskey or low-quality French brandy. Braun wasn't one for mixing it up and stuck with the whiskey as he ordered another large glass. He glanced across; the bar was fifteen metres in length and covered a large area of the saloon. Braun propped himself up at the opposite end to the whores' gathering. The razor-sharp, hawk-eyed vision had passed, and his natural eyesight wasn't great. Still, he squinted and tried to pick out a potential willing participant.

Eight young women seemed preoccupied in grouped and one-on-one conversations with prospective customers. A ninth woman – the eldest in the group – remained alone, lost in her thoughts. Braun tried looking over a couple of times when the opportunity presented itself. It was difficult, as one of the sides of the human sandwich he'd found himself in was a hairy man mountain, six foot five, and nearly as wide.

The huge man, just like many in the room, was inebriated, and Braun had to settle for the odd glimpse when he could see through the man's sea-legged sways. The lady eventually noticed the dodging, and as one of Braun's stolen glances was met, he smiled opportunistically, raising his glass to her.

She reciprocated this act, albeit unenthusiastically, but Braun was grateful for any opening, no matter how minor. He had noticed her earlier on, but his long-time, alcohol-ravaged concentration span and short-term memory had taken over and settled into its regular drunken routine of long, trance-like stares into space. After a short while he'd soon forgotten about her. But standing at the bar and seeing her from close up, he was again taken by her.

She'd arrived with four other women, all younger and prettier, and after watching the older lady for a while, he'd begun to feel sympathetic as cowboys hassled and flirted with other members of the party but ignored her. One by one her colleagues bounced back and forth from upstairs or outside with various randy customers, while she sat on a stool at the bar with some of the other ladies. She had company briefly throughout the night, but mostly she seemed very alone.

She felt like the best option for his motives. She didn't stand out, and he suspected that he could move away with her a little more inconspicuously than with some of the more boisterous and popular members of the group.

Braun couldn't help but like the look of her. She wasn't conventionally attractive. He'd always favoured brunettes, and she had an earthiness that he was drawn to. Her lightly made-up face was very angular, with a long and pointy nose. Had she been wearing sunglasses, it was the sort of look that could give a first impression of unfriendliness, but her kind, sad eyes appeared to contradict the rest of her facial characteristics.

Braun liked her stick-thin figure, and although flat-chested, she was wearing a low-cut, light blue and white striped dress that revealed a tanned chest and a small cleavage. Her legs were covered by a frilly skirt in the same colour, and from the moment Braun had first laid eyes on her, he'd felt an urge to get to know her.

However, he knew that looking at her amorously wasn't in tune with his intentions. He'd identified her as the most viable option for his requirements, and he needed to focus on what he could take from her.

She looked over again, and Braun puffed out his cheeks as he considered how to approach this. Ideally, he wanted to get her up to his room discreetly to waiver the many repercussions that an attempt of public feeding could have caused.

He pondered his new ability constantly and was hopeful that he could figure out a way to control it and not let it get the better of him. Like anything of great power, the first few practice runs could be overwhelming, whether it be trying to tame a wild stallion or an attempt to create a controlled trigger finger for a Gatling machine gun. But he was hopeful that he could somehow curtail it.

The episodes had been played over and over in his mind, trying to figure out how it was able to overcome him. The first time had caught him by surprise so he'd discounted that instance. But he had summoned it on the second occasion, and if he could summon it, then it wasn't unreasonable to think that he could control it.

The large, fat man to his left had grown tired of the drunken swaying and was now asleep with his back rested up against the bar, so Braun could now get a better look of the woman. Again she returned his gaze.

Braun thought, *I'm the only game in town, so maybe she won't be too repulsed by my attention.*

Encouraged by her half smile, it reinforced his determination to hurt her as little as possible. If he could just take enough from her as she slept, she might wake up and put it down to a bad dream.

He noticed that she'd been holding on to the same glass of brandy since she'd arrived. She barely had a drop left, so he decided to order her a fresh one. Not wanting to waste any more time, he took it over and said, "Mind if I keep you company?"

She offered a non-committal shrug of the shoulders. It wasn't the wildly enthusiastic response that Braun would have liked, but he pulled up a stool next to her and took heart that she hadn't said no. He tried to hand her the small tumbler of brandy, but she waved her hand and declined.

"I can buy my own."

Braun, the defeatist, was unhappy straight away and responded, "Sorry, I shouldn't have bothered you, miss."

He was half risen from his stool when the lady apologised. "I'm sorry, mister, I do appreciate the gesture. It's very kind of you, and I will take the drink if it's still all the same with you."

Braun sat back down and smiled as he handed over the large brandy. He offered his hand. "The name's Braun."

She offered her own daintily. "Agnes."

Braun kissed her hand gently and said, "So, you live around here, Agnes?"

Agnes was cagey. "Coming straight at me with your nose, huh, Braun?" She squinted and wrinkled her nose for a second or two before she added, "Umm, no offence, but I don't know you, sir, and I'm not going to tell you where I live."

Braun replied sarcastically, "Sorry, ma'am, I wasn't after an exact address, you know."

She explained, "I'm quite new to this, and I've just had some trouble talking to strangers in the past... especially men." She tucked some loose hair behind her ear. "I live above a shop uptown with the other girls."

Braun nodded and rambled nervously, "I understand, ma'am. You're damn right to be cautious. There are too many bad people around here, and the ones who ain't total rotten bastards are desperate, and that can make them just as dangerous. I've been around it my whole life. Desperation can turn even the most decent folk immoral. Hell, I once caught a preacher stealing pigs from some farmland I used to own. Can you believe that? A man of God, right under my nose, breaking a commandment."

The woman looked a little anxious, despite Braun's attempt to put her at ease. He detected this and changed the subject.

"So, Agnes, did you grow up around these parts?"

"No, I come from elsewhere."

"How'd you find yourself in Ramon then?"

"I'd rather not talk about it, if you don't mind, sir."

Braun held up his hands. "Understood. The past is gone." He fiddled with his tie. "No point discussing it."

Agnes half-heartedly threw the conversation back onto him. "How about you, Braun? I haven't seen you around. Do you have work here?"

Braun was losing interest and reluctant to give her a great deal of information following her unwillingness to share. He pulled up his trousers, using his belt to hoist them up, and responded vaguely. "I'm probably just passing through, but the town is real nice, so I'll see the lay of the land and take it from there."

He noticed a few people looking over. The place had turned quiet, and he felt somewhat uneasy at the thought of everyone listening into them. This brought a stilted approach to his conversation. He was drunk, but not drunk enough to abandon his inhibitions. Tired, weak, and paranoid, it was getting too much. His need to feed was ruling him, and thinking he would venture outside to see what was available instead, he decided to retreat from the conversation as he took to his feet.

"Listen, Agnes, it's been nice talking to you and all, but I'm beat, so I guess I'm going to call it a night."

Agnes touched his arm and said quietly, "Wait."

He sat back down and looked at her. "What can I do you for?"

She said quietly, "Where are you staying?"

He furrowed his brow and scraped at a patch of hair beneath his lower lip with his teeth. He considered the question for a couple of seconds until he felt a minor twinge in his trousers. The second time since his transformation, though the sensation again surprised him.

Decades of heavy drinking had left him with absent feeling in that department.

Part of him, his stubborn side, made him want to respond as Agnes had, following her reactions to his attempts at conversation. However, the activity in his crotch led him along, and established another victory for the nether regions in the balls-versus-brains scenario.

He said, "I got a room upstairs..." He paused, moved his face a little closer to hers, and winked as he embellished in an attempt to entice. "Best one in the house."

She laughed and replied quietly, "Best one in the house! Ha, trying to excite me, huh, buddy? This ain't New York. We're not overrun with luxury around here. Ha ha, I've seen all the rooms, and I'd say they're all much the same. Strange, crusty stains, cobwebs and dead bugs all over them."

Braun got to his feet and sighed. "I no longer want to bother myself with this."

Again, she touched his arm. His sleeves were rolled up, and the soft warmth of her hand brought a second twinge, a little stronger than the first. He automatically sat back down without even pondering the decision.

Braun asked, "You wanna join me upstairs or not?"

She leant in close and whispered, "I'll need paying."

"Yeah, yeah, I may look dumb, and maybe I am a little, but I didn't think that my chances with you lay on my handsome looks and beguiling personality." He smiled "Don't worry, I got money."

She responded, "Lead the way."

Braun was sheepish as he headed out of the saloon area of the hotel. The discretion he'd hoped for wasn't there, and he sensed that all the eyes in the establishment were focused on him. He guessed what they were thinking, and he was embarrassed. This startled him, as his boozy lifestyle had been responsible for countless amounts of cringe-inducing moments and he'd thought he was immune to mortification.

The bar seemed to have doubled in size as he tried to walk as quickly out of the place as his tired body would allow. He made the mistake of glancing over to the card players, when the older guy threw him a wink and produced a prodding hand gesture with his fist. The big-headed younger man laughed and tipped his head to Braun.

Deciding to keep his head down until he exited the saloon area, he neglected to enter into conversation with Agnes, trying to keep as low a profile as possible. But he relaxed a little as they approached the stairs in the lobby area of the hotel, and he smiled at Agnes. She smiled back and they carried on up the winding staircase.

He pointed out a landscape painting of an olive-shaped lake surrounded by cloud free, blue skies, and dogwood trees. Braun admired the picture, and thought out loud, "That place looks awful familiar to me."

Agnes passively glanced at it and said, "It sure looks nice, wherever it is."

They reached the top of the stairs and were met by one of Agnes' friends, a small, slim, and pretty lady.

Braun was quickly put off her when she flashed a full set of dark brown teeth. She was dressed skimpily in a raven black corset, with fishnet panty hose, sitting oddly with workman's boots and a long, unbuttoned man's overcoat. She had a mop of unruly, curly blonde hair that flayed out in all directions, statically out of control following heavy mattress-wrestling sessions.

Agnes addressed her. "Are you done for the night, Heather?"

Heather responded, "Sure am, I'm happy to say. That wasn't easy, though, I tried every trick in the book, but that boy's jam seemed to want to stay in the bottle."

Braun shook his head and looked at the floor. He didn't like women speaking so frankly about sordid details.

Agnes chuckled. "Did you have to do…" She cupped her hands around her mouth and whispered, "…the special thing to coax it?"

Heather laughed. "Uh-huh. I accidentally hurt him doing it, ha ha. So he was pretty pissed afterwards."

She pulled her long blonde hair back to reveal a rosy, red patch that started over her hairline and continued onto the side of her forehead, where the guy had socked her and pulled a chunk of her hair out.

Braun had been intrigued as to what 'the special thing' was, but that interest had now given way to anger as he spluttered into the conversation, "Where is the bastard?! I can't let no sonofabitch get away with striking a lady."

Heather responded, "Steady there now, fella." She pointed to the mark. "This is nothing."

Braun squinted and took a closer look. "It don't look like nothing to me. I'll put something much worse on the piece of crap's face."

He stepped forward. In his rage, he picked a room at random and gestured towards it.

Heather grabbed his shoulder. "Look, mister. If I had somebody roughed up every time a finger was laid on me, I'd soon get a name for being a no-good crying bitch, and no work would come my way. Now, why don't you mind your own business and go and enjoy whatever it is you're paying Agnes for."

Braun was annoyed and said sarcastically, "Hey, sorry for trying to help you out. I'm beginning to wish the guy had given you a black eye to match that ugly damn bruise on your forehead."

Agnes tried to usher Braun away, as her friend squared up to him. "Come on, asshole, you don't look up to much." She pointed to her left eye. "Right here. Let's see what you've got, pecker head."

Braun shook his head. "Never struck a woman."

Agnes attempted to calm the situation. "Come on now, Braun. She doesn't mean any harm."

Her friend contradicted this and spat at him, striking his chin with a gooey chunk of phlegm.

He shouted, "You're a goddamn wild cat!" He turned to Agnes. "Get her away from me. I don't agree with beating on a woman. Not even real dirty whores like this one." He gritted his teeth and pointed at Heather. "But I'd rather somebody punched me square on the chin than spit their disgusting mouth juice all over me."

Heather laughed. "Agnes' saliva ain't less dirty than mine, and you'll be paying good money to have that all over ya."

Agnes scowled. "Heather! That's enough. Go on now. Leave us be."

Heather cackled and walked down the stairs saying, "Now, y'all have a good time together." She waggled her tongue at them.

Agnes and an incensed Braun ignored this and walked to the end of the corridor. Braun muttered his prior remark about Heather. "Goddamn filthy wildcat."

Agnes stopped him as he fiddled with his keys before they entered the room through a four-panelled, lightly shaded wooden door. She was smarting after one of Braun's comments to Heather and asked, "Are you sure you want to spend more time with a dirty whore?"

Braun played down his insult. "That don't apply to you."

Agnes responded sarcastically, "Just my friend then?"

"Yeah, you ain't like her."

"You don't know me."

"No, I don't know you, but I know you ain't like her."

Agnes feigned a weak smile and said, "Are we going in then?"

Braun hesitated for a few seconds. "You go on in, make yourself comfortable. I'm going to head back down to the bar and get us a couple of drinks."

Agnes shrugged her shoulders and Braun turned the key to let her in. He shut the door behind her and looked down the corridor. His room was at one end of the floor, and there were ten other rooms. The stairwell was dead centre and split the floor into two sides. He remembered that Heather had come from the right of the stairs, which was the far side from his room. He stumbled towards there as his mind and body took another sudden turn, weakening him further.

The corridors presented the illusion of closing in, and they appeared to tilt back and forth like a scene from a surreal horror movie. Braun struggled to recognise the separation between the floor and the walls, as a tunnel-like curvature seemed to remove all angles, creating an unbearable claustrophobic effect.

Braun's bad turns had been poking at him for a few hours, but this was the worst yet. Sweat chugged out of his pores at a rate that could have left him dehydrated in minutes. He passed a few rooms, and although he'd only covered fifteen metres, he needed a rest and sat down at the side of a door. He could hear plenty of masculine grunts from inside the room but not too many pleasured feminine sounds. He grimaced at the noises, and after a ten-second breather got back to his feet.

Not passing anyone on his way, he reached room number three. Placing his ear against the door, Braun heard two men laughing and joking together. The nosy side of him tried to make out what they were saying, but he soon retracted and carried on to the next room as the sound of one of the voices appeared to be heading close to the door.

The next room, number five, was extremely quiet, possibly unoccupied. And after twenty seconds of listening intently, he turned to walk away.

The fatigue was energy sapping to the point where his legs were close to giving up. It felt like some sort of debilitative liquid was saturating every fibre of his body. The burn in his chest was minutes away from permanent extinguishment, and the minor adrenaline boost he'd received talking to Agnes had totally left him.

He had passed the room by only a couple of yards when he heard loud flatulence from inside. Approaching the door, Braun's suspicions were aroused when he saw a few strands of blonde hair on the floor just underneath the handle. Thinking these belonged to Heather, he rapped on the door with his knuckles.

A gravelly voice from inside shouted out, "What do you want now, huh? I paid you, Heather, and you're lucky I paid you in full. I've had better skin sessions with the callouses on my left hand. Now, get the bally hell outta here, and don't start this shit with me again."

Braun wasn't too confident that he could pull off a good impression of a woman in her early twenties, so he neglected to respond and knocked on the door again.

The man walked to the door and spoke as he pulled it open. "I won't tell you again, Heather…"

Braun was confronted by a small, stocky, well-built naked man. He could only half open the door, as the bed got in the way. The room was tiny, and two-thirds of the space was taken up by a double bed. A bedside cabinet with two brass candleholders and scattered piles of the man's clothes were the only objects in the room.

The man looked Braun straight in the eye, opened his mouth, and cleared his throat with a disgusting bubbly, retching sound. He didn't excuse himself and the gravel in his voice wasn't altered by the mucus shake as he said, "What do you want?"

Braun removed his jacket, placed it over his arm, and responded, "Sorry to bother you, mister." He pushed the door a little, nudging it into the bed as much as possible. "Mind if I come in?"

The naked man repeated Braun's request. "Do I mind if you come in? Ha-ha, I asked you what you want, and you didn't tell me! I'm in my fucking birthday suit." He spread his arms wide and continued sarcastically, "Oh sure, come on in, total stranger, pull up a chair, I'll fix us up a couple of drinks. How's about that, huh, fella?"

Braun played along. "That's real nice of you, mister. I'd love to join you for a… drrriink." The last word of his sentence came out strained as he pushed his way in.

The man backed up a little, and Braun showed him his back for a couple of seconds to shut the door. As he turned around, the naked man had adopted a slight squatted position and was waving a leather-handled skinner knife. Not the best weapon for a knife fight, but better than Braun's unarmed defence.

Braun said, "Jeez, mister, that was quick. Did you pull that out of your ass or something?"

The man continued waving it and made poking gestures towards Braun. He taunted, "Come on, you stinking bastard, take your best shot."

Braun briefly rubbed his nose against his right armpit and said, "Don't reckon it's me that stinks, son. I got me this new suit, and I bathed just a couple of hours ago. I think it could be your own gasses that you can smell. I heard that damn fart jump out of your ass from the other side of the door."

The man looked ready. His stance and obvious control of the knife indicated a familiarity with this type of situation. But the tiny room didn't have much space for two grown men, and any type of close combat would further benefit the knife wielder in a fight. Braun held his arms up and tried to calm the man down.

"Look, I only came in to have a little chat with you. I know what you did to the girl, and that doesn't sit well with me, it really does not. I don't know if you're a regular, or if you live around here, but you need to know that I'm going to be sticking around for a while and—"

Braun didn't finish his sentence, as the small man, lightning quick, jumped onto the bed for leverage and lunged into him. The human spear effect was led by the tip of the knife tightly gripped in his left hand.

Braun was able to use his advantage at the point when the man crashed into him. His reach was a lot longer than the naked man's, and he initially managed to block him with outstretched arms. But it didn't take long before Braun was overpowered and wrestled to the floor. The man still had hold of the knife, but in his grip and efforts to grapple, it was rested on its side against Braun's chest. It caught him a couple of times on the ball of the shoulder, drawing a little blood.

The two men grunted and groaned. Braun cried in desperation to keep the wild man at bay, but his efforts began to wane as the man's noises built through a determination to stick the knife through his opponent's throat. The mild spark clung on, desperate for reignition; without it, he would have instantly succumbed to the man's superior strength.

Braun kept hold of the man's left arm. He knew he only had a minute at the most to keep the knife from plunging through his neck. The force needed to be summoned, and he attempted to divide his focus between restraining his potential murderer and generating the inner energy required to raise a matchstick flame into the roaring coal fire needed to reduce this man to nothing.

Time was running out for Braun, and the man kneed him in the testicles. It hurt but didn't incapacitate him. The limited purchase garnered through the cramped metre-long space between the bed and the wall lessened the impact, though it did allow the man to draw an extra few centimetres closer to Braun's neck, and a few more knees to the balls would help him reach it.

Braun tried to clamp the man's legs in-between his own, which was hard with the slipperiness of bare-skinned legs against cotton trousers. But it worked in Braun's favour, as an awkwardness was created that made it difficult for the man to attack him this way.

Strained, throaty squeaks and murmurs were occasionally traded between the two men, but despite what was at stake, there was very little noise. Braun prayed, *Please, somebody, anything, help me. I don't want to go out in this stuffy little room underneath this sweaty little naked man.*

The man pushed his knife even closer, and Braun's hand was now pressed against his own throat. The man seethed and dribbled all over Braun's face with foul, halitosis-riddled breath and Braun was disgusted as spittle from his opponent's mouth fell into his and hit the back of his throat. It was icy cold and alien.

The revulsion fuelled more anger in him than the attempt on his life, and the fury awakened the sleeping dragon inside. The mild burn rapidly grew, and Braun felt stronger as he looked at the man's chubby face. He had turned from tomato red to a colour closer to purple, his eyes were bulbously popping out of his head, and his short, tightly curled blond hair was drenched in sweat. The man's face, so full of rage and hate, served as inspiration to Braun's power surge, a reservoir of energy gathering more momentum.

As he managed to push the man's hand back a little to give himself some more time, his adrenal glands began to pump out cortisol at an extremely high rate. His muscles tensed up and his heart rate and blood pressure increased. This was good, and he just needed one big push to unleash a weapon that would make the man's knife look like he'd turned up to a Samurai sword fight with a drawing pin.

The anger was working for him. How could he not be full of hate and anger towards somebody trying to kill him? The man, though, was undeterred by Braun's second wind and he attempted to move the knife to the side of his neck. This suited Braun, as the positional adjustment meant that any restraint would have to be provided by his bicep. This was fresh and meant he could stave off this new approach for a short while.

More anger was needed, and he took a hard look at the crazed face inches from his own. It was hairless, no sign of any stubble either. This detail inexplicably annoyed Braun, and he briefly scanned parts of the man's torso. He couldn't see any indication of follicle hair growth.

I bet he's never had to shave his entire life. The sonofabitch looks like a giant, fat baby, just as damn pink and bald as the day he was born!

Activity was motivated through his heightened emotions, and the flame stoked quickly. Braun could feel a control over it, he was driving it, and within seconds a glow sat on the middle of his chest. *Keep pushing, keep pushing... it's coming.*

Pow! The glow blossomed from his chest and turned into a beam. It struck the man's chest, and the extraction began.

The orange beam was invisible to the naked man, but the effect was scarily clear to him. He dropped the knife in his stunned state but managed to wrap his hand around Braun's throat. He was weakened and couldn't get a good lock to his grip. Braun was nearly out of danger, but he could still feel an uncomfortable level of restriction around his windpipe.

He pushed harder until the man was shoved a little away from him. He kept his hands around Braun's throat, but the push slowly lifted his body, as though a freshly emerged powerful spring pumped out of him.

The man shouted, "WHAT ARE YOU DOING TO ME?"

Braun didn't respond, and it wasn't long before it began to push and pull at the same time as the man's eyes rolled back, and his faculties ceased to work. Braun received the first taste of the man's essence.

It was ecstasy; the energy and new life entering him smoothed out all the aches and groans. The sort of noises usually reserved for good sex moaned from the back of his throat, his lungs purred, and his skin tingled. The feeling, exercising its third run, had created a relative familiarity, and provided Braun with a greater command of the power. He demonstrated this by extending the beam and slowly levitated the man up to the ceiling. When he pulled him back down to a mid-length height, the top of the man's head had cobwebs attached to it, brought down from the dusty ceiling.

Braun bounced him up and down a few times. The change in the pace and force of the beam enlivened the buzz inside him even more.

The man was perfectly still throughout this; his arms remained extended with his hands clutched in a suspended strangulation gesture. His face had lost a lot of its form, and much of the elasticity and collagen had been sucked out it, leaving prune-like skin and a mouth that had drooped to one side, like a case of Bell's palsy. From this point, Braun could have stopped at any moment, but he didn't want to. He was enjoying himself too much, and despite the prolonged toying with the man, he still wanted to view his actions as self-defence. The man had tried to kill him, and if he let him off the hook, he knew that he could be hunted down.

He kept going until the man was completely drained, and as he reached the core of him, it changed. It tasted and felt different and unpleasant, scaring Braun into letting go. He shut it down, and what was left of the naked man crumbled in mid-air into a black soot-like dust which covered Braun from head to toe.

Taking to his feet, he rubbed his eyes and blew his nose before brushing the dust onto the floor. He moved from the cramped space, over to the slightly roomier bedside area next to the door. Stretching his arms out, he thought he seemed taller; his posture appeared to have improved. He looked at the dust pile. It was odd, due to the sheer quantity of it, but he was satisfied that in no way could it be deemed as murderously suspicious.

Upon exiting the room, Braun surveyed the area. He instantly regretted this, as he saw an apparition of the naked man sitting on the bed facing the wall. The smoky blue image gave him the creeps, and just as he stepped out of the room, it turned to him and wailed in the distorted noise he was now reluctantly accustomed to.

Braun hurried from the room and shut the door quietly. Reaching his own room, he turned the door handle, but it was locked. He thumped against the door a few times and shouted, "Hey, it's me, Aggie, let me in."

She shouted back, "Not if you call me Aggie."

"What's it matter?" He sighed and carried on sarcastically, "Now, if you'd be so kind, Agnes, my dear."

She opened the door, and he nearly knocked her over in his enthusiasm to get inside. She teased him, "I half expected you to come charging in with your pants down, Mister Keen."

His physical edge was blunted by his emotional side. He felt odd, inhuman somewhat. The batch had perked him up, but some of the man's deep-rooted nastiness had polluted it. Still, he wouldn't swap it for how he'd felt before the feed.

She noticed he'd come back empty-handed. "Hey! Where are those drinks?"

Braun shook his head and said, "I finished them on the way up here."

"You've got real problems."

Braun changed the subject. "I hope you've made yourself nice and comfortable. It ain't much of a room, but there's a hell of a view out there. Just a shame it's too dark to see."

Agnes removed her shoes and flung them onto the floor next to a wooden dresser. She mumbled, "Uh, huh."

Braun remembered. "Shit, you've probably been in here dozens of times, with all sorts of fellas." He touched the bedcover and rubbed it a little. "I sure hope they keep the bed linen clean. I don't want to be rolling around in some other guy's seed."

He chuckled, but Agnes wasn't amused and wanted to get down to business. "Tell me what you want, and I'll give you a price. I can service you in a number of ways."

Braun sat on the bed, scratched his head, and frowned. "Service me, huh?" He laughed. "Now that ain't pillow talk, as far as I'm concerned."

Agnes responded, her eyes cold, face void of expression. "Okay, you wanna fuck or get sucked then, huh? Is that better for you?"

Braun tapped the bed, gesturing for Agnes to sit down. She walked slowly and hesitantly. Upon reaching the bed, she sat on the other side, facing the window, as Braun stared ahead at the wall in front of him.

He muttered, "Real classy."

Agnes huffed. "Seems like you don't like me talking either way."

Braun swung his legs onto the bed and lay back. Thirty seconds passed without a word spoken between the two before he killed the silence. "Listen, Agnes, the truth is I really don't want anything off you but company." He held his hands up. "And that's all. I ain't spent good time with a woman for years, and I never got to talk with one as swell-looking as you before."

Agnes squinted her eyes suspiciously as she responded. "I've seen plenty of limp-peckered old drunks like you who just want to talk and talk and talk all night. Most of them, they don't want to pay, just whine and complain about how bad their lives are. Well, I'm sorry if that was your plan, but I'd rather go back downstairs and find another customer."

She spun on her heels and stomped towards the door as Braun lit up a half-smoked cigar. He managed to stop her before she turned the handle.

"Now just hold on a minute, Agnes." He pulled out a couple of coins from his pocket, rolled them onto the bed, and continued, "Will this cover me for the night?"

Agnes eyes brightened up and she changed her tune. "Yes, sir. I'll count every hair on your body ten times over for that much."

She walked back over to the bed and lay on her front, keeping her head propped up, with her two hands cupped underneath her chin. She said, "You can talk away. Whatever you want to gas about, I'm all ears."

Braun replied, "When I'm good and ready."

"What! So you don't want to talk anymore?" She laughed. "Gee whiz, you just don't know what you want."

Braun tutted. "Look, I ain't some puppet show ready to roll out routines on command. I just wanna lay here for a while, if you'd just lay with me."

Agnes reverted her position and turned onto her back, adjacent to Braun.

He was very horny and would have loved to get busy with her. He had long written off the idea of being able to get hard again, as it had been years, and over that time he'd lost interest with only numbness in that area. But now it was back big time, and he was dying to use it. Despite his desires, though, he vowed not to act upon them. Over the last 24 hours, he'd thieved, murdered, and he shuddered to think what he'd done to the men in the barn earlier in the day. He wanted to show Agnes respect and not use her in the way she was accustomed to. A couple of minutes passed before Braun broke the silence. "What else do you think is out there?"

"Oh, come on, now you want to talk and you're getting all wistful with me."

Braun carried on regardless. "I just mean that I'm forty years old, and all I've seen my entire life is desert, cactuses, and saloons."

Agnes shook her head and corrected him. "First of all, no offence, but you look much older than forty, and at your age you should know that 'cactuses' is wrong. The plural is cacti."

Braun looked perplexed. "Cacti? Plural? Nope." He shook his head. "That don't mean shit to me. My days getting drunk in Ed's didn't really throw a need for me to talk all proper. Anyways..." He smiled, delighted as he sarcastically avenged Agnes' comment about his old looks. "NO OFFENCE, but I wouldn't have thought that correct speaking would be so important to someone in your line of work."

His confusion then led him to ask. "And just how do you know that stuff anyway?"

"Look, mister, I wasn't born with my legs wide apart. Plural means more than one."

"Go on then, tell me, lady. How'd you get to be so smart?"

"Knowing that doesn't make me smart. Somebody told me about it, and it locked into my brain. If you aren't taught something, then how are you supposed to know?" She curled up the corners of her lips in a cheeky smile and looked right into his eyes. "Unless you are just dumb."

Braun was agitated and raised his voice. "You're rude, lady!"

Agnes shook her head. "After a while, being a fun station for fat, disgusting guys will make you kinda rude." She fanned her face with an invisible fan and continued with some of her own sarcasm. "I appreciate you calling me a lady, though."

Braun reached for his flask atop a cabinet on his side of the double bed. He took a swig and spoke out, "Now you can just leave if you're going to be mean."

Agnes softened and brought the conversation back. "I'm sorry, Braun, I don't mean to make you sore. It's just my way of coping with how badly I get treated most of the time."

Braun's bad mood continued to fester, but he didn't persist with his moans as he simply responded, "Uh huh."

Agnes tried to talk him out of his sulk. "C'mon, Braun. Let's get back to what you were saying."

Braun said. "What was I saying?" He pondered for a couple of seconds and continued as he remembered. "That's it. I was talking 'bout how there is so much out there that we don't know shit about. Those twinkly stars we see up in the night sky and all that land across the seas. You hear stories, but without seeing you just can't think it."

Agnes responded, "Seems like you're a frustrated man. Maybe that's why you drink so much."

Braun hung his head with shame. "Maybe."

Agnes broke it down. "It's good to have questions that stretch beyond your own life. If people didn't look outside of their surroundings. we'd all still be scratching our asses in caves."

Braun replied enthusiastically. "Yeah, that's right. You're real smart. I do think about those things."

"Well, why don't you try and figure some of it out? There are plenty of books out there that would help with your questions. I read plenty of the time."

Braun laughed. "C'mon, lady! You think I can read?"

Agnes didn't join in with the laughter. "If you can't read, it's not because you can't do it. It's what I was just saying. If you aren't given the tuition, then you can't just magic it up."

"Can't happen with me, I'm afraid. I've been drunk most every day since I was fifteen years old. Even if I do learn me something, an hour later..." He clicked his fingers. "...it's gone."

"Well, it looks like you're doing okay." She tugged at his jacket. "You got some nice clothes."

Braun shook his head and dusted down his jacket. "These don't mean nothing. I didn't earn my way into these rags."

Agnes looked confused. "Well, you were chucking money around in the bar, and you didn't have any problem paying for my company tonight."

Despite his drunken state, Braun knew better than to tell her the origins of his financial gain, and he turned the chat back onto her. "So, how'd you get to be so smart then?"

Agnes grew frustrated. "You're repeating yourself. I'm not that clever My father was. He taught me to read and write."

Braun was undeterred and asked, "Can you teach me to be clever? I can pay you. You know I got money."

Agnes shook her head. "You just said you're drunk all the time with a fuzzy memory. You just asked me the same question twice in five minutes! How could I teach you anything? And I'll tell you again, I'm not that smart."

Braun responded, "Even if just a little of what you tell me stays in my brain, then that'd be sumthin'."

Agnes enquired, "What led you to become so dependent on the drink?"

"If I knew that, then maybe I wouldn't be so darn tied to it."

"There must be something you're hiding from."

"Hiding! Ha, I ain't hiding. Everyone in town knew I was a good-for-nothing who couldn't cope without the drink. What else is there to do, though, huh? I took my first drink at seven or eight years old, and I couldn't live without the stuff by the time I was fifteen. I grew up in a town that had a grocery store and a saloon.

Nothing else there. Nothing to do. Nowhere to go. No other children to play with. Every time I would pluck up the courage to take off, try and find some adventure, my pa would frighten me with stories of savages, damn Injuns. He'd tell me they'd pick me up, take me back to their camps and serve me up for dinner. Well! That scared the piss out of me."

He stopped for a few seconds and sighed as he placed his hands over his face. His tone became even more downbeat as he continued to speak through his palms. "I ain't proud of how I turned out. Heck, how can I have any joy inside me when the first darn thing that enters my mind each new day is shame and guilt. How I get past things is to drink. It's a trap that I can't break out from."

"Guilt can come from something that you aren't attached to. I see a lot of sad, lost people around here."

"What d'you mean? What do you feel guilty about? You shouldn't feel bad for what you do to make money."

Agnes shook her head. "I don't feel guilty about that. You don't have any idea why I do this. I mean that it can settle itself in other ways. Maybe a darkness floats through the air and people suck it in. I know from what's happened to me in the past that real bad stink festers, and I think it does for a long time. Anyway, you said that you feel guilt. Maybe your father felt guilty, that's why he acted like such a jackass, getting you all nervy with the Indians. He should have encouraged you to spread out a little. You weren't happy where you grew up, nothing to do you said, but those Indians don't have saloons or grocery stores. They explore, they use the land and what it has to offer. Isn't that what you wanted?"

Braun was irritable. He pursed his lips and blew hard through his nostrils a few times before responding. "Now, that's damn stupid. I'm starting to think you ain't so smart after all. Those damn savages have raped our women, they haven't tried to fit into our ways; that is how it is, Agnes. And I *have* heard stories of them eating some of us civilized folk. They ain't human beings, they're no damn better than animals!"

Agnes responded, "Ever thought that they're pissed off? From what I can gather, the settlers took the fight to them first. Claiming this land as their own because their boats made it here." She tutted a few times. "All the nonsense created by our bloods of the past can burrow that guilt you were talking about. Many others feel it, too, I know they do. Folks complain about what life hasn't given them, but they won't stand up for those who get stamped on. The Indians are too often treated like dirt, and I know that lots of folk would be happy if they were all wiped out." She shook her head again, clearly mulling over what else she wanted to say.

Braun could see that this was something she had mused over a lot, and he thought better than to interrupt her.

She breathed deeply and continued. "Thousands of years of tradition... Craftmanship, spiritual beliefs, all things that shaped them. Most around here would have it all gone..."

She clicked her fingers. "...just like that. Pffft, I don't understand it. But what do I know, huh? I'm just a filthy whore." She shot Braun a mock dirty look.

He put his hands up and pulled his own feigned look of shock.

She smiled and went on, "Maybe I don't know any better, but I do wonder if there is a feeling within some, that instead of trying to live and work together peacefully, they would much rather pillage and kill all the Natives. Claim the land, remove the people, remove the guilt."

She hadn't won Braun over, and he got annoyed. "Now hold on a minute, you can walk on out of this room if you're sweet on those animals!" He looked at her accusingly. "Hell, you probably laid with some. Huh?"

Agnes responded sharply. "You have no business asking me that."

Braun shook his head in disgust. "I'm guessing that you have then."

Agnes growled, "Shut the hell up."

Braun apologised. "Sorry, I just don't like them Injuns."

Agnes sighed as she thought how her words had fallen on deaf ears. "Alright, I gathered that."

A brief period of silence followed before Braun asked, "What you doing tomorrow?"

Agnes shrugged, and Braun pressed. "Or the for the whole of next week, for that matter?"

Agnes was confused. "What are you getting at?"

"I'd like to pay for your services for the next week."

"What do you want from me?"

"I want you to teach me to read and write."

"Look, I'm really not that smart. I can read and write, and I have taught children, but I don't know if I would be able to teach an older gentleman."

Braun instinctively knew that his mind was stronger than ever and his responsiveness to absorbing information would be abnormally fast. He could feel it. He was noticing things that wouldn't normally be on his wavelength and his analytical skills were developing rapidly. This was new but exciting to him.

He wasn't certain that Agnes would be able to teach him anything greatly insightful, but all he needed was a grasp of the basics and he'd be able to do the rest from there.

She considered his offer. She wasn't sure about Braun, but the idea enticed her, and she weighed it up against her regular day-to-day encounters. She'd been on the job for only a short while and she'd managed to avoid catching anything too nasty so far, but she knew she was living with a time bomb. *Plus,* she considered, *when would I receive such an unusual but innocent request again?*

She wasn't confident that she could teach him much in a week, but hoping it could lead on to more of the same, she accepted. "Okay, I'm not making any promises. But I'll do my best to give you a little of what I know. And you've got to understand that I can't go straight into this with Shakespeare. So please don't feel like I'm teasing you with the children's books." She thought for a few seconds. "My friend Sandy has got a four-year-old boy, and I can use some of those books. So, if you can promise that you'll go easy on the drink, listen to what I'm saying, and cover the money I'd earn for a week, then you'll have yourself a deal."

Braun rolled over on the bed and offered his hand. She shook it and he answered, "That's swell. We'll start tomorrow, if that's okay with you?"

"I don't have any appointments. I work on a first-come-first-served basis, although it ends up the other way around, if you'll pardon the expression."

Braun ignored the comment and decided that he wanted to turn in for the night. "Well, I don't know about you, but I'm beat, and I want to be as fresh as I can for my first day at school!"

Agnes rolled off the bed, put her shoes on, and walked to the side table next to Braun. She noticed that he'd placed a few coins on there, and she took one. "I'll take this for the night. We'll settle the rest at the end of the week."

"No, you don't have to leave. You're more than welcome to stay here. I won't try anything. I'd just rather know you were safe in my bed tonight."

"Just looking after your prize, huh?" She crossed her arms. "You know, I'm perfectly capable of taking care of myself. I don't need to stay here with you to feel 'safe'. I could make a few extra bucks if I went back down the saloon."

Braun snapped back, "I told you I'd look after your costs, but go ahead and take off if you want, see what you can get. I didn't see a queue lining up down there for you, but things can change, I guess."

"Listen, asshole! Why don't you shut the hell up, you don't know jack about me." She took her shoes off and flopped back onto the bed. "I'll stay over, but spare me the chivalry 'cause you are not such a gentleman. You've pissed me off more than a few times since we met, and I didn't get that drink you promised when you went missing before. Now, if you want to get frisky, you can. You've paid your money."

Braun rolled his eyes. "Damnit, Agnes, can we just hit the hay for the night?"

She stripped down to a corset, tightly packed over a knee-length, white cotton undergarment. She gestured to the cords at the back of the corset. "Can you lend a hand with this?"

He obliged, and when the chord loosened, he was surprised that from the back he could feel a jiggly motion as her breasts and gut dropped. He had to take a step back and extend his reach to finish the removal, as his erection hardened and stretched to the point where he felt like he'd gained an extra half inch over his regular wood.

She quickly turned around and let the untied corset drop to the floor. She noticed Braun's excited mid-section. "Gee whizz! You should go down and get your money back for the room, 'cause we could pitch a tent with that thing."

Braun managed a chuckle and said, "I'll sleep on the floor; you take the bed."

He pulled a sheet off the bed and Agnes laughed. "It's your room. I'll get in with you, this is a big ol' bed. Just don't poke me in the back, okay?"

He slipped into the covers and turned over. "I'll face the other way."

Agnes blew out the candles.

Chapter Four

Six months earlier, further south on the eastern Californian coast, three young men kicked a soccer ball to each other, not very accurately. The leather-covered pig's bladder was misshapen, and the ball bounced off in all sorts of directions against the bumpy sandy terrain.

Puds shouted for the ball and Henning toed it over to him. It was a rare straight pass that Puds was able to control before punting it over to Christen. It didn't make it that far and the game ended abruptly as the ball landed on the campfire, knocking a recently boiled pan of beans over, spilling out all over the sand.

Christen yelled as the ball smouldered. "Puds! That was the last of the food, you fat clumsy ass."

Puds shouted back, "Sorry, boys."

Christen said, "Would you at least try and rescue the ball? I know it may not look much to you, but it was a gift from my father."

This didn't spur Puds into action as he said, "It was no good anyway. We spent half the game chasing the thing down."

Henning ran over to the fire to try and rescue the ball. Pulling a long stick from the base of the fire, he poked at it until it rolled out. It didn't catch ablaze, but the heat melted and shrunk it, curling the leather into a ruined, less than spherical form, with new angles and corners.

Henning stupidly used his hands to try and manipulate the red-hot shape back into something that would at least roll a little. He yelped as it burned his fingers.

The other boys laughed, and Puds shouted, "What did you expect to happen, Henning? You pulled it straight from fire. Even dumb animals know that flesh can't take that kind of heat."

Water was in short supply, so Henning rubbed his fingers in the night-cooled sand. It soothed the burn a little, but he sobbed as the pain began to throb.

Puds laughed. "You ain't nearly as tough as you think you are, Henning." He snorted hard and fast to release his annoyance and muttered, "Crying like a damn girl."

Henning shouted back in a whiny quiver. "Shut your ugly mouth, you fat blob, or I'll throw you into the flames. Let's see how you like it."

Christen jogged over and sat on a dirty old blanket next to the fire. He reached into a drawstringed cotton sack and pulled out a couple more blankets. Laying them alongside his own, he said in his laidback sedate style, "Come on now, boys, we're all alone out here. Let's keep it nice and chipper, uh huh? Just no sense in getting sore with one another."

His voice soothed the situation, and even the three horses, tied up against a nearby rock formation, stopped fidgeting and appeared to settle upon hearing Christen's words through a deep baritone voice, belying his seventeen years.

Henning and Puds took a seat, and Christen boiled up a tin pot of coffee.

He poured them each a cup and said, "We haven't got too much trekking to go. I'd say two or three more days until we get there."

Puds complained, "You said that exact same thing two days ago"

Henning, not wanting to aggravate his burned palm, neglected to keep hold of his drink for more than a few seconds. He placed it carefully on the edge of his blanket and instead occupied his hand with a stone pulled out of his pocket. He used this to sharpen the edge of a six-inch-long hunter's knife.

Christen answered back, "Are you forgetting the forced change of direction we had to take?"

Puds shook his head. "Look, I know we wandered into Injun land, but I didn't think running away from them for a few hours would set us back by goddamn days."

Christen hit back but kept his cool. "Hey! Are you forgetting that it was your decision to head that way? I said it was a bad idea, I told you we'd run into red skins, but did you listen?"

Henning put his knife down and intervened through his raspy heavy smoker's voice. "Alright, we may have lost a few days, but we've got enough food to keep us going for a while, and if we hadn't swerved off of our route, we wouldn't have found that Injun girl. I enjoyed myself at the time, but now I feel funny somehow."

Puds shook his head. "Maybe you two had a whole lot of fun, but she'd lost all her fight when I got on top of her."

Henning smirked. "Hey, I'm all for some wriggle and jiggle, but the bitch was a little too wild for me. I thought I was going to lose the wood in my pecker a couple of times. And when she bit me... Boy, I swear her eyes looked just like a rattlesnake.'"

Puds was uneasy with this talk and tried to reason with himself as much as with Henning. "I sound like a damn hypocrite, but maybe that innocence we stole from her was eating away at you somehow. Making you see things that weren't there."

Christen joined in, shaking his head. "I don't believe that anyone is made of pure innocence. Even the most noble amongst us have evil thoughts."

Puds didn't feel like offering a counter to Christen's opinion. He walked over to Henning and said, "Let me take a look at that."

Henning pulled down the collar of his denim shirt, tapped the wound, and said, "I haven't felt right since it happened, and it won't stop stinging."

Puds winced as he saw the many shades of red surrounding the bite wound. "It actually looks like a snake bite. The girl must have had some real sharp teeth."

Henning looked disturbed as he offered, "Maybe those Injuns really are part animal."

Christen warmed his hands against the fire and sighed. "I'm sick of hearing all that shit. They're nothing but flesh and blood like us. They don't have special fucking magical animal powers. If she did, maybe she'd have kicked our asses, and she wouldn't be buried..." He pointed northeast. "...way out there."

He shrugged his shoulders. "Now what we *should* be worried about is that her people are going to come for us. It's inevitable. Big Mick used to talk about them all the time out on the fields. He was very clued up when it came to Injuns. They came for his friend and they took the guy's head clean off. I'm not exactly sure what it was about, a dispute over land or something, but it don't matter anyway. What I know, and what's important for us to be aware of, is that even with the most limited information, they can still track people for hundreds of miles wide. We've got to be ready and prepared for that."

Puds said, "Relax, we lost them this afternoon. They aren't going to find us now."

Christen was growing frustrated. "Your confidence is foolish and misguided as usual, Puds. They're determined folk, and your suggestion for us to 'relax' is the last thing we want to do. Granted, we need to rest and get some sleep, but not all of us at the same time. We'll take it in turns to keep guard, and as soon as first light hits, we need to get back on the move."

Christen, Henning, and Puds had been riding horseback aimlessly for close to a month after they were abruptly thrown out of the orphanage that had accommodated them since toddler age.

Henning and Christen were non-identical twin brothers, and children of Danish immigrants. Puds (full name Zygmunt Pudsowski) was an only child and Polish born.

The three boys had found themselves on the same orphan train from New York, following unfortunate fates for their parents. The Danes' mother and father were killed in a factory fire two days into their employment. A worker neglected to dispose of a cigarillo properly, sending the garment factory into flames. The fire injured many and killed fifty-seven of the three hundred workers.

Puds' mother died in childbirth back in Tarnow, Poland. Heartbroken and penniless, his father took his baby son with him on a ship to New York, in search of a better life. Unfortunately, things were just as difficult for the Pudsowskis as they had been back home, and after getting caught stealing two whole chickens from a butcher's delivery cart, Mr Pudsowski was sent to jail, and young Puds was packed onto the same Texan-bound train as Christen and Henning.

The brothers and Puds bonded instantly as toddlers, and after a short amount of time, the two Danish boys regarded the Pole as another brother. The connection was so tight that throughout their time at the all-boys orphanage and during the frequent bouts of rich landowners loaning them out for farming work, they would insist on being kept together. The folks that ran the orphanage soon realised that any attempts to separate them was not worth the accompanying violent tantrums. This kept them from being apart during working hours, and they would dorm together with other boys, some who'd pass through for short amounts of time and others who would stay for many years.

Most who met the three boys were intimidated by them and the impenetrable clique they'd formed. They carried an exotic and unusual air about them throughout childhood, despite their infancy on arriving in the United States. Their attitudes and personalities would confuse many of the youngsters who'd come from several generations of American-born families. Most of the orphans would spend their spare time playing marbles or dominoes, but the three Europeans would shun these games and instead would wind down a lot of hours developing games of their own, most of which involved wrestling, kicking, and punching lumps out of each other. Hours would be spent doing this without resentment creeping in. Painful strikes to the stomach and face would be received without tears or fury. Any anger conveyed would be at themselves, as they'd fester in the frustration of not being able to defend themselves properly.

An instinct and a wisdom beyond the two Danish boys' years inspired all their rough and tumble. They hadn't reached adulthood, but they knew that life was going to be tough for them growing up, and opportunities outside farm work would be hard to come by. Even the agricultural employment was barely enough to survive on and was mostly covered by slaves who had no choice but to do the work for nothing, other than keeping a roof over their heads. Therefore, the boys knew that keeping their bodies well trained and fit was important for future survival. If you weren't a rich landowner or a businessman, the majority of work was reliant on physical graft.

Christen would insist on calling the shots. He had a 'made' gangster's demeanour long before the days of the Mafia's influence on American soil. Just a long, disapproving stare could leave people apologising, even if they didn't know what they'd done to piss him off. He was tall throughout childhood and had grown to his full six-foot four height by the age of thirteen.

Now aged seventeen, he looked older than his years and handsome in a classical Scandinavian sense, his unblemished ivory-coloured skin draped tightly over high cheekbones. His jaw, strong and sharp, and his triangular nose, could have been used years later as a photographed template for a top plastic surgeons' catalogue. His blond, curly mid-length hair had never been properly washed, but after a lifetime of natural scalp-oiled cleansing, it had developed a silky texture as soft as a kitten.

The only obstacle in preventing him from being a stunningly handsome man were his eyes. They were an unusual deep orangey brown colour. But as warm as the colour was, they still somehow managed to look cold and devoid of emotion. And if the eyes are truly the window to the soul, his refused to exhibit any evidence to support this. Although his most unattractive feature, they were his most powerful weapon. He could intimidate, overpower, and frighten people with them, and through this he could dominate, control, and bully his way into getting what he wanted.

Henning had beautiful skin, just like his brother, but that is where the similarities ended. Of average height and not blessed with the bone structure or the platinum blond hair of Christen, he bestowed an aura steeped in the average. Mousey-haired, naturally stocky, and quite shy, he was more approachable than his brother, but held a lot less presence.

Puds was the most likable of the three orphans, always keen to learn new skills, and enthusiastic about life despite the poor hand he'd been dealt. It was unfortunate that any progress or potential he wished to have was permanently diminished by a dim and slow personality. His oafishness was his defining characteristic, and it was this trait that frustrated and endeared him to the brothers in equal measure. Over the years, he provided countless hours of much needed drama to otherwise long periods of tedium growing up in the orphanage and as they travelled aimlessly throughout lengthy stretches of desert.

His nickname of Puds was derived from his surname Pudsowski, but it also somehow phonetically suited his rotund shape. He loved the brothers and would take anything they threw at him, both good and bad, always fully aware of the struggles he'd face without their company. The relationship he had created with them was akin to a canine with a loyalty split between two owners.

At 6:04 am, Christen woke first. The other boys slept in a tent, but if the weather allowed, Christen often opted to sleep under the stars wrapped up in a canvas roll. This meant that he was normally the first to wake, and today was no different.

The sun appeared to rise out of two distant sand dunes and shimmered hazily in the desert sky. Christen glanced in its direction, knowing that any subsequent image for the rest of the day would pale in significance. He delayed waking the others as he wanted to soak in the glory of the sunrise for a little longer. He sat up slowly and squinted enough to be able to protect his eyes, but not too much that it would askew the backdrop, the beautiful view that lifted his spirits going into the new day. His whole body basked in it, and all his travel-worn aches and pains briefly dissipated. Still, he could not fully relax, as he knew the peace would be broken at any second, and sure enough Henning started coughing and hocking up in preparation to release a build-up of yellowy smoker's saliva.

He quickly stumbled out of the tent and rubbed his eyes when the light hit them. Briefly blind to his surroundings, he spat out two gooey chunks in Christen's direction. The first one easily hurdled his brother, but the second didn't quite achieve this and left a salival lump hanging off his right knee.

The peace had been abruptly broken and Christen angrily shouted, "HENNING, YOU GODDAMN FILTHY SON OF A WHORE. I OUGHT TO WIPE YOUR FUCKING STUPID FACE IN IT."

Henning chuckled and hit back, "Hey, don't speak of Mother like that!"

Christen sighed. "It's just a damn turn of phrase."

Henning shook his head. "Maybe so, but it doesn't work when you share the same mother, idiot."

Christen quickly rose to a squatted position and threw his body into a shoulder-led spear, tackling Henning to the ground. Henning thrashed about, but Christen used his superior size and strength to pin him to the floor.

Henning complained, "Get the fuck off me."

Christen ignored him, and his efforts were expressed through grunts and wheezes.

Henning tried again. "I mean it, Christen. You should get off me. Your breath stinks. It will make me sick if you're not careful. Then that spit on your knee won't be such a fucking concern."

Christen slowly raised his knees up to Henning's chest while his arms continued to hold him down. He was careful not to allow the tip of his right knee to brush against his brother's chest, and continued moving it until it reached his mouth. He transferred the saliva from his knee and wiped it all over Henning's lips.

The pressure of the knee against his mouth hurt, and Henning groaned through the pain and discomfort. Christen recognised this and pulled his knees back down. He expected a reaction from Henning, so he persisted with the restraint for a short while longer.

Henning said, "You know, Christen, that came from my own mouth, so it really doesn't bother me that you've just put it back."

Christen retaliated pettily and spat several of his own hocks towards Henning's mouth. Some of it crept in, then Christen climbed off him. He jumped back and laughed as Henning started spitting wildly to remove any trace of Christen's phlegm from his mouth.

"You're fucking disgusting, Christen. I can taste the shit flavour from your mouth."

Christen wasn't bothered by this and carried on laughing as Puds climbed out of the tent. He'd heard the mini row and started the day sarcastically by saying, "Ain't it good to be alive!"

Neither boy greeted him, while Henning directed more anger at his brother.

"You know, Christen, if you weren't my brother, I would have put a knife through your eye by now. And if you keep pushing me like this, I swear that one day you will really regret it."

Christen didn't take him seriously. "You can keep talking like that, Henning. It doesn't worry me, because I know that whatever you think you've got, I have much more."

Puds wedged between them as they eyeballed each other for a couple of seconds. "Now, come on, you two. Stop this. We need to get back on the road. I know you're hungry and we could all do with a good wash. Especially you, Christen, by the sounds of it."

The three of them laughed as Puds continued, "So, how about we end the horseplay and focus on getting to the nearest town? We need to try and get some work and settle down for a short while."

It was unusual for Puds to be the sensible voice of the group, and due to the rarity of this, it weighted the impact and the boys nodded in agreement.

Half an hour later they were back on the road, and after several hours of drifting, they struck some luck and reached the small town of Goaville. The town, if you could call it that, was only made up of a few single-floored shacks of mostly residence-based purpose, but in-between a couple of pole-constructed, stone-based and straw-roofed structures were used as stores.

As the only people who had entered the territory in days, the three boys instantly drew attention. They weren't planning on staying long, and their sole intention was to try and fleece the area for whatever they could get before moving on to a livelier town. With some money in their pockets or decent swag to sell, they could have fun and indulge in the things that interested them, namely drinking and screwing.

Rain had fallen briefly but heavily in Goaville the previous night. It was the town's first shower in weeks, and the formerly dry, dusty terrain had become a gloopy, sticky pallet of mud. The horses hated it and alternated between a frantic canter as they strove to plough through it, and moments of stationary defeat. They grunted and whined throughout the stickier patches, and the boys had to smack them a little harder than usual just to get them through to the central part of the village.

They trotted past a toothless, elderly woman who was sitting on a blanket on the muddy floor, hammering horseshoes into shape. Henning tipped his hat to greet her, and she laughed in response through a witchy cackle that perfectly fitted her appearance. They soon passed her and ran into three young boys standing in a pig pen, filling a trough with a dark brown oily-looking swill that made Puds gag.

He shouted over to them. "What you boys feeding them pigs? Damn, stinks like somebody's pooped out rotting bear meat!"

Christen laughed. "That's pretty knowing, Puds! You smelt that sort of thing before?"

Puds shook his head. "Hell no, but whatever they're feeding that pig might just be the foulest thing that my nostrils have ever had the misfortune to smell."

Christen nodded. "I have to agree. I actually feel sorry for those stinking pigs, if that is all they've got."

The kids, aged between four and eight, looked confused as Puds reiterated his question. "Come on then, boys. Just what is that awful looking and foul-smelling delicacy that you're giving them little piggies?"

One kid – a small, fair headed, freckly eight-year-old – looked down at the floor and pulled at his dungarees as he answered shyly. "Some of it was from Poppa's bed bucket. I think some corn is in there, and food from plates that we didn't finish."

Puds groaned. "Poppa's bed bucket! Aw lord, no wonder the goddamn thing smells so awful. Now I really do feel sorry for those little hams chowing down on that."

The kids didn't know how to react, and two of them ran towards the far end of the pen as the freckled boy continued to pour the swill into the trough. Blissfully unaware, the pigs buried their faces in the muck and lapped up the vile slop they'd been presented.

The boys carried on down the straight path, passing several shacks, most of which were on the right side of the road. The left seemed to have inhabited some sort of dumping ground purpose, and piles of discarded instruments such as buckets, wheelbarrows, and shredded material had been scattered over yards and yards of wasteland. Christen shook his head in disgust as he rode past the mess. This area made up the last of the particularly muddy terrain, and as the horses turned onto a more trotter-friendly, mildly bumpy, but dry, dusty floor, their spirits lifted and their noses snorted pronounced sounds of happiness to punctuate the otherwise quiet town.

One of the few buildings on this side was the best designed, and the last before wilderness again dominated the landscape. The boys had written the town off as nothing more than a run-down pass through when they pulled up outside the place. They were immediately interested when they saw two steps leading up to a landing area outside the small wooden building, upon which hung a wonkily-nailed, plywood sign with the name: 'P. L. Roberts Tobacconist and Groceries. Est 1878.'

Christen took particular interest in the date. *1878,* he thought. *One year ago.* Figuring that P. L. Roberts or whoever worked there was obviously newly established, he became wickedly optimistic. He was in front of the other boys, and he steadied his horse, prompting Puds and Henning to follow suit.

He climbed off the horse, nodded at the sign, and said with a grin, "Time to stock up, boys."

Henning and Puds followed as Christen pushed the door open and entered the shop. Before them was a short and slim, well-presented man in his late thirties, sitting on a tall stool behind a very cluttered counter. Jars of ground tobacco, tea leaves, roll-up papers, and hand carved wooden pipes, amongst other things, were spread across most of the surface. It was all high-quality produce but presented in a very higgledy-piggledy fashion, and without asking the shop clerk, it would have been difficult to be able to find exactly what you wanted.

The clerk wasn't used to seeing three young men travelling together, and although he tried to hide his suspicion, it was written across a serious and wide-eyed expression as he greeted them. "Good morning, young fellas. What can I do you for?"

Christen was pleased with the low-key welcome they received. Naturally defensive and argumentative, he was comfortable when an opportunity to be obnoxious presented itself. Yet, he preferred to build up his intensity, and decided to bide his time with the man.

"Hello, sir. We are fine, thank you."

Puds tapped him on the shoulder and said, "He didn't ask of our welfare, Christen."

Christen felt his blood boil – not with the man, but with Puds for saying his name. He didn't think it would play a factor in this situation, but it maddened him that Puds would use such bad practice and bandy his name around so freely. He'd spoken to him about this several times in the past, and he was at the end of his tether. He made a mental note to give his friend a beat down later and try and knock it into him. He'd call it tough love, but it was more straightforward than that. Clubbing lumps into each other seemed to be the only way the three boys were able to resolve anything.

The man detected a strange vibe from the young men and opted to offer a little more friendliness. "You boys on your travels?"

Christen handled the response. "Yes, I wouldn't say we are travelling to anywhere in particular. We're just wandering until we find somewhere worth sticking around."

Christen fingered through some of the smoking paraphernalia as the man answered with a chuckle, "Well, I don't think you boys will want to be hanging around this place for too long."

Puds intervened, "We'll be the judge of that!"

Christen sighed; again Puds had frustrated him. He wanted to toy with the man for a while before going straight in with a potentially argumentative remark.

The man answered back sarcastically but playfully, "Go ahead then, pitch up here. Plenty to enjoy around these parts. You've got the garbage pile on one side and the pigs on the other. Oh, and you'll be thrilled to know that we had a bad case of dysentery here a few months back. It wiped out half the area, but I wouldn't let that put you boys off."

He smiled, and Henning, sensing a simmering tension between the other two, answered quickly before Puds irritated Christen further. "You get a lot of business here then, my friend? I can't imagine the store is booming in such a little piece of shit town, or whatever the fuck you'd call this muddy, boxed-up patch of land."

The man tried to answer him, but Henning continued to speak. "It must be worth your while, otherwise why would you stand in this dark, stuffy little room all day, huh? Missing so much of the beautiful sunshine out there."

The man answered, "The last few days have been real quiet, but I do okay. A lot of passing trade keeps this place ticking over. Travellers and all, just like you boys." He suddenly became distracted by Christen, who was cackhandedly rummaging through rows of pipes. "Just be careful with them please, son. They're rather delicate"

Christen took a shine to one dark wooded pipe with a large bowl. He held it to the light and asked, "Just what is the end of this pipe made out of?"

The man responded, "I'm not entirely sure, son. I'd assume it's derived from an animal of some sort."

Christen looked confused. "An animal of some sort? Okay, sir. I gotta say that ain't exactly too helpful, you know. For a shopkeeper, and one not holding tons of produce, it should be a relatively straightforward question."

The man's irritation levels increased. "No, just hold on a minute. Look around..." He gestured to the rest of the shop. "...I've probably got several hundred different items for sale in here. Not 'tons of produce', but still all kinds of things." He sighed. "Now you really expect me to be able to know just what materials are used in everything I'm holding here?"

Christen laughed as the other boys looked around the store. He responded, "No, sir. I think it's pretty obvious what most of the other things are made of." He pointed over to the food products before picking up the pipe.

"But this thing is real nice. Seems like I'd call it one of your special shiny things in this shitty little store." He slammed his hand against the counter several times and raised his voice slightly. "You should KNOW what this is made out of!"

Henning moved closer to Christen to look at the pipe. The man was perplexed as Henning weighed in. "I agree, sir. I'm also intrigued as to the origins of this unusual looking material." He pulled Puds into the conversation. "How's about you, buddy? Does this quaint li'l pipe pique your interest?"

The shop clerk became nervous as Puds wiped his nose on his sleeve and joined in with the silly game. "Yes, I must say, it was the first thing I noticed when I entered the shop. I don't smoke a pipe, but the thing is just so damn nice that I'm tempted to part with my money. I can only imagine the admiring looks I'd get chugging on such a well-crafted piece."

The clerk intervened. "Boys, I really don't where are you going with this nonsense but—"

Christen took over again. "Did you hear that?" He pointed to Puds. "My good friend is interested in purchasing this pipe. He even said he ain't a pipe man! However, he is so taken with it, that he'd be prepared to buy it anyway! Now what do you think of that, sir?"

The clerk didn't like where this was heading and changed tact momentarily as he considered whether playing along with the preposterous conversation might be the best way to avoid things escalating. He answered, "Well sure, if he wants to buy it. It's a damn fine-looking pipe. Real swell, son. I'll ring it up if you want it, and... I'll wrap it real nice for you."

Henning looked at Puds. "Half price, huh? Whaddya say, buddy? You want it?"

Puds' facial expression took a very serious turn. "Don't want it no more."

Christen picked it up again. "Changed your mind, huh?"

"Yup."

Christen closed his eyes and shook his head slowly. "Is that because you don't know what materials are used to give it that... hmmm... that real special look?"

"Yup," answered Puds again.

Christen continued, "I understand, my friend." He put his arm around Puds. "Now, I know we've established that you ain't a pipe man, but suppose you took up the habit and somebody, perhaps a potential acquaintance, may ask you about the materials used to construct such a marvellous display of craftmanship."

Puds took up his prompt and responded, "I wouldn't be able to tell them!"

Christen laid it on some more. "Exactly. You'd look like a damn fool and all because this…"

He pointed at the clerk and raised his voice. "… ASSHOLE DOESN'T KNOW WHAT THE DAMN THING IS MADE OUT OF."

Henning sensed things heating up, and he released a faint but excited little squeal.

The man lost his composure at this point. He knew this wasn't going to stop until things got nasty, and although he suspected the boys were armed, he himself had a small pistol holstered up against his right trouser pocket.

The odds were against him, so he neglected any temptation to be hasty as he shouted back. "Look, just what is your problem? This whole thing is so damned stupid. I'm real sorry that I can't tell you what the darn thing is made from. Okay? All I know is that some Injuns gave me a few dozen of these some months back in exchange for food."

Christen immediately dropped the pipe and said, "Eeeww."

Puds started yelling. "INJUNS! YOU SELLING STUFF THAT'S COME FROM DAMN REDSKINS?"

The man responded, "You may have a problem with them, but I sure don't. God made man and I don't argue with his work. Although, I'm now thinking that he must move his eyes from the production line every now and again, seeing as you three managed to slip through!"

Christen said, "Well, your God brought us to your shop today, and do you think he'll intervene if you get into trouble? Or is this your fault? Has your free will led you to this place?" He punched the air and shouted, "AND THIS MOMENT?"

The man fingered his gun a little more, as beads of sweat formed on his forehead. He had never shot a man before, and he was nowhere near confident that he'd be able to outgun three dangerous young men who'd clearly had more experience than him in face-offs. He knew that any chance of getting out of this with, at best, life-altering injuries, were extremely slim. Yet he figured that his best bet still relied on trying to talk to them and keeping his cool.

God had been relatively kind to Patrick Roberts, and he hoped that his Lord Almighty would somehow see him through the escalating tension. He knew the boys were plundering for some action, and they would twist whatever he said into some sort of faked offence.

Patrick had worked hard for this shop; he hadn't just inherited it from a family member. He'd been one of those kids on the other side of the road tending to the pigs. He ended up breeding them and made his money that way. He'd lived on the minimal amount of basic food that his body could survive on, and every spare penny that he could save was put away in his hope to one day open a store, work for himself, and serve the local people whom he deeply cared about. He had achieved his dream seven months prior to this day, and now these little punks had entered his life, ready to take it away.

He needed to channel his God. He needed the Lord to protect him now. He responded as such. "The Lord can be there for you, too, boys. Maybe you haven't had Him in your life, but if you walk out of this shop today without doing me or yourselves any harm, that could be the breakthrough you need. You can bring Him into your lives today. Free yourselves of sin and become better people."

Puds shouted sarcastically, "HALLELUJAH, MY BROTHERS!"

Christen shook his head. "I appreciate you thinking of us, sir, and your efforts to save us. But it don't work like that for me and my boys, I'm afraid. See, this mighty, all-seeing, all-knowing bearded gentleman that everyone talks about doesn't seem to give a shit about my brothers, nor me. If he did, I don't think he'd have left us with dead or absent parents when we were too fucking small to understand anything."

Even through his fear the clerk couldn't resist a dig. "I knew you were a bunch of bastards when you came in. Figuratively, of course, but now I know you qualify on both counts."

Christen ignored this comment and continued. "Anyway. We are nomadic citizens of this planet, and we don't follow 'the rules'. So, all that talk about sin is no good to me. I didn't ask to be born into this madness, yet I am meant to follow these special rules? RULES! to a game that I didn't ask to play? Don't seem right to me."

Henning looked riled and decided it was time to join in. "We grew up in an orphanage, living with a bunch of nuns and a priest. They were meant to be God-fearing, upstanding types. They'd yack on about how this is a sin, that is a sin. Don't do this, don't do that. But it didn't stop them beating the shit out of us all the fucking time."

The man hung his head and said, "Look, I am sorry if you boys had a tough time growing up. I wish it could have been different for you. But that was the hand that God dealt you. Life is a lesson. Some people need to suffer to make them strong. Greatness can come from suffering."

Christen flinched a little; his game playing had taken him somewhere that he didn't intend to go. He wanted to end this and he was getting ready to draw. "The last time we found ourselves in a store like this was about fifty miles south of here." He turned to Puds and said, "You remember that picture behind the counter in that little old shop?"

Puds nodded and said, "Sure, the one with the swell looking cowboy holding..." He pulled his gun out of his holster. "...a gun just like this one!"

He held it up to show Patrick. He wasn't ready to use it, but Patrick raised his hands and said, "Easy now, son."

Puds stared at the gun proudly and said, "I bought this gun from that store just on the strength of that picture!"

Christen took over again as Henning grinned excitedly with his arms folded. "Do you remember asking me about the words, all nicely gathered over the cowboy's head?"

Puds responded, "Sure. I knew the word God, but my reading ain't too good, you see."

Christen prompted his friend a little more. "Go on then, buddy, tell the man what it said."

Puds cleared his throat a couple of times, placed one hand on his chest, and said, "God created man..." He paused for dramatic effect. "Excuse me." He cleared his throat a further time then finished his sentence. "But Samuel Colt made them equal."

The man pulled out his pistol, but he wasn't fast enough. His focus on Puds was set up as a decoy and left him misdirected, as Christen drew first, firing a bullet straight into the centre of Patrick's chest.

He dropped his gun, clutching the wound with one hand, leaving the other hand rallying with instinct as it implored him to reach out for something that wasn't there. All he managed to do was pull a chunk of the goods from the counter onto the floor with him.

Small piles of tobacco pouches, matches, and rolling papers joined him as he struck the floor with a thud, gasping for breath. He still had a little life in him, although he knew it was rapidly ebbing away.

Christen started grabbing boxes of bullets. He turned to his friends and said, "Get ransacking, boys!"

He pointed to a couple of sacks near the door that looked like un-shelved deliveries. "Empty a couple of those sacks out. But don't take too much. We don't want to be hauling too heavy a load."

Puds emptied a sack containing potatoes and started filling it with tobacco, tinned boxes of beans, and bags of oatmeal. In his keenness, he grabbed a couple of eggs from a shelf and clumsily cracked them in his hand. The egg white and yolk ran down his arm, and Christen started laughing.

"It wasn't wise to grab all those eggs now, was it, Puds? Did you think they'd stay whole in that big old sack, tied up against the fucking horse's ass?"

Puds tried wiping the sticky residue off his arm while Christen goaded him further. "They will fry on your arm out there in the sunshine today! But I guess it will give you something to snack on later."

Henning picked the pipe up from the floor and walked slowly around the counter to speak to the dying man. Patrick was clutching his chest and breathing manically through desperate, short, fast breaths.

Henning knelt next to him and quietly spoke. "I'm sure you're dying to know." He stopped and covered his mouth with his hand. "Forgive me, my friend. Bad choice of words. Let's start again."

The man looked at him hopelessly through his instinctive but futile battle against imminent death.

"Okay, just so you know, and as useless as this is. Aw shit, seeing as you're seconds from dying and all, but as it cost you your life..." He held the pipe to Patrick's face, leant in, and whispered right into his ear. "...I'll just go ahead and tell you. Now, I can confirm that your obvious assumption of an animal link to the material was correct. This pretty little thing is in fact clearly made from elk horn."

The man's eyes opened wide, and he said through a weak quivered tone, "Please, don't leave me like this."

Henning nodded. "Oh, don't worry. I'll gladly finish you off, and I'll take that half price deal you offered my friend over there for this. Shall we call it five cents?"

The man whispered weakly, "Please, son, I have a wife to care for."

Henning walked over to the register and placed a coin next to it. Following this, he took the gun out of his left holster and fired four shots into the man. No great aim was produced, and bullets flew through Patrick's left cheek, crotch, and stomach. The man's head slumped to the side.

Puds dropped his sack and protested, "You two always get to do all the shooting. It ain't fair."

Christen snapped back. "Nothing to stop you firing a couple of slugs into him now, Puds. I'm not too concerned with ammo waste now we've hoarded up."

Puds whinged, "It ain't fun when they're already dead."

Puds' petulance frustrated Christen, and he shouted. "YOU COULD HAVE FINISHED HIM THEN. I'm sure Henning wouldn't have minded."

Henning shrugged and said, "Hey, he was all yours if you wanted him."

Christen continued, "But you were too damn busy thinking of food, as always." He looked at the sack which was full of tins and boxes. "We don't need all that stuff, you greedy fat shit. The horses won't be able to carry all that."

Puds, seeing that Christen was getting wound up, submitted. "I'll put some back."

Henning noticed a key attached to a necklace around Patrick's neck. He pulled it over the man's head and got some blood on his hands. He hated the feel of it. It was cold and it left him uneasy. He wiped it on the man's collar and tossed the necklace over to Christen.

"Lock that front door, Christen. I don't want us to have to start shooting any more. We don't need a big stack of bodies to deal with."

Christen obliged, locked the door, and turned the 'Open for business' sign around to the other side, which said 'Sorry we're closed'.

He ordered, "Just get a fucking stick of dynamite up your asses. We need to get out of here."

Puds answered, "There is nobody around here apart from those kids half a mile back. We could sit down and prepare some food if we wanted, especially now that door's locked."

Henning was interested in the back room of the store. It was behind a half-closed door, and he could see lots of boxes. He also noticed a little bird contained in a medium-sized, all-wire, German-style bird cage. A chestnut-backed chickadee was walking back and forth across a branch that had been accustomed to fit inside the cage. The small bird was very quiet, but Henning could hear it release its song through repeated patterns of two short, rapid, high-pitched chirps, followed by a third note that held the pitch for a little longer.

Henning was excited to see it and walked behind the counter to reach the room. Christen was looking around the store while Puds deliberated over weight issues with the sack.

Patrick's body had crumpled into a seated position, surrounded by a pool of blood. His head was slumped to the side, with a hole in his cheek big enough to be able to see his teeth and gums. The space he occupied was at the entry side of the counter. There wasn't a great deal of room between the back wall and the post underneath the counter, so his legs had bunched up in an unnatural way.

Henning could have climbed over the counter, but he decided to pass over Patrick instead to access the back room. In doing this, he caught his right foot on Patrick's belt, sending him to the floor and cracking his head against a tobacco tin. His elbows and knees took the rest against the solid ground. He shouted, "OW!"

This greatly angered Henning and furthered the laughter coming from the other two. He got up slowly, trying to work out where the emanation of pain was at its worst. Deciding to rub his knees first, he suspected that it was the blow to the head that would prove to be the most bothersome in the coming days.

He shouted out to the other boys snidely, "Oh, I appreciate your concern, but fear not, I'm dandy. Though I'm afraid that if my brain starts oozing out of my ear later on, you may have something unpleasant to deal with."

Puds laughed. "I don't reckon there's anything in there to leak out."

Henning ignored Puds' jibe and pulled the door leading to the back room. It was a very cramped and tight space, windowless, with two chairs and a large wooden table just as cluttered as the counter in the shop. Piles of books lay atop; reading material and the sort kept for figures and records. This dominated an otherwise characterless room, and its purpose appeared to be an office space with facilities designed for breaks. On one end of the table, seven large jars were stacked with coins. Henning spotted these instantly and manoeuvred around the table to get to them, ignoring the bird perched in the cage at first.

The bird looked at Henning and tilted her head to one side. She chirped and walked laterally across to the side of the cage where she could get a good look at him. He smiled at her and poured the money from the jars onto the table. Concentrating on the higher value coins, he stuffed them into his near empty coin pouch.

He shouted over. "Hey, toss me over your purses. We've got a nice amount of money back here."

With their pouches just as barren as Henning's, they eagerly complied as Puds requested, "Fill it with dollar coins."

Henning laughed. "I like your optimism, Puds, but it's mostly dimes and quarters here."

He loaded up the other two pouches until they were bursting at the seams and, looking around at the remaining coins, he was satisfied that he'd gathered up those with the most value.

He stuffed them down his pockets and immediately felt uncomfortable with the weight. He was quickly distracted from this, though, as he looked at the bird and made a strange clicking sound with his tongue in the fashion that humans seem to have adopted as a universal communication device for all animals, regardless of species. She was friendly and responded to the attention, staring right back at him as her head tilted from one side to the other.

He wrongfully assumed she was male and said, "Hello there, little fella."

He tickled her beak and she tamely accepted this.

Christen came into the small room. "Henning, can we get the fuck out of here?"

Henning turned to his brother. "Can we take him with us?"

Christen shook his head. "I'll deal with the bird."

Henning's eyes opened wide and his bottom lip quivered slightly. "You aren't going to hurt him?"

Christen was offended. "Of course not! I'm going to let it go"

Henning protested, "You can't let him go! He lives in here! You keep something in a cage, and they don't know anything else. He won't survive a minute out there."

Christen was annoyed. "It's a wild bird, Henning, you idiot. It shouldn't be in this cage to begin with!"

Henning was doubtful. "He don't look wild to me. He was letting me stroke his beak."

Christen shook his head. "Of course it was! It's been tamed and will be reliant on food handouts. I can't believe the man had the poor thing caged up in this stuffy little room. There isn't even a window for it to look out of."

Henning was often easily swayed by his brother and saw his point. "Yeah, I suppose you're right. It does seem rather mean to keep him all caged up in here like this."

Christen reached over to stroke the bird's head a couple of times. "Damn right it's mean. I don't understand it. I reckon that man was pissed at being stuck in this shop all day long. Probably wanted something else to suffer the same fate. Asshole. You ask most people what they wish they could do outside the many limitations we have as a species."

Henning responded, "You mean to able to fuck ourselves somehow?"

Christen slapped his head. "No, you dummy! Though, I understand that coming from you. You don't think like the average person, which is good most of the time, Henning, but it also makes me worry about you when you come out with peculiar things like that!"

Christen wasn't joking, but Henning laughed anyway as he responded, "What d'you mean then?"

"FLY," Christen shouted. "To be able to soar up into the sky, travelling way up there through the wind, tearing through the clouds for miles and miles all day, every fucking day without feeling weary and tired. Enjoying the big and the small with everything in full view."

Henning nodded his head. "Yeah, that would be good."

Christen agreed. "It would be incredible. But how can people restrain something that is able to achieve such a magnificent thing? They capture it and keep it caged up, forbidding it from doing what nature intended its very purpose for. They remove that natural essence from them. It really pisses me off. Do people feel so alone that they want to impound others that are free and attach them to their own fate?"

Henning could see his brother getting wound up and said, "We've done some cruel things of our own, Christen, but I agree that we need to take him out of here and watch him fly off into the clouds."

Christen smiled and put his arm around Henning. "Come on then, let's get ourselves, and the bird, out of here."

Christen took the cage from the table, and they passed through the door to the main room of the store again, joining a bored looking Puds as he sat on the floor next to a couple of sacks.

He asked, "What's holding us up, boys?"

Christen pointed to the bird and walked towards the door with the cage. "Our new feathered friend is going first."

A few yards before he reached the handle, the boys heard a knock on the door and a female said through a raised voice, "Patrick. Why have you locked the door? You know I don't have keys."

The three young men froze and looked at each other. Puds put his index finger to his lips, gesturing for everyone to keep quiet.

Christen placed the cage down on the floor and raised his hand to the other two, beckoning them to leave the next move to him. Puds sat back down on the sack, and Henning moved to the side of the shop to stand next to him. They both looked at Christen, waiting for directions, as the woman knocked on the door a few more times.

"Come on, Pat. It's windy out here, and the dust is making me sneeze." She duly followed this comment by sneezing a couple of times and continued, "I don't understand why you've closed the shop."

She knocked again a few more times. "Patrick."

Christen knew he had to react quickly. He didn't want her queries to prolong and potentially face the prospect of her taking off to enlist the help of others.

Patrick's wife Agnes had been teaching children throughout the morning in a one-room shack down the road. It was such a tiny space that they could only fit a few kids in at a time. This didn't pose a lot of problems, as the small town only contained two dozen children, but it meant that she and her teacher friend had to rotate the classes with different groups of kids taught at scheduled times. Her friend had just taken over for the afternoon, and Agnes was coming back to the shop to help out.

She rapped her knuckles against the door a few more times and said, "Patrick, I'm getting worried. Will you open the door now, please?"

It was at this point that Christen acted and turned the key, purposely rattling it around a few times in the hole, in a way so she could hear. Once unlocked, he pulled the door across fast and he was instantly grateful that Agnes was stood right against it, leaving him able to place one hand over her mouth while his other arm was long enough to reach around her small frame. He pulled her tightly into him, muffling her screams.

Chapter Five

Agnes couldn't snap out of a psychological shock – a manifestation her body developed the instant she was so violently pulled into her husband's shop.

The buttons from her blouse had been ripped off, and the top half of her body was exposed with four fingernail-produced cuts, three on her left breast, the deepest and ugliest in a jagged pattern over her right. They were a souvenir of the life-altering violations that she had no choice but to succumb to, and now she was left in a completely despondent state.

Her mind struggled to compute the storm of emotional turmoil that the last half an hour had given her. The grief of losing her husband, the man she had fallen in love with twenty years prior, the man who had always vowed to protect her but had been unable to live up to that promise. His corpse watched helplessly as those boys did such terrible things to her, and all she could do now was lie and stare into space as her friend Margaret stood over her, trying to offer reassurance that she would be okay.

She didn't know whether to feel grateful when Margaret, her husband Peter, and Rupert the local lunatic had turned up to interrupt the boys' actions. The horror felt fully realised when they arrived and bust down the door. Shock had immobilized any ability to fight back and drifted her mind to a place of numbed nothingness. And although she was acutely aware of the fat boy slapping her across the face and grunting throughout his forced penetration, this defence mechanism had somehow almost left her paralysed from top to toe, and she was able to experience a full body shutdown that took away some sensory awareness.

The duration of the horror had been spent with her imaginative and loyal brain helping her out, conveying the thought that what was happening was not real and merely the product of a bad dream. This helped her to survive the ordeal, but the illusion was slaughtered when the familiar faces entered the fray.

Immediately, reality set in and ended the underwater sensation she'd been cocooned up in the whole time, incredibly distressed but able to breathe somehow. Peter and Rupert bust the door down, and she was abruptly pulled out of the imaginary water by her hair. Her heartbeat began racing at an uncontrollable pace, easily enough to put a less healthy person into a coronary. The stupefied state that her body had placed her in had changed to the harsh and unforgiving reality of the situation.

Peter shouted, "What in the Hell's going on here?"

She instantly felt the fat boy slide out of her, and the screaming began for the first time since her initial cries for help. The tall blond boy had stopped her that time, and she'd self-imposed a refusal to allow any screams, wails, or cries throughout the humiliation that had been inflicted on her.

Agnes had only ever been intimate with Patrick, and the act had always been something she'd associated with love and tenderness. Even after their attempts to bear children had been met with two stillbirths, it didn't deter them from regular lovemaking, and knowing that they could not add to their family only strengthened their dependency and devotion to each other. Now she was left with a whole new experience of the act – one of violation and violence. What was once only known to her as an uncontrollable urge to feel love and connection had been destroyed, and it almost seemed painfully symbolic that the death of this feeling was watched over by the dead, empty vessel of the man who'd once made it so perfect.

The three boys, the two men, and Margaret were armed, and the situation quickly entered into a stand-off.

Shouting and negotiation attempts were thrown back and forth, but to Agnes, it all sounded faint and hopeless. She didn't care how it panned out as she lay on her side thinking about how incredibly unfair it was that three strangers could have left her life in ruins. How could such coldness exist in people? That they'd be prepared to take a man's life and a woman's dignity? It would probably be a fleeting moment in the lives of such evil. Something they might discuss and laugh about over the campfire with complete disregard for the real devastation, that they'd just ended a marriage and years of happiness for the sake of a few minutes of sick and depraved gratification.

At one point, the first boy likened it to having sex with a corpse. Upon that remark, Agnes had a disconsolate will that he would kill her. If that's how he felt, it wouldn't have made much of a difference to his pleasure gauge, but no, he just carried on anyway.

Despite the two rapes, it was the tall blond boy who she held the most hate for. He declined the opportunity to have his own session and merely sat on top of a crate next to the door and calmly read a book as his two buddies had their fun. She looked at him, sitting there, seemingly without a care in the world, patiently waiting for his friends to be done, looking over and smiling at her occasionally as though he were pleased that his friends were getting what they wanted while she was thrown into the worst private hell she could have imagined. He seemed the most twisted of the three. The others were at least operating on some sort of primal urge, but he practically facilitated the whole process. She thought that she'd even possibly struggle to identify the two rapists. She kept her eyes off them as much as possible, although the fatty was of a large size that was unusual for the time. But the other boy, the overseer, she would never forget him. And she knew that his face, his icy, brown button eyes would be imprinted on her mind for the rest of her days.

A gunfight ensued between the two parties. A few shots were fired until the two men and Margaret retreated out of the shop to withdraw their attack.

The boys grabbed what they could and exited. Agnes, as she was lying down, caught sight of part of Patrick and could see some of his right leg, arm, and shoulder. She couldn't bear to see him swimming in such a thick, gloopy pool of blood, so she turned to the other side. Then she saw the caged bird. She recognised the cage as being an old keepsake of Patrick's mother's, but she didn't know where the bird had come from.

It trotted from side to side, and she noticed that its left wing hung lower than the right. Clearly suffering from an injured or broken wing, Agnes briefly moved away from herself in sympathy for the bird.

Chapter Six

The boys managed to get out of the town mostly unscathed, although Henning lost an earlobe after one of Margaret's bullets just missed her intended – right between the eyes – target. This didn't bother him too much as his concern was preoccupied with the bite mark on his neck inflicted by the native American girl. He'd been long feeling it, but he'd received a shock when he noticed its appearance through a small mirror in the shop. It was getting angrier and expanding as it now formed a strange, cobbled, light purple and green pattern over one-third of his neck.

A weird bitter smell was produced from the mark, and every so often Henning swore that from the corner of his eye he could see wavy lines of vapor floating away from it. He'd convinced himself that the girl had fixed this, and that the vapor release was designed as a scent track for her friends to follow them. He kept this thought from the other boys for fear of being branded crazy.

On a couple of occasions he was close to shouting them over when he thought he could see the vapor, but every time he'd turn to look at it properly, a sudden evaporation occurred, as though the wound was playing tricks on him. It became all he could think about. High anxiety pestered and probed him, and he struggled to enter and join in with conversation. He covered the wound with a bandana, but the vapor sifted through the fabric.

He was swarmed with paranoia by the worsening of the appearance of the bite and its surrounding area.

He couldn't live with the peculiar look to it and needed a second opinion, but Christen and Puds played it down and acted as though it wasn't that bad. This didn't reassure Henning, and instead he was left thinking that they were either deliberately passing it over to try and relieve him of his obvious distress, or the other scenario was that he was losing his mind and seeing things that weren't there.

After riding north for fifteen miles, Christen was confident that they were not being followed, and although he struggled to persuade Henning, the fatigue was so overwhelming that it was a case of them having to take a break.

They found an inconspicuous spot, right in the middle of a cluster of prickly pear cacti, and aside from a small Greystone chapel a few miles away, it was a very remote area. They sat down, extremely tired, and quiet following their brush with death. Christen thrived on adrenaline surges, and sailing close to the wind exhilarated him, but the reality that they'd just found themselves in was different. He was amazed that they'd managed to get out of the shop without major harm. Bullets had flown everywhere from both sides. They'd hit the broad, grey-haired fella in the leg, and somebody had hit the other man in the head, but the older woman got away, and he was sick that they hadn't managed to finish off the shopkeeper's wife. He was convinced that she would be able to identify them; no question. They didn't blend into the crowd with their Scandinavian looks and Puds' square head and round nose.

Christen was demoralized, as he knew that much of the next few months would now be spent trying to get as far away from the scene as they could. Their travels would need to take them further than he'd originally intended, and the journey was going to have to venture up to San Francisco and beyond. To add to his bother, a pang of shame was gnawing away at him. This surprised him and he didn't like it. He knew that if they'd shot the lady as soon as they'd pulled her into the shop, they'd have gotten away clean and easy, and he wouldn't be feeling stomach knots of remorse.

He had no problem with ending something. Once it was gone, that was it. If something ceased to exist, then what was the point of holding penitence against it? But to leave something behind, an energy that had to live with the consequences of their actions made him feel rotten. His damn stupid randy companions had caused this. He'd wanted to end the lady quickly and get out of there, but he hadn't pushed it enough. He'd been complacent and not thinking about the aftermath; he'd even become relaxed about sticking around. As a result, Henning and Puds' salacious appetites for emptying their balls had now made them marked men.

He was pissed with himself. He couldn't write this off as immaturity because he recognised it, and those who are immature rarely recognise it. No, it was sloppy, and it didn't fall in with his childhood fantasy of answering only to himself. If they weren't extra careful, this would mean trouble and having to surrender to others. The grim nature of the forced sex, twice in a couple of weeks, was getting him down. It made him think about the bird in the cage that they'd left behind. The freedom he'd dreamt of through an outlaw life, all the romanticism that he'd played out in his head countless times as a child, could not be fully realised if they were imprisoning others in such a way.

He liked having a little fun at their victims' expense, but this was too savage. They were behaving like animals, and even throughout their criminality, they had to maintain some civility. Otherwise, what would become of them? The desensitized detachment of holding no boundaries when it came to others would soon wind up with imprisonment, if death didn't come for them first.

The other two boys knew better than to disturb Christen when he was clearly in a ponderous mindset, and they sat around for a short while in silence. Puds and Henning were lost in a mixture of their own thoughts and exhaustion. Several minutes passed until Henning, not wanting to linger on the bite wound, decided to shift his moans to something else as he complained about his missing earlobe.

"I'm going to look like some kind of freak with half of my ear missing." He used his right thumb and index finger to fiddle with the small, jagged line of skin hanging from the cartilage that rimmed the ear canal.

Christen and Puds, sick of Henning's whingeing, ignored the complaint as he continued to finger the damaged area.

"It hurts and it feels just so horrible." Needing reassurance, he turned to his brother. "Tell me honestly, Christen. How do I look? Am I hideous?"

Christen was fed up and teased him. "Yes, Henning. That earlobe was your best feature, and now without it..." He covered his eyes with his hand. "...I can hardly bear to look at you."

Henning was dismayed. "Really? Is it that bad?"

Christen shook his head; he could see that his brother was very troubled, and he decided to call time on the wind up. "No, Henning. It doesn't look bad. It just looks like you've had your earlobe shot off. If it's going to be something that bothers you, just grow your hair and cover it. Okay? But trust me, brother, I don't think you're going to be kidnapped next time the circus comes to town."

Puds lay on the floor with his head rested on his hands. He said, "I'm surprised that we're all pretty much intact, apart from that soft part of your ear, of course, Henning. But we got away lightly with the number of bullets that flew our way." He sighed with relief and added, "That was real fucking close, boys."

Christen started to relax, stretching his long legs out as he shuffled his backside over to a less rough part of the ground. "Yes. I don't think Henning's unfortunate ear injury was too much of a price to pay, given the circumstances. I didn't think we'd all make it."

Puds enquired, "Where are we heading next then?"

Christen answered, "We need to keep heading north. We've got to make some serious ground over the next few days. We have plenty of rations and enough money. The key now is to stay quiet for a while. We may even have to split up at some point. Try and get work separately in different towns."

Henning momentarily forgot about his injury. He stopped messing around with the affected area as he said, "No! That will not happen. We do not go off on our own. We always need to stick together, Christen. You've been saying that to us since we were small children."

"I'm not leaving either of you," added Puds.

Christen sighed. He was only too aware of how vulnerable the boys were without him, but he was also mindful that the reason for much of this reliance was of his own making. He decided to downplay it, although he knew it was highly likely that they would have to compromise their companionship at some point in the very near future.

"Look, I'm only saying that so it doesn't come as a shock to you. We'll be hunted through the idea of the three of us being together. So, if we let the dust settle for a short while and wait for the heat on us to wane off a little, which it will with time, then we can get the gang back on track. And who knows, we may even meet a couple of others that we can bring in and form us a real strong posse."

Puds spat on the floor, laughed, and turned to Henning. "Oh, now that's wonderful, isn't it, Henning? Your brother is already thinking of making some new buddies, and we haven't even gone our separate ways yet!"

Henning placed his head in his hands and cried. Puds looked at Christen and shook his head.

Christen was frustrated, but knew he'd have to try to console his brother. He walked over and sat close beside him, ready to offer a few words, when he heard something in the distance. It was quiet initially, but a sound that lifted by the second. "Can you hear that?"

Henning turned his back to him, still upset, but Puds answered, "I hear something. Like a herd of animals."

Christen agreed. "Yes, that is what I thought. I don't like the sound of it, though. I think we need to get moving."

Puds climbed to his feet as Christen gathered up the bags.

Henning remained seated, sulking. "Well, seeing how you want us all to take off on our own, I'm going to leave you boys to it." He flicked his hand dismissively. "You move on, and I'll sit here for a while."

Christen strapped the bags to his horse and listened intently. The sound was very faint, but he was convinced that it was the noise of charging rabble. He perceived a hollering of some sort on top of the rhythmic stampede.

He couldn't dither around Henning's petulance any longer, and he grabbed his brother by his shirt collar. "Get up! We haven't got time for this shit. I hear something, and my gut tells me it isn't good!" He pushed Henning towards his horse. "Now, stop being a fool and get your ass onto your horse."

Henning, riddled with paranoia, could see the vapour puffing from his wound at a thicker density. He was no longer trying to write it off as a state of delusion; it seemed very real, and now he knew they were coming for him. He briefly considered splitting off in another direction from Christen and Puds to remove them from trouble.

They want me. I can spare the other boys. It's the bite, the mark of the girl. They sense it.

Full of angst, he didn't linger on this thought, and obeyed his brother as he scrambled onto the horse. Puds followed, and Christen climbed atop his big grey stallion.

Puds turned around and, coming from the south, he could slightly make out a cluster of horses surging towards them. He said, "We gotta get going, boys."

Christen turned to see sand clouds, as a widespread area of kicked-up ground descended towards them like a spooky fog. It emptied every few seconds before starting up again, and through a clearing he saw an army of natives charging towards them. The airborne lump of sand led the pack, as if it magnetically pulled them along.

The boys whipped their horses wildly and fired them up. The animals recognised their masters' fear and responded by instantly picking up an impressive pace. They cleared a few hundred yards in no time, and Henning and Christen charged out. But Puds lagged behind. His horse was travelling at a decent rate, but as well as his extra weight, his fitness levels didn't allow him to infuse the animal with the gusto and energy needed to get anywhere near its top speed.

They rampaged through the barren desert land, passing dry, yellowed plants as they edged closer to the Greystone chapel that was now apparent to them. Yet despite the mighty pace they were setting, Christen became dispirited when he briefly glanced behind to see that the army was closing in on them. Wild chanting and whooped yelps glided through the air on top of reverberant sections of eerie, mournful hums. Christen interpreted it as the sound of death coming for them, and he wondered if the other boys felt the same.

The only hope they had was to head towards the chapel to try and create a bunker for themselves. From there they could attempt to battle their way out. He knew that if they made it, and providing they shot well, they'd easily have enough ammunition to take out the natives.

The other boys were on the same wavelength, and as Christen turned to his right, he could see both sets of their eyes fully focused on the chapel. Although, frustratingly, for each metre they advanced to the haven, the natives gained several more on them.

For the first time in his life Christen began to pray. All his dismissive comments subscribing to the idea of a God no longer mattered, and in his desperation he reached out to a higher force.

'I'm sorry, God, if you are there. I truly am. I know I don't deserve your help... But I'm still going to ask for it. I have not bothered you with anything before, so if you could show us some mercy and let us make it to your house out there on the yonder. I give you my word that I'll never speak ill of you again. I will repent. I will reform. Just, please, please, please, put a fire up the asses of these fucking slow horses."

The chanting, the lethal hypnotic drone that lay underneath it, was now within a zone that rendered their chances hopeless. Yet still, all they could do was keep going. Puds' horse was tiring with the weight, and his lag left Christen in no doubt that he was seconds away from being swarmed by the rabble.

Henning shouted, "CHRISTEN, I'M SCARED, WHAT ARE WE GOING TO DO?"

It broke Christen's heart in this desperate time that Henning was so reliant on him. It briefly brought him back to a moment in childhood when they had been sitting together at ten years old in the orphanage dormitory, bouncing a ball off a wall to each other – a game they often played as they tried to relieve boredom. The game had ended abruptly when Henning had a strange episode after he took his turn, throwing the ball as hard as he could at the wall, hoping it would sock Christen right in the face as it bounced back. For reasons unknown, this action brought on a fit and Henning hit the floor shaking wildly. His eyes rolled back, and his nose snorted in short, fast bursts.

At the time, it was the most frightening moment of both of their lives, and Christen had felt just as hopeless then as he did now. He was convinced at that time that Henning was going to die, and he very nearly did when his airway became blocked by his tongue. Christen had screamed for help, but it didn't arrive until it was almost too late. Big Mick, the orphanage handyman and friend of the boys, had eventually heard Christen's cries and charged into the room. Immediately and instinctively, he'd pulled Henning's tongue back into its natural position.

Mick had cradled the boy for two minutes until the fit slowly dissipated and Henning came back around, although he was full of confusion and forgetfulness for the several hours that followed.

The nuns were convinced that a demonic entity was responsible for Henning's seizure, and this meant an increase in the beatings dealt to the boys, especially to Henning.

The vulnerability of Christen that day changed him and constructed a tough exterior and inner fortitude. But now, on this day, at this moment, being charged by two dozen men all focused on orchestrating their demise, he was brought back to that time seven years ago. The incorrigible wall of attitude he'd perpetuated was now crumbling, and standing behind the wall was the ten-year-old Christen, unable to do anything today as he hadn't all those years back. His heart ached with every beat, and he was more aware of it than ever, as if it had swollen to twice its normal size, pumping out a sensation of pain into his blood flow.

He couldn't do anything to help his brother or Puds, and every fibre of him was anguished with devastation.

The truest and best words he could find were also the simplest, and he said to his brother through a lumpy throat, "I love you, Henning."

Henning welled up; his head dropped a little. His silence indicative of resignation.

Christen turned to look at Puds. He looked terrified, and his eyes were so bulbous, as though a little tap to the back of his head would send them tumbling to the floor. His red face gasped and panted with exhaustion.

Christen quickly turned away again. He couldn't face looking as a vision emerged through the dustcloud of three, full head-dressed natives caked in warpaint.

They closed in. Ten seconds later, Christen heard Puds shouting as a young native to the right edged his horse towards him with a level of skill and aplomb that demonstrated an almost spiritual command of the animal. He moved as close to his target as he possibly could without the horses clashing.

Puds fumbled for the gun in his right holster. But before he could get it, the native began hacking into his right forearm with a thick and freshly sharpened tomahawk. The screaming started, and even through the deafening noise of the stampeding horses, Christen could only hear the gruesome sound of steel plunging in and out of raw meat.

The native's friend, a much older man to the left of Puds, joined in. Chopping away, he ripped Puds' shoulder and torso apart with his tomahawk.

Christen heard members of the tribe farther behind shouting, as though instructing Puds' attackers to stop. He couldn't look. The squeals from his friend and the tinny swooshes and squelchy thuds of the tomahawk against flesh painted a picture that Christen couldn't bear to see played out. Puds was as helpless as a carcass on a butcher's slab, and Christen had to carry on charging, getting ever closer to the chapel.

He continued to glance sideways at Henning who, unlike his brother, was frequently looking behind. Christen shouted, "Henning! Stop looking back, dammit. Keep your eyes on the chapel."

He didn't answer, but he'd heard, and they both fixated on their goal.

Seconds later, arrows began descending, and four flew towards Henning. Three ended up a few metres to the right of their target, but another whizzed close enough to graze the side of his horse. She whimpered but carried on running. The surface was very flat and soft, sandy terrain overwhelmed small patches of yellowed grass.

Frustrated by the near misses, the natives opened the floodgates and rapidly fired out arrow after arrow. Speed and quantity of output was the only approach they could take. Any sort of focus on accuracy was not possible at the pace they'd set on their incredibly fit horses. Countless arrows flew over the heads or fell short of their intended target, and the odd one came within a hair's breadth to Christen. But he could see the vast majority were aimed at Henning, and he knew it was only a matter of time before the aims were met with success.

The three natives had stopped ganging up on Puds and had retreated slightly to fall back into the pack with their friends. Christen turned around. It wasn't going to be pretty, but he had to check to see whether his friend had any kind of fighting chance. He was instantly sorry he'd looked, as Puds was in such a ruined state.

His right forearm had been sliced from the elbow, with only a thin layer of skin keeping it attached to the rest of his arm. It was useless and flapped back and forth while his left arm (also weakened after flesh blows to his shoulder) desperately clung to the horse. Both sides of his head had been bludgeoned too. His entire face was layered with a crimson mask, with dark, near black congealment present on both sides. The blood acted as an unwelcome hair product as clumps of his hair almost formed into pigtails. His right leg, sliced to ribbons, merely flopped around, unable to create any sort of clamp on the horse.

Christen looked at him, and Puds stared right back, his eyes empty as the last drops of adrenaline faded away. Seconds later he lost control, and his body slowly dripped headfirst from the horse.

The suddenness of Puds' big body dropping into the horse's path proved to be a hurdle that it couldn't overcome, and the animal tumbled down with him.

The ten metres that Puds' attackers had pulled back couldn't form enough ground for them to avoid the obstacle, and they folded into the carnage and commotion. An almighty pile-up ensued that several others behind them also fell foul to.

With the fallen, injured, or worse, Christen and Henning were dealt a much-needed shred of hope through the despair they felt for their mangled friend. Other natives withdrew from the pursuit to tend to their wounded.

The brothers were so close to the chapel. They would make it if they could just avoid the arrows that relentlessly chased them, although Henning was clearly the next intended target.

Christen screamed, "Henning, keep going. We are so close."

Henning yelled back, "We have to make it for Puds."

They surged ever closer. Christen glanced to the rear, seeing a mess of piled-up figures in the distance. From his position, all he could see was a blob of brown and grey shapes smothered in sand and dust. But many of the natives had managed to pass through successfully, and despite the reduced numbers, it hadn't dampened down their battle cries or chanting.

Within four hundred metres of the chapel, the structural formation of it began to emerge. There was an inviting appeal to it even without the motive for getting there. The building consisted entirely of wood, and it had recently undergone a fresh lick of white paint. A small and square building, it had a wonkily positioned triangular roof underneath a very long watchtower. It was moated with a small, also newly painted, grey wooden fence, with the chapel set back twenty metres from the fence. A few graves inside the land were scattered with pebbles and stones, perpetrated to differentiate the sacred church grounds from the surrounding desert land.

With the chapel now encompassed in such a visible form, Christen's will to get there increased ever more, and this want transferred through to his horse as it rampaged ever faster. This gave Christen a rush that lifted him a little from the immense sadness following Puds' demise.

The boost was short-lived, though, as the natives' aim of the arrows improved. Christen decided to edge a little closer to Henning to try and put them off, as evidently they wanted to keep one of the boys alive.

Closing in on his brother, he heard a whoosh, and moments later the pain hit him as he realised that his left calf had an arrow sticking through from one side to the other. He was grateful that it hadn't cracked through bone, and although agonising, his body acted quickly and pumped more cortisol into his bloodstream.

The arrowhead was very small and wedged into his calf muscle with such power and pace that the wound around it was compacted against the wood of the arrow. This created an immense tightness and, mixed with his body's natural response, it was bearable. Although he knew it would be a different story when he tried to walk.

Henning's horse had been struck a couple of times and was crying and whimpering in pain. An arrow had lodged deep into the side of its stomach, and another had pierced its left buttock. It carried on running but was thrown into a frenzy. The pace and direction were compromised by distress, and it awkwardly zigzagged its way to the chapel.

Henning roared, "She's not going to make it, Christen." He pulled at her reins, but she was slowing down and thrashing about, wanting Henning off her back.

Christen had no choice but to career off to the side and form some space while Henning's horse moved in strange, drunk-like patterns. He steadied his own horse before he moved too far ahead of his brother.

Wondering if it was the presence of the arrow that was bothering the injured horse more than the pain, and whether removing it could settle her down a little, he called out to his brother, "Can you reach the arrow in her side?"

Henning turned to his right to see if this was possible. It was at this point that an arrow struck him. It torpedoed through his upper right cheek and passed upwards through his brain and skull.

Christen screamed as Henning fell off his horse. He knew for certain that his brother was dead, but he still wanted to tend to him. His instinct was to protect Henning.

Pulling at his hair, he tore a small clump out of his scalp in his shocked state of grief, and anguished noises that he had no control over pushed out from the back of his throat.

He yelled despairingly, "HENNING! HENNING! MY BROTHER! NO, NO, NO, NO!"

The natives had gained a lot of ground and arrived within twenty seconds of reaching their target.

Christen was mostly insensate, but his spirit commanded him to carry on towards the chapel. In the first couple of seconds that followed seeing his brother perish, all he had wanted was for hundreds of arrows to rain down on him. They had shared a womb and entered the world as a pair, surely it would be fitting if they left it together? But that thought didn't hold for longer than an instant, as fight or flight grabbed him by the scruff of his neck and demanded he turn his horse and run it like the wind.

Impulse pulled him along like a marionette as his brain tried to unscramble the last ten minutes of his life, and in his traumatised state he managed to get to the chapel within fifteen seconds of turning the horse back around.

He reached the waist-high fence, expecting his horse to easily clear it, but frustratingly, at this crucial point, it refused to jump. Christen slapped him a couple of times, but the animal wasn't going to budge, and without time to waste, Christen got off its back.

He tried to put his left leg down tentatively, but the pain socked him hard the very second he placed his foot on the floor. The weight on the injury shot waves of hurt up his leg that he knew would be intolerable beyond more than a couple of steps. He let his right leg do the work, and his left foot scraped along the ground as he dragged his wounded limb.

The natives soon closed in, and just as Christen walked past several gravestones on his way to the chapel door, five horses cleared the fence. As they arrived at the chapel ground, they began to steady, approaching Christen slowly.

The rest of the tribe remained outside the boundaries of the fence and stood aside their horses. All eyes were fixed on Christen, and the five who'd entered the chapel grounds created a semi-circle around him as he backed onto the chapel front.

He pulled at the door. It was high, double-fronted, and made from heavy duty wood. The fact it was locked deflated him; it was too heavy and thick to break down. He pounded and kicked it with his good leg.

He yelled, "HELP ME, PLEASE. THEY'RE GOING TO KILL ME."

Only one of the Natives close to him wore full headdress. It was his crown, made up of eagle feathers and a braided headband at the base, assembled from plant fibres. The tips of the feathers were coloured in reds and blacks. White warpaint masked his entire face, with three lined blue streaks spread across the nose. His skin was dark brown, closer to cocoa powder than the rest of his tribe's predominantly dark caramel shade. Thick, long, treacle black hair ran halfway down his chest. It looked heavy and chunky in its matted, dreadlocked style. He was unusually well muscled, with hard, oval-shaped pecs and arms that ousted the scrawny native frame that Christen was used to seeing out on the road and in books. He was the chief and looked every inch a leader. His four tribe members had less warpaint smothered across their faces and no headdresses, but they were bare-chested like their leader, with buckskin loincloths covering their midsections.

Christen pulled the gun from his holster. It was fully loaded, but he knew that if he began shooting, they would likely charge and pummel him with their tomahawks. Still, he had a weapon and a potential bargainer. He waved it across the five of them.

"Back off, you animals, before I start shooting."

One of the men momentarily gestured forward before the chief reached an arm out and grunted a command, clearly telling his friend to stay back.

They could have easily mounted a quick attack, but they were reluctant. Several of the men outside the fence began chanting again and tapped the fence over and over with their weapons. Within a few seconds they'd all joined in, and a unified beat was created. The rhythm was improvised, but they quickly picked up a tempo and a sequence of one, pause, two, three, four, five, and repeat.

Christen was lost for words and merely continued sweeping his arm across the full direction of those in front of him, berating them all with his gun, seeing it as his only hope to keep them at bay. But he knew they were fully in control. He was the toy for a change, and it gave him a sense of what he'd put others through in the past.

The chief walked two steps closer, and Christen took two steps back, placing himself right against the door.

He shouted, "STAY BACK THERE OR BULLETS WILL BE FIRED."

The chief's face showed no sign of fear. He was calm and curious in the experience of the occasion. He didn't venture any further, and slowly squatted to a crouch, his eyes fixed on Christen as he placed the tomahawk to the floor. Using the dirt, he drew a circle around it with his finger.

Christen was unsure what he was trying to say, but it became clearer when the chief jumped back upright from his squat. Outstretching his arms, his palms faced upwards to appear innocuous, with his weapon on the floor. He grunted and nodded at Christen to do the same.

Christen was reluctant to comply with this request and kept hold of his gun. But despite the weapon advantage, he felt captive to the man's presence. As he faced his adversary, an inferiority complex gnawed at him – not through the gap in the years between them; it was much deeper than that. He was looking at men made up of warrior, hunter, and spiritual embracer DNA. The fabric of their being had been defined through centuries of knowledge, wisdom, and survival methods, passed down from generation to generation, and all kept within their tribe.

His connection to his own heritage had been severed when he was too young to know anything about it; firstly when he left his country, and secondly when his parents died. He didn't know anything beyond what the nuns and Father Loughlin had taught him, and most of that was about a single man who may or may not have lived two thousand years prior.

He tried to muster some fury as he pondered the chief's responsibility for Henning and Pud's deaths, but the anger wouldn't come. His tense muscles relaxed as he looked at the tribe with no more bitterness than he'd feel towards an avalanche of snow that had taken those he cared for. And that was how this man and his tribesmen now looked to Christen; as part of the Earth, and as important as a flourishing forest. A forest that had been cruelly damaged when he, his brother, and his friend had desecrated a beautiful young tree, uprooted it, and buried it out in the desert.

Christen recognised that he'd betrayed nature, and now it was after revenge. Yet, he would not surrender. It was not in *his* nature to do that. To betray the nature of others was bad enough, but to forsake his own would render his life totally worthless. He owed it to Puds and Henning.

The chief gave Christen a few seconds and gestured several times with his arms for him to place the gun on the floor. Each time he was a little more animated than the last, until he knew he wasn't getting anywhere. He attempted to speak to Christen through very limited English.

"Girl, you take."

Christen didn't want to lie and decided to offer the man and his people closure. Now he was on his own, his attitude was different. "Yes." He patted his chest. "Me..." He pointed out to the desert. "...and my friends. We took her."

The youngest of the five men surrounding the chief surged forward with tomahawk in hand and ran towards Christen. The chief reacted quickly and jumped into his path. Stretching his arm out, he clotheslined the young tribesman, sending him to the floor. The other four surrounding natives remained still and watched, as the fence drumming stopped.

The young native rose to his feet and smacked the chief in the face with the handle of the tomahawk, busting his nose. Reams of blood instantly spurted from his nostrils and poured down his face, smearing deep red across his lips and chin. The warpaint now looking more like clown make-up, and with his leader briefly indisposed, the young man took the opportunity to move towards Christen again.

The other tribesmen surged forward to tackle him, and Christen stretched out his arm to direct the gun at the furious man storming towards him. He shouted, "YOU ARE GOING TO DIE IF YOU GET ANY CLOSER."

The man paid no attention, and as he reached within six yards, Christen quickly fired off three bullets, all of which struck the man in the chest.

Unbelievably, the native remained on his feet and continued moving. His friends couldn't catch him, and Christen missed with a fourth shot as the man closed in. Within two yards, he screeched and sprang off the floor to launch himself at his target.

The tomahawk connected with Christen before any part of the man did, and a small chunk of scalp was sliced off before any sort of grapple ensued. It hurt, but Christen remained stood and gripped the man's shoulders with both hands. They were sweaty, and it was hard to keep a tight hold. He bucked his knees a bit, and in his lower position he slid his hands down to the top of the man's chest.

He was able to fend him off a little more with a sumo-style approach, but Christen was stunned by the man's strength despite the three bullets he'd taken.

The man thrashed his tomahawk around wildly, connecting a few times with several knicks to Christen's torso. The wounds were more than paper cuts, but not deep enough to create serious injury.

The chief soon pulled himself from the floor and reached out to the man, shouting in his Navajo tongue, "He can take us to Yanaba!"

Hearing his love's name made the native cry, but he carried on swinging through the tears as Christen began to tire.

Christen spoke solemnly in strained tones. "We shouldn't have taken her from you."

Two of the other men joined the chief and pulled the frenzied native off Christen. Just before they could put a full restraint on him, he dealt one last swing of the tomahawk and it was a sweet one, catching Christen deep on the left of his chest. Such was the force, the weapon wedged its way into the flesh.

The sound of the squelch and the sickening feel of metal ploughing so deeply into his body knocked Christen out instantly.

The chief yelled at the young man and slapped him across the back of his head several times, furious until he noticed the severity of the bullet wounds. The young man, seeing the concern on the chief's face, looked down and gasped. In his emotion-fuelled rage, he hadn't flinched. He loved the girl and had wanted to marry her.

Instinct had superseded his chief's command, and his sole intent was to kill.

Now he glanced over at Christen. Satisfied that his wish had been fulfilled, his consciousness turned back to himself as the holes in his body became all too apparent. He fell to his knees for a few seconds before toppling over fully into the dirt.

Two of the tribesmen ran over to tend to him. The chief tapped the youngster with his foot but received no reaction. He pointed towards the fence, instructing the tribesmen to take him away.

The chief slid his hand over his face in frustration when the door of the chapel opened slowly to a narrow gap. He turned to look, and the two remaining tribesmen in the chapel grounds moved forwards to join him.

A pair of eyes and a Mexican-accented voice emerged from the dark gap. "I am the priest of this chapel and I live for peace. Please, I don't want any more blood spilled. This is sacred land. I'm sure you and your people can appreciate that, High Chief."

The two men either side of the chief looked at him and gesticulated with their knives, symbolically asking questions. The chief shook his head and outstretched his arms sidewards, directing them to stay back. He recognised the voice and moved closer to the door to peer through the gap. He looked at the man inside and grunted loudly.

The man noted the neither friendly nor threatening noise and continued. "Okay, Chief. As I said, I'm not at all comfortable with violence, and I know we look at some things differently, but we are men of God. That we do share."

The chief responded in grunt again.

The man behind the door, Salvador Villegas, was the priest of the chapel. It was also his home, with a couple of rooms behind the altar at the rear of the building used for living quarters. This was the first trouble he'd encountered in the United States since he'd moved north from a Mexican border town. He'd turned away from Mexico to avoid this sort of thing, and when the commotion and gunshots started outside his chapel, he initially chose not to get involved. But now it had quietened down and with people injured, he felt it right to get involved.

Salvador thought for a few seconds. He was optimistic that the situation could be resolved amicably, and his intuition, which had rarely let him down in the past, told him that the chief was merely inquisitive and negotiable. He decided to slowly open the door.

The chief recognised the priest's white-tabbed, black clerical shirt and black trousers as representation of belief. Faith in a higher presence. He respected this and bowed his head to Salvador.

The priest joined his hands together in a praying position, and reciprocating the bow began, "Chief—"

But the chief interjected, beat his chest with one clenched fist, and said, "Bidziil."

Salvador responded, "Sorry, Bidziil." He pushed the door a little more to get out into the open. Noticing a heaviness against it, he recognised that this obstructive weight might be something that he shouldn't push too hard against, so he squeezed out of the small gap.

Once outside, he quickly peeked to the left to see a young man slumped against the door with a tomahawk stuck in his chest.

Before Salvador reacted to this, he offered his name, but he was uncomfortable at the thought of reaching out to instigate a handshake. It was unlikely to cause offence, but he didn't want to potentially create tension if the Native American felt that the handshake was coercive conformity. Instead, he just wanted to tend to the boy, and immediately turned his thoughts to the story of the Good Samaritan for inspiration.

He pointed to Christen for a second or two, then gestured to the door and said, "May I take him inside, Bidziil?"

Bidziil shook his head. "He take girl." He pointed to his tribesmen, all watching silently as he struggled on through limited English. "We need... He take to girl."

Salvador pleaded, "He has a weapon stuck in his chest. If I don't get him inside soon, he will die, and I can see you don't want that. Just look at him. You haven't done a good job in keeping him alive so far."

The chief nodded, pointed at Christen, and tried to communicate with the few words he knew outside of his own language. "He take girl. Girl gone." He looked up to the sky and wiggled his fingers.

Bidziil looked quite angry following this, through a mixture of linguistic frustration and an imagination that constantly nagged him with unwanted scenarios of what the girl might have been put through.

Salvador, though, was resolute in trying to keep the situation as calm as possible, despite the circumstances. "I understand. The boy has clearly wronged you and your tribe, and he's taken somebody very special from you all. That is none of my business. That's between you, him, and God to work through. But what is my business is that you are on my land, and this boy, whatever he has done, has arrived here at my door, and I have to help him."

Bidziil recognised that Salvador was trying to be a good person, and he responded to this. Although one of the two tribesmen behind him started to grow impatient and said in his native tongue, "Oh, strong one. Tell this man that the boy is coming with us!"

Bidziil shouted back, "Do not tell me what to say, Hashke. The boy is hurt. This was not our plan, but Tsohanoai has decided. This man of God will tend to the boy, and we will return for him."

The native stepped back, accepting what his chief had to say.

Bidziil turned to Salvador. "You make boy live?"

Salvador nodded and said, "God willing, I shall do my very best for him."

"We back..." Bidziil pointed to the sky and drew a circle in the air with his index finger.

Salvador understood and nodded. "Full moon."

Bidziil repeated, "Full moon."

Salvador pointed to Christen. "I can't make any promises, and I shall need to get help. But I will work night and day to keep him alive."

Bidziil understood and said, "Thank you. We come back. If boy not here..." He pointed at Salvador. "... bad for you."

Salvador nodded, accepting and understanding the threat.

Bidziil turned and walked away as his two tribesmen followed him out of the grounds. They joined the rest of their men to head back out to their camp 40 miles east.

Salvador was left with Christen. He scratched his head. He hadn't thought any further than getting Bidziil and his men off his land. Left with the boy, he began to worry that he wouldn't make it. He hadn't noticed the arrow in Christen's leg until now.

The boy was sitting with his head slumped to one side and his legs wide open. Salvador was surprised by how peaceful he looked and wondered how he'd ended up here today. He looked so pure and innocent, with soft, tawny blond hair, and sublime, very lightly tanned cream skin, young and free of blemishes and lines.

The intrigue spurred him to help. He wanted to discover why God had delivered the boy to him at this time. His hour of need.

He crouched and felt for a pulse. It was quite strong considering the condition he was in. Not wanting to waste time, Salvador picked him up slowly and draped him over his shoulder. He tried to be careful by not putting too much pressure on the boy's chest, avoiding any further push of the weapon. At the same time, he was preoccupied with manoeuvring in such a way to avoid aggravating the arrow in the boy's calf. This was difficult, and he felt the handle of the tomahawk press against his back a few times as he pulled the door open, entering the chapel.

Salvador was of average build but naturally strong, and he didn't struggle with Christen as he hurried down the mid-section of the chapel, passing through the benches and pews until he reached the altar.

To the left of the altar was a door leading to the living quarters. The door was stiff. He considered placing Christen on the altar while he opened the door, but he was put off by thoughts of sacrificial imagery.

Turning the door handle, he used his free shoulder to barge through. The time was 10am, an hour before the first visitors to the church would normally show up. How he wished it was an hour later and he could have had some assistance.

He placed Christen down on a wooden bench that had formerly been in the chapel. One of the parishioners had knitted some woollen throws as a welcome present when he'd taken up occupancy at St Joseph's chapel. He folded them up and padded out the bench to make it a little more comfortable.

Wetting a cloth, he placed it on Christen's forehead to try and cool him down. Beyond this, he didn't know what else to do. Without any medical experience, he didn't want to meddle around with anything he had no clue about. He looked at Christen's shirt. A large circle of blood had formed around the wound, but it had dried, and the moisture no longer looked particularly fresh. This gave Salvador some hope that the blood had stopped leaking.

Without wanting to waste time, and once certain that the boy was as comfortable as he could be, Salvador passed back through the church to see Christen's horse. He had a horse of his own, but Christen's was more athletic and a physically superior animal. He climbed on and began the short ride out into town.

He returned to the chapel twenty-five minutes later with Michael Rosen the town doctor. There was no time to waste as Michael immediately started rummaging through his bag for suitable instruments and medication.

He said to Salvador, "Would you clear that table, please, Father?"

Salvador took off a few unwashed plates and candlesticks, and they picked the boy up together, placing him upon the wooden table. The table wasn't very long, and Christen's legs hung off the end.

Dr Rosen hastily unbuttoned Christen's shirt halfway down, until tearing to the point where the material was gathered around the weapon.

He looked at the tomahawk – a long, hatchet-type blade wedged four centimetres deep into Christen's right pectoral – and pulled it out slowly. Christen flinched a little and his shoulders shimmied several times.

The doctor instructed, "Hold him down."

Salvador pinned Christen's shoulders against the table. The boy remained unconscious and settled back down.

Spurts of blood gurgled from the wound, and the doctor placed both hands on it to little effect, as the blood continued to ooze through his fingers.

The doctor, already frustrated by Salvador and his lack of initiative, noticed how uncomfortable the priest was as he winced squeamishly at the blood.

He said, "Get the bottle of whiskey out of my bag and pour it over my hands."

Salvador immediately complied and poured a generous helping of the bottle's contents over the doctor's hands.

Allowing the whiskey to sink in, the doctor briefly moved his hands out of the way to enable some of the alcohol to rinse further into Christen's wound. It helped a little, but the blood still pumped out at a worrying rate.

Salvador lugged the heavy bag of medical apparatus onto the table. Although the chest wound was clearly most important, he realised that the doctor hadn't even acknowledged the arrow in the boy's leg.

The doctor could see by Salvador's newly ashen complexion that he was not comfortable with all the gore, so he gave him a break and left one hand on the wound as he reached into the bag with the other to pull out some bandages. They looked a little yellowy and not too clean, but they were the only ones he had.

Dr Rosen folded the long bandage nice and thick and placed it against the wound.

He asked for Salvador's assistance again. "Father, keep tight hold of the bandage against his chest."

After checking the tomahawk blade, he was satisfied, once he'd drummed his fingers over, that it was nice and smooth, and he was able to dismiss the likelihood of shrapnel entering the wound.

The bandages stemmed the flow a little, but he knew that if he didn't stitch his patient up quickly, the amount of blood loss would cause Christen serious problems. So he used a thicker hooked needle than he was accustomed to.

It didn't take him too long to sew the crevice up, and after doing his best to clean the damage, he was pleased with his handiwork as he applied the bandage properly.

The arrow in the leg was treated in much the same way and he was satisfied afterwards that he'd done all he could for the boy. Tired from the emergency call out, he shared a pot of coffee with Salvador.

The priest said, "He's been out for quite a time now."

The doctor scratched the back of his head and grimaced. "He could be out with shock, or it could be a reaction to the pain he's suffered. It's not unusual for a prolonged unconscious state to occur after the kind of experience he's had."

Salvador nodded and looked over to Christen. "I'm just grateful to the Lord... and you as well, of course, Doctor, that we were able to give him a chance."

The doctor said, "He's got a fine chance. He's in great physical shape, and he has youth on his side. I've tended to people a damn sight worse than that during the war, and many of them pulled through."

Salvador sighed. "I just hope that he isn't some kind of beast when he comes to."

Dr Rosen put his hand on Salvador's shoulder. "I can ask the Sheriff if he could send a couple of men out to watch over him, if that will put you at ease, Father?"

Salvador shook his head. "No thank you, that will not be necessary. The Lord has assigned me to tend to him, and he will protect me from any opposition I may face from the boy."

"He won't be fit to do anything for a long while after he comes around, so I don't think the Lord's protection will be required straight away."

The doctor twirled his grey, upturned moustache. It was moist with coffee, and he wiped it dry with his sleeve. He fidgeted with his face further, rubbing his forehead and scratching the back of his neck. This habit of touching and rubbing would always follow any tending to others, a need to reconnect his hands with himself.

Taking to his feet, he said, "Well, I'm happy that I've done all I can for the boy, and now I'll be on my way, if you think you can take it from here. Margaret worries if I'm away too long. I think she forgets that my occupation forces that on frequent occasions."

Salvador stood up next to him. "How much do I owe you for your handiwork, Michael?"

The doctor laughed. "Now, come on, Father. What kind of man would I be if I took money from a servant of God? Especially in such awful circumstances. You're a good person. Most people would turn their back on a dying man these days."

Salvador shook his hand. "God bless you, Michael"

The doctor left, and Salvador waited for the young man to come around.

Chapter Seven

As Braun's mental and physical tuning took him into new realms of consciousness, he quickly discovered that where rewards grew and bloomed, the roots of the darkness that had bubbled under the surface began to sprout poisonous shoots.

Side effects; visions of other times and of unrecognisable places, began to plague him. Most of them provided what he could only imagine were glimpses of the future. More often than not they were unremittingly bleak or just plain weird. Basic sensory activity was all that was needed for the curtains to open for these scenarios. A particular scent or the touch of live and inanimate objects could throw him out of his present and into a virtual reality. His surroundings would cease in motion, and time would pause.

Braun's first fully interdimensional transcendent experience occurred four days into his settlement in Cheston. He'd been talking to a railroad worker who was busy fitting parts of track into smoothed out land, as the town was being equipped for the train station.

Braun was nosy and wanted to know all the ins and outs of what the man was doing. He was clearly busy but was content to speak to Braun. Halfway into the conversation, Braun wanted to get a closer look at some of the man's work. He trod onto part of the completed track and the very instant his foot hit the wood, it was as though the world was lit by a giant candle that was suddenly blown out, leaving Braun stranded in pitch black. He'd experienced blackouts before, with a few fainting episodes, pass outs, and the many times he'd been knocked unconscious through clumsy drunken episodes or getting his ass kicked. But he'd always been aware of the drop before he hit the floor.

This time was different. There was no collapse or snap into unconsciousness, and he remained standing for several seconds, totally confused in the dark, before he felt himself being pulled along with his feet dragging on the floor, not by anything physical, but through a magnetic field with a line of force attracted to his chest. And it was his chest that led the rest of him to be dragged through the black for just over a minute, until he saw an opening that appeared at first to be the size of a penny, but expanded slowly as he drew closer. After a few minutes he reached a large circle, and he fell straight through it into a murky grey sky.

The pull didn't stop, but the motion of it changed as his body cartwheeled and tossed throughout the sky. He was bewildered but not scared. The inability to influence the situation left him with no choice but to succumb, and once he stopped thrashing around and surrendered to the force, he briefly found some inner peace through the experience. He was far above the clouds, but they weren't formed in the way he'd been accustomed to. The fluffy, marshmallow blobs of white that he'd spent so many hours gazing up at throughout his life had become tatty, torn, and flimsy, like flotsam and jetsam. They were nearly as grey and murky as the sky.

After being tossed around for a few minutes, the inevitable fear crept up on him as he started to feel frustrated by the lack of control. The view wasn't anything to enjoy either. He couldn't see too much under the clouds, just the odd smattering of green amongst more greys. He was too high up for birds, and his situation was made worse when he began to struggle with his breathing. The atmosphere was so thick that he could almost feel it entering his mouth and nostrils as he tasted grimy, unclean air.

The whole thing lasted for only a couple of minutes, and it ended suddenly as a black hole opened through a void in the sky. He was sucked into it, and his consciousness re-entered what he'd previously thought of as his true reality, finding himself back from where he'd been taken, standing next to the rail worker. The man was still talking away to him, seemingly unaware of what Braun had just been through.

Braun quickly wrapped up the conversation and walked away, scared and concerned. He forced himself to write it off as a side effect to a bad feed he'd taken from a drunken brawler the previous night. It had been an easy draw, as the guy was heavily inebriated and falling all over the place after having his ass handed to him in a one-sided fight. Braun had watched him like a hawk, and as soon as he got a little close to him, he'd ripped a strip off the guy and sucked it up. Half an hour passed, and he felt like crap; his head cracked like thunder all night and gave him little sleep.

Two days later, it happened again, as he sat reading the Cheston Gazette next to Leonard, the resident barber at the Redmond saloon. He was waiting for his turn in the chair while a large, fat man's scruffy six-inch beard was trimmed and tamed. Braun was engrossed in an article detailing the influence of the Gatling machine gun during the civil war. Close to finishing the interesting piece, the blackness descended on him again, and he was thrown back through the mysterious tunnel into sky. Only this time he didn't hurtle across; he plummeted alongside two metal cylinders nearly as long as him. He went into freefall and followed the cylinders all the way down into the eye of a huge explosion as they hit their intended target.

He didn't know whether he was invincible or if he was even there at all, but all he could do was watch helplessly as motion slowed down just before he passed through the roof of a small building, with the cylinders leading the way. He braced himself for impact once he hit the deck, but this didn't happen. Instead, eight metres from the ground, he found himself suspended in mid-air, front-faced like a skydiver. He could not see where he was, as destruction unfolded around him in a higher frame rate that belied what the human eye should be able to detect. This gave him an unwanted chaotic detail, as bricks, mortar, furniture, and limbs and heads of women, men, and children flew off in all directions, like a medley of fruit hitting the blades of a powerful blender.

Just as the destruction peaked and he was left floating in a cloud of dust, blackness descended from the sky and swallowed him up like a blue whale sucking up krill. He was thrown back into the Redmond, shaking so violently that Leonard refused to take a blade to shave his neck for fear of slicing his throat.

He pondered this one heavily afterwards. *Was he going to be there? Had he been there and travelled back? Or was this thing that lived inside him a separate entity that would be present elsewhere in the future?'*

He was confused and resentful of what he'd hoped was a gift. Over time, numerous other visions would bedevil him, many of which could be so horrifying that he would toy with the idea of not feeding, but the hunger was so powerful, necessary, and hypnotic that it always superseded such thoughts and distracted him from conscience grapples.

The following day, he was out of sorts after a deep, thirteen-hour undisturbed sleep. He rolled out of bed and opened the window for fresh air. Two middle-aged railroad workers were passing, and he released the beam from his chest and fed from the healthier looking of the two. The hunger had set in, and the oversleep was his body's response to not getting what it wanted.

It was all over in a matter of seconds, and the only indication of something happening to the man was when he stumbled a little, as though an invisible rock had tripped him. It was so minor that neither he nor his friend mentioned it.

Braun instantly felt better, and although haunted by visions of the previous day, he decided to revel in the moments when he did feel good and not dwell on the darker hours. He didn't want to let it stop him from spending time with Agnes. Two weeks into Braun's reading lessons, he'd made advancements that staggered her. She had never taught an adult to read or write, and she'd been certain that it would take a lot longer and more effort would have been required with the sponge-like child mind long gone. But it was as though she only had to tell him something once and that was it. He'd instantly process and programme the information and they could move on. The repetition that she'd worked so hard to master with the children was not needed.

It didn't make sense to her, but she figured that she must have been doing a solid job. The gratification and the experience of sharing knowledge with a willing participant had given her the best three weeks she'd known since her husband Patrick had been killed. The thought of being able to do something worthwhile again had not entered her mind until the chance to reignite her teaching vocation had presented itself. Picking herself back up from rock bottom had been tough. She'd been so cruelly shunned by the people of her old town, Goaville. Regarded as soiled property in their eyes, they didn't want her near their children once word got around about the assault.

She was sitting in a quiet corner of the saloon with Braun thumbing quickly through dictionaries and thesauruses from the local library, rapidly absorbing each word and its meaning. All the while, she was on the receiving end of the odd scowl and catty remark from the ladies hoping for someone to pay for their services. They were bored, sitting at the bar sharing drinks with what little money they had. Most of them had not received the opportunities that Agnes had been given, and their comments were rooted in jealousy.

Agnes bit back a few times at first, but she felt sympathy for them. She'd at least had some years of happiness, but for many of the girls, it had been abject misery from birth. She quickly discovered that ignoring them was the best way to avoid getting into petty arguments that resolved nothing.

Following Agnes' teaching and imprinting into her student the understanding of words, grammar, and everything else that comes with basic language and literature, Braun merely had to touch a book to digest everything that was inside, such was his ability to extract. But he loved being with her and hung on her every word. He didn't want to draw attention to what he could do with his roided, mnemonic device mind, so his approach was that of an enthusiastic student with a keen eye and a high capacity for information retention. Yet, the play down of his ability was pleasurable to him.

He loved the feel of the thin, delicate paper between his fingers, and he gained as much satisfaction as the most avid reader if he chose to slow down and take his time with the reading. He flicked through a thesaurus to try and find suitable words for his latest assignment, to write a short piece based on how he would have done things differently, and what he was going to do to try and move on from the past.

Agnes did have an agenda with this, as she was fishing to find out a little more about him. Braun's company had left her with a multitude of responses. Getting to know him firstly in a teacher-and-student relationship, things quickly blossomed into friendship – one that was based on curiosity on her part initially, but gradually over the time that followed became something more. Yet, she was reluctant to get involved with him. He left her with so many conflicting emotions. She felt safe around him, yet he still made her uneasy. She had become attracted to him in a physical sense, but she was also disturbed by his appearance.

He was so smart and healthy looking in a way that completely belied how she'd found him on the night they met. Her own dull, uneven skin tone seemed right for her age. But Braun was a little older than her, and Agnes was bemused how all the crags and lines in his face had been smoothed out, his skin free from any blemishes, with one consistent lightly tanned colour running across his entire flesh, just like a small child.

His hair seemed to have a permanent layer of shine, and it was soft and tawny. Despite this, he still looked like an older man full of wisdom and experience that seemed to increase by the day.

She couldn't fully understand what was so absorbing about him. She didn't consider him to be wildly charismatic or breathtakingly handsome. There was just something different in his whole demeanour and it went beyond exotic; he moved in a strange but interesting way. She was constantly aware of his breathing, and he pulled air in and out in a very focused rhythm, as though it was pleasurable to him. She had not got too physically close to him, but they'd held hands a couple of times. On both occasions she'd noticed a smidgeon of something that she knew was running through him. His hands gently pulsated, and through each throb she was acutely aware of something passing from him and into her. It was nice, and once or twice he'd looked right into her eyes and it felt stronger. A shared electricity that made the hairs stand up on the back of her neck.

She sipped from a glass of water as he wrote away as though his life depended on it. He was already very advanced with his writing, and he'd read and enjoyed many books. *The Last Man* and *Moby Dick* were two of his favourites. Next to him were several volumes of the *Alienist and Neurologist* that he was working through. He had dozens of books in his room on all different subjects, non-fiction and fiction, picked up from a small library in a nearby town. He would pull all the information from the reference books in seconds, but with a lot of the classics and the great fiction he preferred to read them through and live through the stories.

He was disturbed briefly when Dan, the saloon and hotel owner approached. "Good day to you, Mr McCleary."

He tipped his head to Agnes. "Madam."

She smiled back at him, and he continued talking to Braun. "What about that new painting, huh? Did you see it? I put in your room yesterday. I know you like animals, so I thought you'd appreciate it."

Braun shrugged and said, "Bison are beautiful creatures, but sorry, Dan, I don't care for it much. Far too much oil was used. It just makes it look too…"

Dan finished his sentence. "Too blob-like?"

Braun laughed. "I was searching for more of a befitting word, but what the Hell, I'll take blob. Damn, I'm doing all this reading and all, but I've still got a way to go."

"Sorry you don't like it, sir, I'll take it down straight away."

He turned to walk off, but Braun called him back. "Dan, forget about it. I can live with it. It's just a damn picture. It doesn't matter, man. It's your hotel but, hey, how about you take it easy. You're fussing about in my room all the darn time! I need space please, my friend." Feeling himself getting wound up, he pursed his lips and blew some cool air onto his knuckles to calm himself, then lowered his voice as he continued. "You got that, Dan? Space. I like space, alright? Just cut out the snooping for a while."

Agnes noticed that Dan was visibly upset, and his whole demeanour changed from his regular jolliness. "I wasn't snooping, Mr McCleary. I would never do that, sir. I just want to make sure everything…" He paused and composed himself as he whimpered the end of his sentence. "…is real nice for you."

Braun sighed, put his pen down, and humoured Dan. "I told you to call me Braun, Dan. Enough of this Mr McCleary and Sir crap now, okay?"

Dan was close to crying as he closed his eyes and bit down hard on his bottom lip. He nodded before Braun carried on.

"I appreciate you looking after me and all. You're very hospitable. It's just..." Braun sighed. "First, we had the new curtains. Very nice, they are, but I didn't ask for them. Then all the vases, trinkets, and crap..."

"All from my quarters," Dan added.

"All from your quarters. Again, I appreciate your efforts, but I don't understand it, expect it, nor want it. I'll come see you if I need anything from you, Dan."

"Anything at all."

"That's wonderful, Dan." His tone verged on condescending, and he put a hand on the man's shoulder.

Agnes watched as they both closed their eyes for a split second, and their bodies shuddered as though something passed between them. It all happened within the blink of an eye then Dan walked away out of the saloon, back towards the hotel reception.

"That man is in love with you," said Agnes.

She wasn't joking, but Braun treated it as such. "Well, who can blame him?" He buried his head back into his writing.

She looked out the window. She had seen a lot of this since Braun had entered town. It wasn't quite sycophancy, because people didn't appear to want anything from him. But there was an over-the-top eagerness to the way people would behave when they were around him. And as much as he seemed to be glowing, a lot of folks in Cheston were the opposite and didn't look so good. Most of them hadn't looked wonderful to begin with, but whenever Agnes went for a stroll, she was always startled to see so many pale and ghostly, lost individuals walking around.

It was very peculiar, but the malaise hanging over the town had not extended to her. Maybe this was because she had grown so close to Braun and knew how highly he thought of her. But whatever was going on, it was clear that he had brought something strange and chilling to the area.

She tried bringing the subject up occasionally, but Braun would just look perplexed as she struggled to find the right words to try and explain what she could see. It was so buried under the surface that outwardly accusing him of anything would suggest that it was she who had a problem. The reluctance was also affected by the kindness that Braun had shown her, and she was feeling something for him. Although not in the traditional sense, the longing was something that she didn't want to jeopardise.

Braun looked up from his writing. Distracted by a flickering motion, he turned his head towards the cluster of tables in the middle of the saloon. With a good mood firmly in place, he enjoyed the supernatural image for a change and smiled as an elderly, tattily dressed, happy looking couple danced the waltz. No music played but they danced. They were clearly in another dimension, yet he could see them. He pondered this aloud as he turned to Agnes.

"Your eyes, my eyes. Ya reckon they see things in a different way?"

Agnes glanced at him with a purposely, obvious fake smile. She was tired and dropped her head a little.

She liked his adventure but wasn't always in the mood to see where he took it.

Seeing her reaction, he laughed and carried on undeterred as he pointed to his eyes. "Other than I. No man, no woman, no animal ever has, nor will, see the world through these. Where I turn, what I look at. Each moment is my painting. I frame everything and each picture belongs to me."

Agnes shrugged and playfully punched his arm. "You have a real knack of trying to turn the obvious into something else."

He yearned to tell her more, but he was happy for once as he savoured his exclusive look at something beyond. Not caring for a change, he stood up and folded his arms, watching as the ghosts moved beautifully. Their eyes were shut, fully immersed in the dance. It was a style unfamiliar to him, the only 'dancing' he had attempted or witnessed before, was far less graceful and usually followed amounts of booze that only allowed rhythmless stomping and arm swinging.

Agnes wondered what he was looking at but, more than used to his odd behaviour. she decided better than to ask.

He had the feeling that as long as he looked, the perfect waltz they were immersed in would continue. He didn't want to return to his writing, as he had too much going through his mind, and he said, "I'm just going out for a little break. Stretch the legs and pick up some jerky from the store."

Agnes replied, "Don't be long, I'm a little tired and I'd like to have a nap."

"Sorry, I've taken up enough of your time. You conk out for as long as you need. I'll be in my room later if you want me."

Despite any reference point of her own, she sniggered along with several others as he mimicked the ghosts and waltzed with himself out of the saloon.

Another oddity she'd noticed about her new friend, he'd often talk about food, but she never saw him eating anything. She knew that he must eat and eat well, judging by how healthy he looked. But they'd spend many hours together and she'd not even seen him dip his hand into a bowl of nuts.

He walked out of the saloon, breathing in the fresh air. Looking around, he thought, *Who's looking juicy today?*

Firstly, he encountered a couple of little girls skipping. Most of the time, their essence was the best, uncorrupted, with bolder moistened colours, as though they weren't yet fully saturated. He smiled at them, and they waved back. Strong temptation was roused but he would not take anything from them.

A week earlier the allure had gotten the better of him and he'd taken some from Martin, a buck-toothed, pudding bowl-haired, eleven-year-old boy. Braun had spoken to his father, Raymond, a couple of times and he had got to know the boy a little. But he wasn't keen on him. The kid constantly darted in and out of the saloon, annoying those who just wanted a quiet drink. Martin was hyperactive, constantly demanding attention, and when he was too tired to run back and forth, he felt entitled to entertainment from the nearest person. He was a nuisance, and although the hair colour was different, he quickly became the annoying ginger-haired stepchild to the Redmond regulars.

He would constantly knock against or full-on clatter into people, breaking numerous glasses in the process.

Kieran the barman would lose it and shout at Raymond, 'GET THAT KID OUT OF HERE!'

His pleas mostly went ignored. Kieran would lose his rag, but with Raymond being one of his best paying customers, he wouldn't protest too much. And Martin kept coming back, pestering fellas who were in there with one focus, to let the whiskey soak up their problems.

This went on for a while, day after day, and each time he'd come in with a different toy. Balls, skittles, and soft toys that he was a little too old to be carrying around. He'd constantly wave one of the things in some lonely, sad old drinker's face, wanting to play. Raymond wouldn't do anything and just allowed the boy to run wild. He wasn't concerned that his boy was bothering people. He was just grateful for any break from him and would happily let other people humour the kid.

Braun couldn't bear the boy and tried hard to ignore him. But Martin recognised this, and it became a game for him to prod and poke at Braun until he succumbed and played along with whatever was exciting him that day.

One day the previous week, Braun had become really tired of it. He'd been firm with the kid for hours and asked his father to have a word with him. Raymond threw a couple of half assed 'Settle downs' the kid's way, but not with the kind of authority that the near feral lad needed. Kieran was busy flirting with some of the better-looking whores, and Braun was left with extra unwanted babysitting duties. He was a little low on resources that day and had been struggling with another attempt to wean himself off the feeding. The cold turkey bouts would ultimately fail as the threat of severe illness or death would present itself. The apparitions – objects as well as humans – would increase and symbolically indicate to him that he was close to becoming one.

During these interim periods he'd drink heavily, more so than his usual intake. The power had not removed his addiction, but his capacity for its consumption had increased. It didn't debilitate him like it always had in the past, though. Instead it served as a good way to nuance his heightened senses and stopped him from running completely amok with his dangerous capabilities.

Martin was charging around the saloon like a demented baby rhinoceros, not looking where he was going, weaving in and out of the tables on his way to Braun and then back to his dad. Back and forth this went on. Braun turned his chair around to face the wall, and that's when Martin stopped and began bouncing the ball against Braun's back. It was only a small rubber thing, and it didn't hurt, but it augmented an already irritable mood into a downright pissed off one. Braun shouted over to Raymond who was talking to a patron on his neighbouring table.

Raymond just laughed and said, "Hey, why don't you try catching it? Put the damn thing in your pocket. That's the only way you'll stop the little asshole."

Braun was seething at this point. He hadn't been in town for long, but he'd quickly gained levels of respect from most people. Raymond and his boy didn't seem to follow.

He hadn't drunk from Raymond before; the man's colour was off. He was wasted most of the time and stank to high heaven. Braun figured this was why he wasn't under his spell like most of the townsfolk.

The disrespect spurred him on, and in a one-and-a-half second flash he pulled some of the spark out of the boy. The colour immediately drained from Martin's face. His eyes opened wide with fear, staring straight at Braun. He knew something had happened, but it hadn't fully registered.

Braun was close to mastering control over his enforced anatomical tenant and could fire off the beams from his chest at lightning pace. So fast that the human eye couldn't detect it, but Martin felt peculiar, and he ran back to his father, crying and shouting that he wanted to go home. Raymond looked over at Braun, who shrugged his shoulders, always trying to present the illusion of calm on the outside while a roaring fire ignited inside.

The buzz was sensational, and when Raymond put his arm around Martin to take him outside, the boy looked around at Braun who responded with a wave and a sinister smile that said, 'That'll teach you'.

For the rest of that day Braun basked in a surge of power. He could have beaten up, outrun, outgunned, and outsmarted any person that came his way. Just knowing that he could take on all and sundry was enormously satisfying, and he felt better than ever.

This was ruined the next day when he discovered that Martin had taken ill in the evening following the extraction. The local doctor was baffled by his condition; there was nothing unusual about his temperature or any record of a previous injury to indicate the kid had something wrong with him. The boy slipped into a coma when he went to sleep that night and didn't come out of it for two days afterwards. Eventually he made a full recovery physically, but in the few times that Braun saw him afterwards, Martin didn't seem like the same annoying kid that he'd been familiar with. His face, which had previously been extremely animated, had lost a lot of its elasticity and he just manoeuvred between a handful of sombre expressions. With his spark no longer present, he stopped coming into the saloon. Braun didn't mind this, of course, but Martin was now terrified of him and would run the opposite direction if he ever saw Braun the boogeyman coming anywhere near him.

Ruining the child devastated Braun, and it gave further indication that whatever festered inside – as wonderful as it could make him feel – wasn't good for others.

So, on this day Braun walked his usual circuit around town looking for prey and approached Timothy, the tailor who'd sold him his suits. He was an old guy, and his colour was often dull and didn't do a lot for Braun. But his green and blue looked a little shinier than it had in a few days.

Braun passed him and tipped his hat. "Morning, Timothy."

"Braun! I was hoping to see you," replied Timothy, as he reciprocated with his own tip of the hat.

Braun answered, "You were hoping to see me, huh? Hey, I'm not a hard guy to find, like most around here. The saloon would be a good place to start."

Timothy laughed. "Yes, that I do know. However, the Redmond is not the place for me. See, I am not too popular in there." He raised his fists and chuckled some more. "I've always been great with a sewing needle, but I can think of at least five of the big drinking boys that would love to stitch me up good and proper."

Braun didn't want to know the story and asked, "What can I help you with?"

"I have some beautiful drawings in the shop, and I would be thrilled if you came over and took a look at them."

"Drawings, huh?"

"Yes. They are pictures of new suits. The best I have ever seen, and..." He punched through the end of his sentence. "...They... Are... Due... To... Arrive... Soon! The detail is exquisite, perfect shading and close-up sketches of the finer details. I just know you'll be interested. They are based on new European designs. One is an incredible black woollen suit that just screams to be worn by your good self!"

"Black wool, huh? You fucking serious? Huh?" He cleared his throat. "Don't you think wool would pump me full of sweat out here in this heat?"

Timothy looked hurt by Braun's dismissive response but carried on the sales pitch regardless.

"No, Braun, you see, it's a very thin, springy..." He closed his eyes and took in a deep breath to demonstrate the end of his sentence. "...breathable wool."

Braun had quickly become Timothy's best customer, after buying five suits during the short time he'd been in Cheston.

"I'm a little busy right now, Timothy, but come by the saloon later with those drawings and I'll take a look at what you've got."

"That is wonderful, Braun! I haven't sold much over the last few days, so I'll be closing up early today. I'll see you in there. Is three o clock befitting for you?"

"Sure, Timothy. Three."

Braun was a little irritated that Timothy had dropped his poor sales for the week into the conversation. He just about stopped himself from thinking aloud as he pondered, *He's had plenty from me. 'Bout time I took something from him.*

As the tailor passed, Braun demonstrated a proficient control over his gift as he quickly secreted his beam like a spider releasing silk from its spinneret gland. He took a little bite of his prey, and it was all over in less than half a second. Timothy momentarily jolted but didn't notice any time lapse within that half-second period.

This gave Braun a nice hit, but he still craved more, and as he continued his scavenging pursuit, he made a mental note to leave Timothy alone for a while. He hadn't taken much from him, but he knew that it would leave the older man weary for a few days.

He decided not to take more than he needed and to spread it out across the town. This could be frustrating for him, as some tasted a lot better than others, but if he feasted too much on a handful of people regularly, it would weaken and eventually kill them. This way he could keep them alive by spreading it out, allowing subtle recovery bouts in-between.

Two more people passed, and Braun withdrew from them just as quickly as he'd taken from Timothy.

He'd extracted several different colours; the third person he'd fed from had pink, brown, and maroon. This spirit multivitamin of varying hopes, dreams, dread, anxiety, and disappointment gave him the usual heightened mixture of emotions.

He carried on walking to the end of the town, passing more people on the way. Most would nod or say hello, and many would want to engage him in conversation, but often their words would fail to register as all he could see, smell, and hear was their energy. The scent from a good person was an amalgamation of all his favourite smells – freshly baked bread, woodchips, and good quality aged whiskey.

He was mostly repelled when he'd see darkness in someone. It had happened a few times, mostly through visitors passing through, running from something and with plenty to hide – not unlike himself. He often wondered about the prevalence of dark residing inside him, and he didn't want to feed on those who displayed it.

Still, Braun could see melancholy in the darkness. The browns, blacks, and dark greys glistened with dewy verve. The vibrancy of the darker-led citizens was no less than that of those who displayed a lighter and softer look. Though what really separated the dark from the light was the horrible smell, with strong skunky and horse manure notes. Yet still, Braun wasn't totally turned off by it. It smelt like shit, but the odour was fresh and earthy, and he was more drawn to it than a depleted case, the sort that he'd taken too much from or those that didn't have much to begin with.

Where there wasn't much to extract, where he'd need to really scrape the barrel for any remnants of sediment, in those instances it was difficult to detect any smell. The colour they may have once displayed had lost its pop and shine, and instead would be nothing more than a faded, unappealing pastel colour.

During his first few days in Cheston, he'd drawn too much from the townsfolk and drained most of the people of nearly everything they had. He'd noticed a shift three days into his arrival as a malaise poured over the town. The bakers and the production turned; the saloon was full of the regular drinkers, but the minimal atmosphere that was conjured up on most days just wasn't there.

Even the whores didn't seem bothered to drum up much interest that week. It was strange, and although Braun felt amazing, with ecstasy constantly pouring through his body, he knew that it wasn't sustainable. The supplies were low and seeing the people looking so confused and out of sorts ruined some of the buzz for him. He knew he'd have to ration what was available, unless he took it out on the road, but he didn't want to. He was settled and quickly falling in love with Agnes.

She'd noticed how people would act funny and how they were not quite themselves. She would ask questions such as, 'What's gotten into everyone?'

This concerned Braun, especially when she'd make comments that pointed directly at him.

'People have been acting awful funny since you turned up around here.'

She'd normally follow this with a laugh, but he'd catch her looking at him suspiciously. He briefly considered telling her what lived inside of him but thought better of it. He didn't want to scare her off and jeopardise any future happiness that he knew could be fulfilled with Agnes at his side.

Now he thought of this after his feed for the day had settled, and he headed back to the saloon. Agnes had cancelled her afternoon nap. Intrigue got the better of her and she wanted to see how Braun acted on his return. Seeing him coming through the long narrow windows of the saloon, she thought, *He always looks different when he comes back from those little walks.*

Braun bounded back into the saloon and Kieran automatically poured him another whiskey.

He walked over to Agnes with his drink. "Hey, you're still here. How's about we call it a day, huh?

You must be hungry; you've eaten nothing since we met up this morning. What do you say I grab some food for you, and we can sit down by the lake. I can get a carriage to come and take us in half an hour."

She answered, "You seemed a little restless today, Braun. That walk sure has put a spring in your step now." She looked at the time on the clock behind the bar – 3:25pm. She put her pencil down on the table. "Right then, school is over for the day and you've been working hard, so no homework tonight. I will go down to the lake with you, but only if you buy me a slice of that scrumptious cider cake from the bakers."

"I'll get you two slices!"

As he ran out of the saloon, Agnes shouted, "Don't forget to get yourself something to eat—"

Braun didn't respond, and Agnes muttered, "Not that he will. Strange, funny little man. Doesn't eat a crumb of food, but he's got the energy of an eighteen-year-old."

An hour-and-a-half later Agnes was devouring the last few chunks of her second slice of cider cake at a nice spot next to the lake. Braun had been quiet since they'd got there.

Agnes asked, "Is everything okay, Braun? You don't seem happy; you haven't touched any of that jerky. Seems the whiskey is okay, though, of course. You drained that flask no problem."

Braun walked over to the small lake, which wasn't much bigger than a large pond. The grassy land around it sloped in a steady decline straight into the water, with no real border to speak of other than caked slabs of mud splattered across the sides. He removed his boots and socks, rolled up the trouser legs to knee length, and began paddling in the water.

He closed his eyes. "Feels real nice against my old pins." He looked out over to the other side of the lake and smiled as he saw two blue herons trying to grapple and peck each other over a fish.

He shouted over to Agnes, "Which one are you throwing down your money for?"

She'd stripped to a white silk underdress and was tanning her legs and arms. Her face was hidden under the rim of a straw hat.

She barely looked up as she replied. "I don't know, they both look the same to me. I'll take the blue one."

"Me too," said Braun laughing. "Why don't you come and join me in the water?"

"I'm not going near that water now your smelly feet are making it all dirty."

"Hey, a mud bath is real good for your skin. Those pigs ain't so dumb, you know."

"Take the rest of your clothes off then."

"Okay, I see what you're doing! Now don't use this as a ploy to get me naked!" chuckled Braun.

"It isn't a ploy. I just thought it would be a good excuse for you to get a proper wash. You know, that smell doesn't just stop at your feet!"

"Well, thank you very much! I'll have a word with my stink and tell him to go easy on everyone for a while."

Agnes smiled and shook her head. She knew that he didn't smell bad. She pondered, *He really doesn't smell of anything. Yet another peculiarity of my friend.*

She thought about this for a moment until she decided that she was focusing too much on something that didn't hold a great deal of importance. He was a nice man, wonderful to be around, and she could see herself being with him. But nagging thoughts about his very nature, as undefinable as they were, kept chipping away.

"Owww!" shouted Braun.

He pulled one foot out of the water and hopped about on the other as he looked for the source of the pain. Something had bitten him and chomped a nick out of his foot, just to the right of the heel. Blood gushed out from the small wound. He'd seen plenty of his own blood during the many drunken accidents he'd been involved in throughout his life, but this time it looked strange to him – still red but edging towards purple, and it was thick and gloopy like a syrup. He wasn't alarmed by it, given the multiple changes to the inner workings of his body, but he was surprised at the level of pain that the nip had produced. It zapped right through him, and his eyes gushed as he winced. *Probably just a piranha, but boy did that hurt.*

Agnes rushed over. "What happened to your foot? Has something bitten you?"

Braun played it down. "Don't worry, Agnes, it's nothing."

She saw tears on his face and the blood that ran through his hands as he held his foot. The colour was odd to her, but she put it down to the light, as heavy sun rays beat down and shimmered against the water.

"It doesn't look like nothing. Let me look at it."

"IT'S FINE, AGNES, HONEST. PLEASE STAY WHERE YOU ARE."

"SORRY FOR TRYING TO HELP!" she yelled, before changing her mind. "Actually, no I'm not. The only thing I'm sorry about is that the critter didn't take your whole foot off!"

Braun snapped back, "I just don't like a big hoo-ha over nothing, and that's what it is. Look." He put his sore foot back in the water for a few seconds to wash off the blood.

Agnes shouted, "My God, I thought we were making progress with all the reading. You've come on at a rate that has made me question whether you were telling the truth about being so dumb in the first place, but now I've just watched you put a bloody foot back into the water! That critter will be back for second helpings. And this time, he'll bring a few buddies with him."

Just as she finished shouting, Braun confirmed her prediction as he yelped, "AAAAHHH!"

He charged out of the water and dragged a trail of blood along the lightly coloured sandy mud that led onto the bank. He didn't get too far before the pressure of the wounded foot against the floor became too much and he dropped to his backside.

Agnes hurried over with two handkerchiefs she'd taken from her bag. "My word, is that a lot of blood." She looked at the jammy magenta coloured stain that smeared across the ground. "I won't take no for an answer this time. Now give me your foot."

His eyes were closed as he held his injured foot with both hands, trying to stop the heavy stem of blood.

Frustrated with his ignorance, she slapped one of his hands. It dropped to the side, and she looked at the lateral part of his sole. Flaps of flesh hung off through bites that had ripped his skin deep into the tissue.

Without much medical knowledge beyond tidying up and dressing small cuts, she was at a loss when she saw the magnitude of the bitten damage. She reached over for Braun's hip flask and poured what remained of it onto the marks.

He shouted, "DAMNIT, AGNES, just give me the handkerchief."

She handed it to him and said, "Suit yourself, but we'll have to get you to Dr Trundle straight away. That doesn't look at all good, Braun."

He placed the cloth on the wounds with the intention of tying a knot around his foot, but it was a well-worn handkerchief made of very coarse cotton and it hurt. He tossed it to one side.

"That's too much. I'm just going to let this breathe for a minute or so. Just let the sting ease out a little."

"I don't think the stinging will tail off any time soon. Have you looked at it? Your skin is horribly mangled down there."

"That's real helpful, Agnes, thanks," replied Braun scornfully.

She picked up the flask and filled it up with some water from the lake. "Just let me run some of this water over it. The alcohol must have sunk in now."

He was reluctant to let her near his foot and he took the flask off her. He said, "I'll handle it."

She huffed and threw the flask in his lap. "You don't mind taking my help when I'm showing you how to get through a book, but when it comes to tending to you when you're hurt?"

She turned her back on him and sat facing the water as he muttered, "I'm perfectly capable of pouring some damn water over my foot."

This pissed her off even more, and she turned around quickly to give him another piece of her mind. But as she looked at his foot, it didn't look half as bad as it had earlier. The cuts appeared to be more graze-like, and the bleeding had stopped.

He saw her looking and decided to acknowledge it before she did. "See, they ain't so bad now I've cleaned them up. Just a few little bites."

"No," she said, and moved closer to him. She grabbed his foot, and Braun resigned himself to her determination.

The flaps of skin that hung off so limply had closed into the foot and appeared to be weaving their way back into the epidermis level of his skin. She knew he was trying to conceal this, but the secrecy had become too much, and it was at this point that she realised just how much she cared for him.

Braun twisted his foot into a direction out of her sight. He was no longer in pain, but to keep up the pretence he winced and sounded out all kinds of 'oohs and aahs' as he rubbed the handkerchief over the foot, which was only minutes away from turning back to its normal state.

Agnes had suffered a fair amount of pain throughout her life, and she could easily detect that he was now feigning it. She pointed to his foot, "Okay, mister. I know that a big chunk of your foot was hanging off when you came out of the water—."

Braun interrupted and tried to play it down. "Don't exaggerate. It really wasn't so bad."

"Yes, it was! It was a real ugly wound, and all I could think about was getting you to the doctor. But once you fell to your ass, all you seemed concerned about was hiding it from me. Part of your foot was gone and now…" She pointed to the foot. "…it just looks like you scraped it against a rock."

Agnes stared at Braun for an explanation. He knew she wouldn't accept any more of his nonsense, but still he attempted to carry on the pretence.

"I don't know what you think you saw..." He stopped for a second as Agnes continued to glare at him, then composed himself and tried to start again. "Now listen, I've been..."

Suddenly, he felt exhausted, his head dropped, and he couldn't continue.

Agnes reached out and held his hand. Her hand was soft and her touch tender and gentle. This made him cry, and he slapped his free hand across his eyes, sobbing until his throat made strange noises. They both knew that he had to wait for this to ease off before he could talk.

When Agnes felt he was ready, she said softly, "Show me your foot, Braun."

He nervously removed the handkerchief from his foot and turned around to face her.

She couldn't suppress an astonished reaction as she gasped. The only indication of injury to his foot was the strangely coloured bloody substance that had dried into his skin. Underneath this, his flesh was as unblemished as it had been before he'd got into the water.

"Why has it gone?" was all she was able to muster as she let go of his hand.

Braun, still crying, had to release some of his torment. "A lot of strange things have been happening to me, Agnes. Real... funny stuff. I wish I could tell you what it means and why it's happening, but I can't."

"That isn't right. You aren't right. Your foot was ripped to shreds and now... nothing."

Braun looked dejected. He wanted to tell her the full story, but he was so upset by the way she was looking at him that he didn't want to give her too much and scare her away. He loved her, and he'd recently started to think and hope that she might have felt the same way. Despite the concern, he noticed an overwhelming sense of relief as he opened up, even if only addressing the tip of the iceberg. He didn't understand it, so he struggled to articulate it.

"The last few weeks have been odd, to say the least, and it's damn hard to explain something when you don't understand it yourself. But something, call it an imposter of some kind, is living inside of me." He stopped for a second. "I'm sorry, Agnes, you must think I'm nuts."

She shook her head. "Go ahead, Braun, I'm listening."

He sighed and carried on. "You see, this thing that I'm talking about is now... Damn, this sounds crazy... This thing is, it's part of me, and it's controlling me. Part of my soul has been stolen, and I don't know who or what I am anymore."

Agnes looked concerned. "I don't understand, Braun."

"Okay, let me try. It's, it's... Umm, okay... Imagine containing the lifeforce of one hundred people. Everything has improved but beyond what I, or anyone for that matter, should be able to do, you know? I can see things from a distance that I shouldn't be able to. I can smell all kinds of things at any one time – and let me tell you, that's not too great in the saloon. That's why I sit so far away from the bar and that disgusting spittoon..."

He pulled a face expressing revulsion. "Even from my table, I can tell you what different flavours of tobacco are in there, and what all the guys in the bar had for dinner the previous evening. It's damn disgusting."

Agnes tried to make a joke. "I'll have to start bathing more regularly."

He failed to see this, and continued, "No, you smell great, but I can't say the same for most of the folks back in town. Anyways, there are all sorts of other things I can and will tell you about, but most of it is beyond my small mind. And if there is something I should be doing with it, I don't know what it is!" He gritted his teeth with frustration and tried to produce a better rhythm with his breathing. "I wish I could tell you more, and I pray to God I haven't scared you off..." His lips quivered. "Meeting you has been the best thing that's happened to me since, well, ever." He smacked himself quite hard on the back of his head with a closed fist. "Damn, I've said too much. You probably think I'm a monster now."

Agnes responded, "Too much! You haven't told me anything! Now, I knew there was something queer about you. Each day we've spent together, it's as though you're gaining strength all the time, but I see others around you, in town, they seem to weaken. You're just so much different from the first night we met. You even look different. Somehow... I can't put my finger on it but, no offence, sort of cleaner and shinier, and that funny walk you've got like you've pooped in your pants."

Braun laughed. "I know I looked like shit the night we met. But I *was* real drunk. And while we're on the subject of shit, I must tell you, I haven't shit my pants since I was knee high! Well, only a couple of times. There was my friend Ron's wedding night, and that one time when I drank some bad beer... Uuurrgghh, I can still taste it now. It must have been sitting at the back of Ed's cellar for probably ten years or so..." He snapped himself out of trying to recap any other incidents and shouted, "Anyhow! I do not have a silly walk!"

Agnes laughed. "Sorry, I guess you've just got a funny way of moving. And I wasn't saying that you looked like hell that first night, but you did look different, and you can't blame the drink. You haven't stopped guzzling hard liquor since the moment we met. I know there's a lot more going on than you're telling me, but I see it's hard for you."

He tried to play down some of her probing. "Do *you* feel weaker since you've met me?"

"Well, no, not exactly, and I can't answer for other people, but so many seem to have lost something since you came to town."

"Have you seen me hurting anyone?"

"Not directly, no."

"People are friendly with me all the time. I've been around two weeks, and I'm already on first name terms with half the town."

"Yes, that's the other thing, and again, please don't take this badly. But... okay... you're a sweet guy, but I wouldn't say you have the most extraordinary personality."

Braun laughed. "Thanks a lot."

"Well, come on now, be honest. You aren't Mister Life and Soul."

Braun half smiled and shrugged in response as Agnes continued, "Yet people can't get enough of you. Dan would refurbish the whole saloon if you asked him and the girls. The way they look at you."

"Come on, those girls bat their eyelashes at anyone who looks their way."

"Uh-uh, it's not the same with you. I know the difference, believe me. I see them staring at you, I mean really gawping at you, like you're the only guy in town."

Braun knew what she was talking about. The relief of being able to talk about this with another person and someone he really cared for had released so much of his anxiety, but he was still reluctant to divulge all the parts of the transformation that he could express. Agnes had reacted well so far, which had surprised him, and his love for her had intensified in the process. He was encouraged to open up a little more.

"I don't care about anyone in that town apart from you. And it's you that stops the bad inside me from taking over."

"We've all got some bad inside of us."

"No, not like this. This... whatever it is... it urges me to do wrong, God-awful terrible things. I have a constant battle with it. I know that to truly release its power I would have to let the evil pour all over me. And, God forgive me, I have let it get the better of me at times."

She shook her head. "That explains all that money, I guess."

He was annoyed by her assumption. "I didn't hurt anyone to get that money! Anyway, what I'm trying to say is, I have to work real hard to stop this getting the better of me. It's a constant mind struggle, because I want to be a good person and I know that it doesn't want me to be. Sorry, this probably ain't making any sense to you. But I know that in another person, a truly bad soul, this would cause all kinds of terror and horror."

"Look, I know you're trying, and I do believe there's something real different about you. Heck, I know there's something different, but this is all so vague, and I think you're holding back. But I'm not going to push you. It's your business, and I can see this is upsetting for you. You are a peculiar man, Braun McLeary, but you're decent, you make me laugh, and I can tell you have a good heart. This... erm, condition you talk about does make me look at you in a way I'd rather not, but I also know how so much is unexplained, things that we don't know about, and things that people know about but won't talk about. You're a good person. You've been a gentleman to me since we met, and I know you care for me. I didn't know what to make of you at first, and the truth is I've started to care for you too. But..." She held a finger up to him. "...I need to be sure that this thing won't get out of hand."

Braun reached out and put his hand tenderly on her shoulder. "I care deeply for you, too, Agnes. Since the night we met, you have been the angel protecting me. I don't know where this thing would have taken me otherwise. If you will be my wife, I will provide for you and repay what you've done for me."

Agnes was shocked and totally unprepared to receive the proposal.

Braun wasn't feeling too confident when he studied her perplexed expression. He took his hand off her shoulder before he added nervously, "Sorry. A little strange to jump into that after telling you what a damned freak I am. But of course, don't feel you have to give me an answer now. All I'd ask for from you is that you'd just please consider it..." He smiled hopefully. "And let me know when you're ready."

"I didn't expect it, that's all, Braun. It is very sweet of you." She turned away and looked out towards the lake. "I need you to know something about me now."

"You can tell me anything, Agnes. I want you to know that."

He winced as his internal voice ticked him off, *That's enough now, you big wet sonofabitch.*

She said, "I have been married before."

Braun looked at her sombrely. "I know you have, Agnes."

Her face was wrapped in confusion as she turned around suddenly to face him again. "What? You know? How do you know? I've not told you anything about that."

"I heard what happened to you. Your husband. Back in Goaville."

She could see the upset in his face as his head hung, his eyes fixed on the ground. Anger rose inside of her as she shouted, "WHO told you?"

He carried on staring at the ground.

"Look at me, you bastard!"

He obliged, and his eyes hovered on the lower part of her face. His reluctance to make eye contact enraged her further.

"I've never told anyone in town anything about me, is that clear?" She didn't wait for an answer. "And how dare you snoop around asking questions about me! HOW DARE YOU! Huh? Just who the hell do you think you are?"

"Honest, Agnes, I've not been prying into your business. I wouldn't do that. People talk, and somebody told me about that terrible... That godforsaken awful thing that happened to you."

She grabbed him by his collar. Anger and pain-induced tears cascaded down her face. "Who told you? And why haven't you said anything?"

"Does it really matter who told me? I wasn't fishing for anything on you. Honest, Agnes. It's goddamn meddlesome people with nothing better to do. They can't help themselves. It wasn't my business to ask you about it, Agnes. I figured that if you wanted to talk, you would. But now you've mentioned how you've been married before, I didn't want to... just couldn't act dumb. Wouldn't be right, and I don't know if I have the whole picture." He sighed. "The amount of lives that must have been ruined or ended through idle gossip."

She was furious that people had been talking about her, and her thoughts were soaked with recollections of her time in town. She processed and played out dozens of scenarios rapidly as she tried to work out who may have been prone to talk about her in such a way. She quickly decreed that it was pointless and concluded that Braun was right; gossip hounds fester in every town, and the concealment of such an emotionally agonizing experience was never going to be realistic. Drifters, travellers, and those looking for work passed through town all the time, and anyone could have recognised her from Goaville. She had to accept that through no fault of her own, people with nothing better to do could pull you down and cover you in dirt before moving on to the next person.

She looked at Braun and could see the want in his eyes as he anxiously awaited her answer. She'd known him for only a short space of time, but the way he was looking at her, like a puppy wanting some affection, drew her in. A lesser man could have been cruel to her with the information he had. But he had respected her and waited for her to be ready to talk, if she'd wanted to at all.

This won her over, and the warm glow of love blossomed inside her as she said, "I will marry you, Braun. As long as we can leave town and start a new life somewhere else."

Braun climbed to his feet and jumped with excitement. His leap reached an impossible height as he briefly levitated three metres above the ground, delightfully punching the air with a hang time that Michael Jordan would have been proud of.

It was a supernatural movement of restrained power, and Agnes was once again torn by a strange emotive juxtaposition, as the passion was replaced by an unnerving sense that she so frequently felt in his presence. She knew that Braun was good, but he had a second entity inside of him, and she worried what it could be capable of.

Chapter Eight

Salvador held the door open as he waited for Christen. The young man lagged as a limp slowed him down.

Christen shut the door behind him, and Salvador threw a batch of oak chunks onto the stone fireplace. A swarm of dust bounced back into his face, prompting a bout of coughing.

Christen called over, "I will get you some water, Father."

He filled up a tin cup from one of the several water buckets in Salvador's kitchen area and took it over to him. The priest had a swig and managed to say through his spluttering, "Coffee."

Christen brought a pot of coffee to the boil over the fireplace and sat on a rocking chair next to Salvador, who'd unselfishly opted for a far less comfortable tiny wooden stool, more suited to a child. "You must be tired, Christen. It's been quite a day for you."

Christen struggled to catch his breath. He was shattered and had not yet recovered fully from his injuries. The extra effort he had to put into his walking, plus the strain brought on by the wound to his chest had drained him. This was a feeling he'd became accustomed to, as good quality sleep had been hard for him. The horror of his past actions nagged his every non-distracted moment, and he was grateful for Salvador's company. They had very little in common, but just being able to talk to someone, a relative stranger, provided respite that had stopped him from putting a bullet in his own head.

Still, most of his conversation was dominated by philosophising about what he had done, what he was going to do, and what was going to become of him.

"I have no choice but to wait for it to happen now, Salvador? You know, what the chief said?"

Salvador put his tin on the floor and checked the coffee. "Pay no attention, Christen. I only agreed to that to spare your life."

"He told me a spirit, a skin walker, is going to claim me... my... my soul, and take it back to his tribe. I have never placed any belief on that kind of talk, but he didn't just believe it, he knew it. And I believe him, Salvador. Something inside me is slowly draining. I feel it."

Salvador could see Christen's anguish. He handed him a fresh cup of coffee and said, "You don't need to be afraid here, Christen. You are recovering, getting stronger every day in the best place..." He spread his arms wide. "a house of God."

Christen looked around at the surroundings: a large room, encompassing a kitchen, dining space, and several sitting areas. He counted eleven wooden crosses of varying styles and sizes scattered across the walls, some with Jesus nailed down, some without. Pictures of the Virgin Mary with child, and painted depictions of saints, covered much of the wall space, mostly wooden, a lot of which had begun to rot.

"All those crosses and faces staring down at me. They do not provide a shield from my fear. That man and his tribe, I spoke to him and several others on our trek in great depth. They speak the truth; it pushed its way into me. The truth. *They* are the truth, Salvador."

Salvador picked up an old dusty Bible from a small shelf next to the fire and jabbed it with a finger. "All the truth you need is in here. They have theirs, but the true word of God, what a man needs to live by, is all in here, Christen."

"Yes, so I've been told all my life. Nothing but. Do you know, the only reason I was taught to read at the orphanage was so that I could follow this book?" He took it from Salvador. "One book! I wasn't allowed to look at any others when I was a child. Do you think that's correct?"

He didn't wait for an answer and continued, "It didn't stop me from reading others when I got older. I'd get hold of them somehow, and I read many. But yes, there is a lot to follow, and some of it *is* beautiful. But with the written word, you can make anything sound beautiful, and I do know the book has offered comfort to so many throughout the centuries. It's just... I suppose some of us aren't as intoxicated by it as you, Sal."

Salvador winced. He didn't like being called Sal and had asked Christen several times to call him Father.

Christen continued to express himself. "The book has brought out an ugly side of humanity, no question. It's right there from the beginning. The very first man in the book was bound by rules to follow, set by an imposed higher authority. And so, it began, the temple was created."

Salvador looked frustrated. "No, Christen. Adam was punished because he took something that wasn't his to take. Much like you did. The young beautiful girl that we dug up today!"

Christen hung his head in shame. "I will despise myself for the rest of my days for what I did, but please don't use the book to condemn me, Salvador. I've fought that all my life, and every day I was called a sinner, thanks to your Jesus."

"I'm sorry that you were mistreated in the name of the book. People, they make it to suit their own agendas and desire for control. I know this. I have never feared God like so many others. I respect and love the Lord, but to be constantly scared is not what God wants. I have always taken more of a reasoned approach with my teachings – some like it, others do not. But I have to be authentic, you know, and I am appalled by those who constantly look to shame someone because they want to see the sin in everything. I believe that Christ died for the sins of mankind, not man. How mankind treat their own. How rulers and those with responsibility abuse their power and use and take from people; it could be within a family, or someone of privilege wanting to expand an empire with no regard for anything but their own greed and ego."

"I do respect that, Salvador, but I also respect my right to independent thought. And I think that we have more to learn from the chief and his people Their wisdom is based on the ground below and the sky above, animals, trees. It is life that does not waver from its path, a path that was designed for them—"

Salvador interrupted, "By God."

"Yes, maybe, but not by your cruel God! They are guided by the Earth. What are we guided by? Pages of stories based on speculation and hearsay..." He pulled at his black and white checked shirt. "Look at the clothes we wear! It's not real, but we, many of whom are Christians..." He stuttered and briefly lost his thread as he tried to put across his thoughts. Salvador waited for him to expand on something that was clearly important for him to talk about.

He wiped his sweaty forehead and continued. "After what I did to that girl, we, we take over and run them out, we ruin what little they've got, and we call them savages! Where did it all go wrong, huh?" He took the Bible and chucked it into the fireplace.

Salvador watched sombrely as the book slowly caught the flames amongst the wood. He stood up and walked over to a drawer in the kitchen area, taking two cigarillos out. He put one between his lips and handed the other to Christen. He struck a match against the wall and lit up. Christen didn't wait for the matches and stoked his up through the fire.

The two men sat in silence as they savoured the initial drags of the cigarillos. Christen thought he would get a reaction out of Salvador after his disrespect of the Bible, and although his action had not been pre-meditated, in the seconds that followed he'd secretly hoped that the priest would lose it with him. Salvador had shown Christen only kindness since he'd nursed him back from the brink of death, despite his unreasonable and trying behaviour in the weeks that followed.

Salvador enjoyed his smoke for a little longer until he put it out against the wall, with half remaining. He looked at Christen and said, "I have plenty more Bibles, but I'd rather you stick with the wood for the fire please, Christen."

He smiled, and Christen half smiled back. He found the soft tones of Salvador's voice very comforting and soothing. Only a faint hint of a Mexican accent was there in a voice that was somehow distinctive in its indistinctiveness.

He carried on, "Life was tough for me growing up, not too south of the border. A little pueblo, a village called Concha, which is Espanola for seashell." He shrugged his shoulders. "Miles away from coast, but that was the name. It also means something else, but as a religious man, ha-ha, I will remain silent."

"Concha," repeated Christen, managing a slight smile as he pondered over the other meaning.

"Concha was, and I'm certain still is, not somewhere that I would recommend as a place to spend too much time. Perhaps one drink in the cantina, but it is just somewhere to pass through. No work there, no money to be made. One end of the pueblo was particularly bad. You would see very poor and hungry people just walking up and down, up and down, to the end of the buildings and back again. This went on all day and night, many of them no stitch of clothing, naked. Children, men, women. Terrible place. I would call it uncivilized, but they didn't have the opportunity to be civilized. I lived with my padre at the better end of the village. Now when I say better, I mean we could eat most of the time at least, and we had clothes – not always shoes, but I could cover my ass with something."

He struck another match and lit the second half of the cigarillo. Taking a long drag, he continued, "My padre was very good with his hands. He would take any work he could get in town. Anything, repair work mostly, but he would also do what he'd call favours for money. Now, for this he would not tell me. Always a secret, but I knew they were bad things. You see, Padre was mean, drunk, and angry. Very angry. Most people in town feared him, and for good reason. I was terrified of the man. But he provided for me… most of the time. Not always, but yes, most of the time. Sometimes, I would go hungry for a couple of days. I was always second best to the animal he kept behind the house. Now, she would never go hungry, no. And if it was a choice between me and Eva, she would get the steak, not me—"

Christen interrupted, "Animal? What was it?"

Salvador laughed at the thought. "Eva was a Jaguar. You know this animal?"

Christen slowly nodded. "It's a cat, right?"

"Yessss." Salvador grimaced. "But not a little pussy cat. She was biiiggg. Yellow with spotted markings and thick, sharp teeth. You know the name jaguar means 'he who leaps once'. I don't know where that comes from, but you get the picture. She was long and muscular. Stood on her hind legs, stretched out like that? I'm thinking bigger than you."

Christen whistled once quietly in acknowledgement as Salvador continued, "Strong and scary. I never knew a time without her. Right from my earliest memory, she was there."

Christen asked, "What about your mother?"

Salvador's voice dropped. "Yes, I was just going to tell you about that. I never met her. Padre did not tell me one single thing about her, and the few times I did ask, he would react so angry. He would fold up his leather waistcoat and slap me, always trying his best to catch me right where it would hurt the most, on the elbows or the knees. See, you wouldn't believe it now…" He clenched his hands around two clumps of fat around his stomach and jiggled. "…but I was a very skinny boy. Bones sticking out everywhere. I can still feel the waistcoat striking me.

"It was a different kind of pain, you know. I think the betrayal of someone who is supposed to love you giving you hurt like that, it makes the pain worse. I don't know, and the smell... his smell when he'd get so close to you, the whoosh of the strike brought it out. Not pleasant. Rotten, just like him. Still, sometimes I would be relieved if he grabbed the waistcoat. He couldn't always find it, so he'd use his fists to beat me down instead. I pray for him, but he was a sick man, my padre. And when the children out on the street would tell me that Padre had fed Mama to Eva, at first I wouldn't believe them, but after a while you know..."

Christen wide-eyed, shook his head, and said, "Children make up all sorts of things like that."

"Yes, but when you are a child and you hear it over and over again, it starts to take on a life of its own. The turning point for me was when Padre put a swing up behind the house. He said it was for my birthday. Ha-ha, he didn't have a clue when my birthday was; some years I would have two, others none at all. This swing was tied up between two trees, with a wooden slab, just big enough for a child to sit on. I must have been around five years old when he did that for me, and I can honestly say it was the first time I'd felt true happiness. It wasn't much, just some old rope threaded through a piece of wood. But he was proud of himself. I remember the day he did it so clearly, too clearly in fact. He couldn't wait to get me on it, and I was excited, not to get on the swing but by Padre's attention."

Salvador took a few seconds; he hadn't spoke at such length to anyone about his past and he was surprised he was doing it now. Momentarily he was taken aback. He filled up his mug with more coffee and nodded to Christen, who bowed his head back, keen for a top-up.

Salvador took a few swigs of coffee and sucked out the last remnants of his cigarillo. "It was only when I sat down on the swing and Padre started pushing me, that something didn't feel right. I was directly facing Eva. She was chained up in the corner of the yard. There was a little slack on the chain, but she didn't have a lot of movement. No, no, she was choked by that thing. Padre said he loved her and, yes, he would go hungry to feed her, but that chain? No, that was not kind. If he'd truly loved her, he would not have kept her tied up like that.

"The joy was taken out of the swing when Eva started to get involved. I became a toy for her, and she would watch and jump as I flew back and forth. Her mouth looked so big from that height, and I could smell the raw meat on her breath every time I got near her. And I did get close. Too close. I told Padre that I didn't like it and I was scared, but he wouldn't answer and just kept pushing me. I would turn around, but he wouldn't look at me, and would stare at Eva each time she leapt with the giant mouth snapping open and shut. I don't know what he was getting out of it, but he was getting something. Something I would never want to understand. He knew she couldn't get me, but the look on his face as he'd stare at her, it was peculiar. His lips would twitch very fast, like this." He imitated it, his lips gurning and moving rapidly into many shapes.

Christen thought it looked funny, and his attempt to stifle laughter failed as he spluttered into chuckles.

He apologised. "I'm sorry, Salvador, your face just looked so odd with your little moustache bouncing around like that."

Salvador wasn't bothered and carried on from where he'd left off. "He'd pull this stupid face and make strange noises. I can picture him doing it now, just like it was yesterday. It felt like he was willing her to break off from the chains and get to me."

"Did she ever attack either of you?"

"No, she didn't manage that, thank the Lord. But Padre? Things changed between them. At first, he would pet her and she would respond. Not with purrs. I don't think she could do that, but it was more of a grrrrr. But still somehow friendly, you know. She would give back the affection that he'd show her. But after a while the chain must have got to her and the growl stopped being so friendly. She'd still communicate but you'd get more of a 'Stay away' message from her.

"Now Padre could be a gentleman on occasions – not too often, but if he really liked someone, he'd show a different side. People around town, passing through, they'd talk to him and some women were taken in by him. I suppose he wasn't a bad looking man. But, as I say, on the inside? Not so great looking. He could turn nasty just like that." He clicked his fingers. "No warning, just this ferocious anger would take over him, and he would do something horrible."

He closed his eyes and bowed his head for a short moment. "One night I was asleep. We lived in a hut about..." He looked around. "...Imagine this place split into four pieces."

Christen nodded. "...Just one piece of the four, okay, that was our hut. Very small. Not enough room to swing a cat. Never mind a jaguar, you know." He laughed.

"He had a woman with him this night. They were both drinking, kissing, cuddling. Acting like I wasn't there, you know. I was probably nine, maybe ten years old, and most of my time inside the hut was spent playing with a small piece of blackboard and chalk. I would make stories through drawings. Little adventures that would be lost every time I'd rub out the picture and start again. But I would remember the good ones and do them many times.

"I would have these adventures on the blackboard until I fell asleep, and that's what happened this night. I was out until... Snap!" He clapped his hands once. "The woman screamed, and I'm awake. I look up and she is sitting on the floor, her back to the wall and her legs spread out, but not how you would sit normally. Her head was turned to one side. Padre, he sees I'm awake and looking. He runs at me and... Bang!" Another clap. "He smacks me over the head with something, and I'm out straight away.

"The morning comes and the woman, she has gone. Now this wasn't unusual, as Padre was bad and people wouldn't like to stay for too long, you know? But this day I knew something was wrong. That scream and the way she was sitting when I saw her. Not good. And when I saw a little piece of clothing, just a tiny square with flowers on it, right outside next to where Eva was resting..." The pain of the memory struck hard and stopped him in his tracks.

Christen laughed. "The jaguar couldn't have eaten a whole person in one night."

Salvador agreed. "No, of course not. But Padre was funny for the next few days. Maybe he had her somewhere and he was feeding Eva bits at a time, I don't know. Still, going back to how he started getting mean with Eva, it wasn't nice, you know. He would poke her with big sticks. Why he liked to torment her like that? Very peculiar to me. Another one of his favourites was to put food on the end of the sticks, and just as she was about to take it, he'd pull it back to him. He would do this until her mouth started bleeding. It must have been her tongue or something else inside, with the bite coming down again and again.

"He liked playing cruel games like that. One day, though, he got it back. He was drunk and acting stupid, singing and dancing, getting close to her. I was playing outside, skipping or something, when he slipped. He must have spilled some of his tequila, and he landed right in front of her. She didn't hesitate; she'd probably been waiting years for the chance and her mouth went right for his neck. He tried to shout to me for help, but his throat must have been that torn up. All I could hear was blood being gargled through whatever was left of it."

Christen was perversely enjoying the story. He thought back to the bird in Patrick's shop as he asked, "What did you do, Salvador? Did you set her free?"

Salvador shook his head. "This might sound ridiculous to you, but you see, I think that finally getting to Padre gave Eva the strength to break free. I swear on the Holy Bible—"

Christen interrupted and pointed to the fire. "You mean that book keeping us nice and warm, Sal?"

Salvador sighed. "I know you don't care right now, but you will, Christen, trust me you will."

Christen laughed and said sarcastically. "If you say so... Father."

Salvador looked sombrely at the book crackling through the flames, its leather-bound cover slowly melting as the corners curled up with the heat.

He got back on track. "Eva pulled herself up. She stood upright, which I hadn't really seen her do that too often, but she was determined. She roared and ripped the chain out from the wall with this almighty strength. It wasn't just raw animal power; I know it came from somewhere else. That chain was practically part of that wall. The years that had passed had proved how tightly moulded it was.

"It was strange, because in that moment, I had no sadness for Padre as he lay there. Only joy for Eva. I felt something you know. If you really want a good... umm... a correct thing to happen, you might have to wait a long time and go through so much pain. But if you don't give up, it will happen. I saw it, Christen. She'd been tied to that wall for the whole of my life and I don't know for how many years before that. But removing the cause of her pain set her free. There she was right in front of me. She could have ripped me apart in seconds, but I felt no fear. She looked at me, and her eyes, they sparkled in a way that I hadn't seen before.

"We stared at each other for, maybe ten seconds. I smiled, and this sound came from her, it was soft, and I understood. We connected in that moment, and she was saying goodbye. She moved past me and jumped over the back wall. I watched her running out into the desert, right until I couldn't see her; just every now and again, I'd hear the chains hitting a rock. It was something, you know. She'd spent most of her life just pacing up and down and she must have been very old, but when she got the chance... whoosh, she was gone. I mean really fast. I hadn't seen that kind of speed before. It took my breath away."

"Where did you go from there?" asked Christen.

"I didn't want to stay in Concha. I picked up blankets, boxes of Padre's matches, and filled up two flasks from the well. I didn't need food. I'd gone days without even a grain of rice. But I knew I had to leave. You see, I felt something that hasn't left me since. It was God's hand on my shoulder. And with my guide, I walked and walked and walked in one direction for days, only stopping once or twice a day to rest. And I would sleep besides bushes or rocks, just for shelter, you know.

"I had God's protection, but the nights were frightening. I was eleven years old, and the sounds I would hear kept me awake most of the night. I would find a bush somewhere to lay down with a fire to keep me warm. But the sheer black surrounding me and all the strange animal noises stopped me from getting sleep. All I had were a few sharp sticks to defend myself. But I kept going, and at some point, after three days or so of walking, I crossed into Arizona.

"I was finished, and I was down to the bottom of my flask. I was starving, tired, and the thoughts in my head were driving me crazy. I passed a few cowboys heading in the other direction. A couple asked if they could help, but I didn't trust anyone out there. I must have looked death-bound. I can still picture the shock on their faces as they passed me.

"I nearly didn't make it and fell down more than a few times from heat exhaustion. But God pulled me along until I found a chapel, and that is where Father Herman found me. And I've told you what that wonderful man did for me. He saved my life, and now you are here. Much the same way, you have found me, and I want to help you just as God and Father Herman saved me."

Salvador smiled at Christen and patted him on the back a couple of times.

Christen looked at Salvador, he looked so tired. Reliving painful and pivotal moments from the past had taken it out of him. His appearance belied his thirty-two years. Paunched stomach, receding hairline, and a well spread bald patch aged him greatly.

Christen pulled his own tobacco patch from his pocket and rolled up a smoke. He offered to roll one for Salvador, but the priest shook his head.

He stared into the fire as the Bible began to crumble, glancing at Salvador, who also watched. A pang of guilt hit Christen, and he toyed with grabbing the brass stick from the side of the fireplace to pull out what was left of it, but it was pointless as the damage was so severe.

He smoked away and carried on gazing into the flames as he said, "I'm sorry about the Bible, Salvador, that was wrong. I should not have done that. But I'm afraid that is my problem. I have an impulsive nature that implores me to do... bad things. I don't like it but that is me."

He shrugged his shoulders and carried on, "I know your intentions are good, and that was a beautiful story. I especially liked the part where the jaguar ate your daddy's throat." He laughed and briefly turned to Salvador.

But the priest didn't see the humour as he looked straight ahead, like Christen, eyes focused on the fire.

Christen continued, "You are wanting to make this a passing of the torch. A torch burning for redemption. You see me turning up as symbolic, and you think it is your turn to impart your wisdom onto a poor, misused adolescent. But there is a difference. You were a child when Herman took you in and not old enough to be fully tarnished by life's cruelties, like I have been."

Salvador answered, "Yes, but Christen, this is... You are my opportunity to pay back the kindness that God deemed for me."

Christen was angered. "Your opportunity! So, that's how you see this, huh! I'm a special token for you? A new character for your precious book. Ha! Not so, Salvador, that is not the fucking case. Don't forget, I was brought here through theft, rape, and murder. I'm a bad person, and neither you nor anyone else will be able to change that. I don't have this magic inside of me that is screaming to be awoken. Only bad lives in here.

"I'm sorry, I know your intentions are with honour, but I must make it clear and help you to understand that not everyone is going to adhere to how you or all your religion-obsessed friends want things to be. Perhaps man has created the idea of God. Is it a tool to try and make sense of the confusion we feel just through being alive? Tools can be used to fix, but they can also be used to construct..."

He paused for a few moments and drew on his cigarette.

Salvador looked hurt by his comments, but it didn't stop Christen from laying it on further. "The deeper the pain, the more we produce the legend of God for our own comfort and hopes. The original intentions of the myth, I'm sure were good, but when all is said and done, God is merely a device formed by man to avoid the agony of dealing with our inner torment and knowing that this is it. We need to convince ourselves that the illusion is real, just so we aren't cursed by our minds, and knowing when we are at our youngest and fittest that all we have waiting for us is a lifetime of struggle. Some may make enough money to stop when they are old, but what do they have to look forward to with the rest of their time? All they can do is watch helplessly as their bodies deteriorate and sag, pulling them closer to the ground."

He stopped and briefly managed a bitter laugh. "It's been a long day, Salvador, and after seeing that girl and reliving what I did, and of course remembering what I'm capable of, I'm afraid I feel thoroughly depressed. But I do want you to know that I will repay you for what you have done for me—"

Salvador interrupted, "Surely that shows there is goodness in you?"

"No, not out of goodness. I am not arrogant enough to completely dismiss the idea of God. Anyone who does should not be taken seriously. But I do not believe. I do, though, think that evil exists, and now the chief's curse has started to eat me from the inside out. I will succumb to it, out of hatred for what I am and for what I have done to other people, my brother, and my friend. It would be cowardly to end myself, much as I want to. It would not be right; I deserve to feel every moment of the slow hollowing of me."

He paused for a few seconds as he considered how to present a request to the priest. "Now, if you are agreeable, Salvador, I shall serve out my penance at the chapel. I know that remaining here could hide me from trouble. And I will help you out in return, wherever I can be of assistance. I can keep the church clean, tend to the crops and help wherever you see practical. I know you have much beauty and forgiveness. You know what I've done and what I'm capable of, yet you tended to me when I faced death, and now you listen to me. That is not something that I'm used to."

He bowed his head. "I give you my word that as long as I am here, I will not let you down. Something happened when I was buried in my sleep for all that time. You kept me alive, but a big part of me died. I hope it was some of the rot that has misguided me since I left the orphanage, but I fear that it could be resurrected if I get back out there. I want to stay here with you, Salvador, and all I'd ask from you as well as food and shelter is that you continue to be my suppressor of wrongdoing."

Salvador reached out, patted Christen on the shoulder a few times, and said, "Christen, I don't agree with much of what you say, but you are a thoughtful young man and that is without much help from others. Very good. It's just a shame that you took the wrong path."

Christen responded. "Do you not think that intelligent people existed before formal education? Greek philosophy wasn't influenced by an establishment; they weren't all brought up on the chosen few books that education has been designed against. Everyone learning the same way! Pfft, I feel advantaged that my thoughts have not been clouded by the modern system. You are the same, growing up poor in Mexico. Just because I didn't have the privileges that others are born into, it doesn't mean that I have not tried to build a relationship with my brain. I had plenty of time to think in that place; that's all I did throughout childhood when I wasn't trying to entertain my brother and Puds. I tried to discuss ideas with them, but they just wanted to run around, fight, and fist pump their peckers."

Salvador smiled and shook his head.

Christen chuckled. "Dumb bastards. But that was how they were, and I had others to speak to, out in the field. The slaves." He looked at Salvador, who frowned. "Yes, slaves. The Civil War didn't free them all up, you know. Talking too much could get them a good whipping, but it didn't stop us having some very good conversations. It was so boring and tiring being on your feet all day in the heat. You had to talk, or you would lose your mind. Coming over here from Denmark so young, it wasn't my choice, and I resented my forced place in this country. But when I spoke to them and heard how they were captured and removed from their homes like wild animals, and what they went through on the ships..." He pursed his lips and blew air. "...I had no right to complain. I truly felt for them, Salvador."

He looked sad, and his eyes briefly filled with tears. "Yet I still took that girl from her people. That is all the proof that I need to know that I am commanded by evil."

Salvador patted Christen on the shoulder again and stressed, "Yes, but you recognise this, Christen, and you want to work things out. I know you do. That is progress, my son."

Christen hung his head, with shame written all over his face.

Salvador, as shattered he was, could see how tired Christen was. It had been a troublesome day for him, and he was alarmed by how different the boy's face looked since they'd returned from the barren desert land. The boy was naturally very thin, but the pupils of his eyes were wide and closer to a dark grey than black. They seemed to be set further back in his face. His cheekbones were already angular and prominent, but the collagen in the skin underneath had lost its shape, and a sunken effect had developed. He looked truly haunted, and for a split second Salvador wondered whether the chief had bestowed a curse on him.

Just being in the chief's presence had left the priest in no doubt that spirituality was at the forefront of everything he did. And if he believed so adamantly that he had cursed Christen, then could the energy of that thought have forced its way into reality? Or even affect someone to the point of ruin, just through power of persuasion? He shook it out before he started to think about it too much.

Christen was clearly in a disturbed state of turmoil, and Salvador knew he had to close the door to stop any of it heading towards him.

He fixated on his breathing for half a minute and his regular sense took over again. They had experienced a deeply emotional and harrowing day, and he knew it was time to get back to his daily routine.

He pushed down on the arms of his chair to suggest he was ready to move on, as he added his final comment. "Christen, what I do see within myself and others, is if they have faith and belief in something, they grow stronger. And for that, I can only see that something beyond our limitations responds and pulls us forward." His legs were stiff, and he was starting to feel too hot. "I must move, Christen. I'm getting too warm next to the fire."

He headed to the far side of the room and Christen followed. The priest pushed through a door that separated the chapel from the living quarters, leading them into a small corridor, either side of which took them to an end of the altar and into the chapel. They passed through and Christen stumbled as he misjudged the large step to the corridor floor. He flinched as his foot hit the ground, the impact of the misstep jarring his wounded leg. He made a reactionary pained throat rumble.

Salvador heard this and commented, "That is the first time I've not said 'watch the step', and look what happened."

Salvador laughed, but Christen didn't. Instead he felt sorry for himself, and his limp briefly became as severe as when the arrow had struck his calf a fortnight earlier.

They carried on around the corner. The sight of the chapel cheered Christen up as it did almost every time he'd spent time there. He had found comfort in this space when he first came around after the injuries and the subsequent infection that had nearly killed him. It was the stillness, the smell of frankincense, and the fact that no matter how warm or cold it was outside, the room seemed to have its own perfectly regulated, constant, and consistent climate.

He remained standing at the opening of the corridor with a full view of the chapel, as Salvador sat on a stool just to the left of the rickety old wooden altar. Christen looked around and began to understand that a big part of its charm lay in the randomness of its design. Salvador had been assigned to the chapel ten years ago when the building was empty and only fifteen years old. But it had ceased operating as a place of worship for six of those years. The small town that it represented had pretty much packed up and left. Its inhabitants had either died or moved on for pastures new. The lack of work and any kind of exposure for the town had made it difficult for people to remain there.

Salvador had been reluctant to take up a post in such a desolate area, but with developers aware of the industry created through the aftermath of the Civil War, the town of Pendle became something they were interested in. Much of the infrastructure was already in place, with young unoccupied buildings aplenty and plans for Pendle to feature on a train line.

Despite the optimism for the town, Salvador was only afforded minimal funding for the chapel which had been gutted following its original closure. All the fixtures and fittings had been removed, and Salvador was left with an empty shell with instructions to arrange for the place to be re-conditioned on a measly budget. He appealed to priests and clergymen in nearby areas for anything they could spare, from pews and pulpits to candleholders and chalices.

It wasn't long before deliveries came pouring in, and such was the generosity of the donations, it reached a point when he was having to turn carriages away. Quantity didn't prove an issue, but quality did, and the items and furniture he received were in most cases riddled with issues, from woodworm-infested benches to leaky holy water stoups. But he dusted off the best of the bad bunch and enlisted the help of the stronger early settlers in the newly emerging Pendle.

The day it was finished, Salvador was immensely proud of the enormous amount of work that had gone into getting the place up and running, but he couldn't help but feel embarrassed when he surveyed his new surroundings. It was very haphazard; bent nails held together misshapen wooden benches and steps leading up to the altar, tapestries displayed across all four sides were mostly ripped or stained, and the look of the chapel held no cohesive aesthetic.

Large pastel coloured fabric wall hangings with Latin Psalm quotes sat awkwardly next to much smaller and brighter coloured styles. Benches of all shapes and sizes, made for two wonky looking sitting areas, flanking the stone-floored middle nave.

The first day Salvador opened the doors to the public, he was apprehensive. But to his delight, people liked how quirkily put together everything was. He noticed a few sniggers from the younger worshippers, but he knew it was mostly good natured.

The chapel quickly amassed a small but devoted following, and a few years into his tenure he'd acquired enough money to give the place a real spruce up. To his surprise, people reacted badly to this and the overwhelming opinion was that it should stay as it was – an ugly duckling that had won the hearts of the local townspeople.

He made a few necessary changes here and there and always kept the place very clean, but for the most part it still looked and held up the same way as its initial makeover a decade before. Salvador had grown to love it and he wouldn't have left it for the grandest cathedral in the country.

This very same thing had happened to Christen, and now two weeks in, he had developed a strong fondness for the place. It felt somehow alive to him, and he saw Salvador as the main reason for that. The chapel was an extension of the priest, and looking out as Salvador closed his eyes in silent prayer, Christen was momentarily numbed from the pain.

Chapter Nine

Braun was trying to live with his hallucinations and visions as best as he could. It was extremely difficult for him to stay rooted in the present, with most of his head trips throwing him into what he could only ascertain as belonging to another time. He would touch things and see something that he figured was future-related.

A weird happening presented itself on a typical day, as he spent time in an outbuilding of the saloon to feed Maggie the cow. He loved petting her, placing his hands on her head. She was always so grateful, and her cold hide would warm up rapidly under his hands.

Early in the morning, one day when his mind was particularly effervescent, he topped up Maggie's tray and gave her the customary head rub. It felt different this time, though, and the warmth wasn't present. It was fuzzy and static. He couldn't remove his hand, and he knew the second he blinked he would be taken somewhere else. He tried to fight it, refusing to blink for as long as he could hold out. If he'd been able to detach his hand, he would remain where he was, but he couldn't. And after a minute, the inevitable blink occurred. The room darkened, and he briefly found himself in a large, clinically decorated and putridly lit room.

He was pinned to a wall, unable to move as though stitched to it, and all he could do was watch as dozens of grossly oversized humans, young and old, stuffed their faces with thick, circular chunks of meat wrapped in oddly coloured and weirdly formed bread. He shouted for people to speak to him. He wanted to ask why they were so hungry, and why they were so determined to maintain or add to such massive size. But no-one could see him, and he realised that he was a ghost, just like the apparitions that had haunted him, lost in a different place at a different time.

Flashes of imagery suddenly filled his head like a rapidly changing slideshow: big people, sickly human beings, in all sorts of different scenarios, charged through his mind so swiftly that he couldn't focus on one event. Such people were not familiar to him, and the fact that it was presented as a collage and programmed into him left Braun in no doubt that a problem was imminent. He was unsettled to see so many people looking such a way that he was not accustomed to.

Further nightmarish visions ensued. He could only stand by and watch as acres of forest was ripped apart by men controlling enormous vehicles designed for destruction. Their metal necks stretched out like dragons as they ploughed into trees, leaving only stumps behind. Thousands of the trees were burnt to the ground to be replaced with crops. He looked on, always inaudible and always unable to move far. If he wasn't stuck to something, he was left in a restrictive vortex, with invisible walls preventing him from moving beyond a very limited patch of land.

The crops were taken to feed the cows that were in turn feeding the extremely large people. He would feel immense tension, as though two powerful hands squeezed his temples as hard as they could. It hurt, and he could feel the pressure that was being placed on the planet and the enormous bodies of the people. His thoughts moved towards quite a paganistic contemplation process, as the notion of those who disrespect nature will in turn lead those to disrespect themselves. It dawned on him that the health of the planet could be seen through the collective health of the people, and if they were not being looked after adequately by those with great power and influence over the world, then the planet could only suffer.

Braun closed his eyes for a few seconds. The pain was real, and just as his head was about to cave in on itself, he opened his eyes and found himself back in the barn, standing next to Maggie. She stared right at him as she mooed over and over. She recognised the state he was in, and she didn't like it.

He filled up her trough and re-assured her softly, "It's okay, Maggie."

That night he went to bed thinking, *How could something that felt like a wonderful gift turn into such a horrible curse?*

The potential foresights could pull him out of any momentary situation, but to others his transportation would go unnoticed. When removed from the present, everything around him would pause, and upon being thrown back into his reality (if that's what it was) a comment was rarely made outside of the odd remark about the weird expressions on his face. It must have been over in a blink of an eye for those in his presence, but for Braun the episodes could last hours.

Days, even weeks would pass without Braun experiencing anything, but when they came, they left him depleted and incredibly hungry. He understood parts of most of them, or what they were getting at, but some would be totally bizarre and left him seeing shapes and colours in strange unoxygenated atmospheres. He was unable to breathe in these scenarios, but he didn't need to, as he saw monolithic blobs building structures from textures he had not seen before. He didn't know if he was even human in these moments, as they were beyond human comprehension.

He worked on switching off completely, closing his eyes, and shutting down as much negative mind energy as he could. This helped a lot, and through this he could ask the questions and throw them into the ether. The method provoked some response, and his visions started to gain some more clarity.

He could never participate in the scenarios, though, and would not been seen by others. But he started to hear other people. The clearest example hit him in a dream two weeks before he was due to marry Agnes.

He found himself outside a building, the sort he was mildly accustomed to seeing through other mind journeys. It was the usual tall, grey, boring structure that repelled any design appreciation.

This time he wasn't locked into one spot. Instead, the invisible wall was behind him, only it moved when he moved, but also stopped when he did. This forced him to move forward, and he could only turn his head so far to look behind. What he noticed through the corner of his eye was a street with what looked like a park on the other side to the building. He couldn't see much, but from the little that did come through, he noticed it was spotlessly clean.

He didn't want to enter the building, but he also didn't want to remain on the steps, so he walked up to the building front and pulled at the door. His hands felt numb against it. He was aware of a formation at the end of his hand, but his sense of touch was unable to register anything of matter. As he tried it again unsuccessfully, he was joined by two people. One was a very healthy-looking woman in her early thirties, with a blonde pixie-cut. She was dressed in a designer suit, well fitted to a gym-toned frame. Alongside her was a tall and skinny young man, also suited, fresh-faced and boyish, with dark brown mid-length, wavy hair. They didn't look his way, but he tried to greet them anyway and offered his hand. He figured that they wouldn't be able to ignore a man dressed in clothes from another time if they'd been able to see him.

The lady placed her thumb onto a small box next to the door. A click locked out a mechanism, and a flap opened in the middle of the door. Behind the flap was a tiny screen.

The lady was tall in her high heels, and she crouched down a little, moved her head towards it, and a flash was produced at her eye level. This produced a second click and the door opened.

She said to the young man, "We'll get your recognition security set up by the end of the day."

The door opened and Braun followed them in.

He found himself in a very quiet lobby, where a pristinely presented receptionist in a suit sat behind a desk and typed away on a computer, while four heavy set and armed security guards flanked the big stone reception front. Two doors were either side of the desk, both of which were manned by a pair of the security guards.

The two visitors walked towards the receptionist as Braun was pulled along too. He cleared his throat loudly to test the water, but they couldn't see or hear him, and he was just grateful for the extra mobility and audibility that this scenario provided him. He looked around. There wasn't much to look at, but he was briefly distracted and confused by two flat boxes strapped to the walls containing moving images of humans.

A man and a woman, both wearing the type of boring suits he was now familiar with, sat behind another giant desk, as a bar of information ran along the bottom of the two boxes. It was quiet and he didn't really listen to what they were saying, but he briefly became distracted by the statements on the screens. It was all miserable: murders, countries at war, and names of those who'd been scandalised.

Like all his previous visions, his lack of awareness of the place and time frustrated him, but a sense of alienation was enhanced further by his attire as he paced around in a tailcoat and spurred boots. The receptionist wore a clean, groomed beard, not much shorter than his. The woman and her companion chatted to him, and the young man was passed a few forms to fill out. He leant against the desk and started ticking boxes as the lady chatted to the receptionist about the weather and how busy she'd been. It was all very boring to Braun, and after a couple of minutes waiting for something to happen, he got fed up and sat on the floor.

He shouted, "Come on! Throw me out of this one, please." He pointed to the security guards. "I'm guessing they have to stand around here all day. Urrrgghh, I sure feel sorry for them."

He threw his arms around. "Look at this, nothing but white. White Floor, white walls. It's real strange how something so plain can look so damn… horrible. Could they not be given something to look at? Maybe a picture of a lake or fields, just to remind them that the world can look pretty sometimes. Hell, even that terrible oil painting that Dan put in my room would be better than all the white nothing. Makes me want to puke."

He put his fingers to his lips. "Hey, maybe that wouldn't be such a bad idea. I could spray some up the walls, and they could put a frame around it." He mumbled, "After all, isn't that where the best art comes from? Deep inside and all."

The young man finished filling out his forms and handed them to the receptionist, then the woman led him towards the door on the right.

The man said, "Where does the other door lead to?"

"I'll tell you another time," she snapped back.

The man nodded, knowing not to press it anymore.

The security guards moved aside as she placed her thumbprint onto another recognition device attached to the door. This door had a big, bank vault-style, wheeled handle. It was strong and robust, but neither of the security guards stepped in to help her, as they knew she could handle it.

The door opened, and Braun charged through with them quickly, as the guard seemed keen to shut it as soon as he could. He squeezed through and followed them down a windowless corridor, again, very non-descript, white-walled, tunnel-like in shape, with rounded angles conjoining the walls, ceiling, and floor. The lighting was dim, and they passed a few doors either side to make their way to a door at the far end.

The woman chatted to her companion along the way. "So, have you settled into the campus okay, Karl?"

"Yes. My house is amazing. I can't believe I've got a cinema room, a games room, and a gym."

She smiled and said, "You're on row thirty-three, aren't you?"

"Yes."

"They put me there when I signed up ten years ago."

"Where are you now, Sofia?"

"I'm on row nine."

He looked impressed. "Wow, row nine! All the houses from row fifteen down are huge!"

"It's more than enough room for my husband and me. But I still hope to get to row five one day. You've got to aim high, right?"

He responded, "Why not shoot for row numero uno?"

Karl saying 'numero uno' annoyed her, and she said, "Technically, it isn't possible for me to go beyond row five. Four to one are strictly for the family."

"Right." He laughed and tapped his nose with his right index finger. "And we don't talk about them, of course."

Sofia sighed internally and thought, *Not the best start. Who vetted this chump?* Then she remembered that he was the nephew of a man she respected, and she took a deep breath.

The corridor was long, and Braun just wanted to get to the end room. Despite the sterile surroundings, he was beginning to enjoy the distinctness of the vision.

Before they reached the door at the corridor end, they surprised Braun and turned to the last door on the left, again actioning the thumb-eye, identification-verifying process.

Just before they passed through to the room, Sofia held the door open and said, "Don't worry about being stuck on campus for eighteen months. It sounds like a long time, but honestly, you'll be learning so much during probation that it'll fly by."

Karl nodded. "It's not so much being confined to the campus that bothers me. I mean, it's got everything – multiplex, bowling alleys, designer shops. I've already had a night out with a couple of the other apprentices, and the bars are cool."

"Let me guess, it's the psyche tests?"

"Yes, I hear they're pretty heavy, and one a month! I don't know, that just seems a little intense to me."

"I know. That is the suckiest part of being here at first, but it's only during probation. People think it shows a lack of trust in our new club members, but we've really had to take these measures, especially after we had a couple of near incidents a decade ago. But just think of the rewards afterwards. And as for the confinement you'll go through, you said it yourself, it really isn't that bad. There's plenty of room around here, green spaces, and we've got lakes one and two if you're into water sports. We do everything we can to keep you from getting bored. We've even had a couple of bands playing at the campus recently."

"Yes, I heard Flying Saucers played here a couple of weeks back. Man, I'd loved to have seen that. Dave Growl must be well into his eighties, but that guy can still rock hard."

"Yes! Paul, my husband, and I went to see them. They raised the roof. I can't believe he can still scream like that!"

"I'll be sure to check them out if they come back. It's awesome that the club organises that sort of thing.

It won't be too much of a stretch to stick around here for the foreseeable future. I know that there could be lots of international travel opportunities after probation."

"Sure, I've lost count of how many countries I've visited. Some of them I didn't even know existed! But most of that was done in my twenties. I still do a little international presenting, mostly in Europe and the Far East, but I'm really settled to life in the campus, and I don't really leave for anything unless I have work commitments."

An alarm-like beeping noise came from the door. It hurt Braun's ears and he shouted, "JUST GO THROUGH THE GODDAMN DOOR, WILL YOU?"

Sofia ushered Karl through. "Quick, it will lock us out!"

They skipped through, unaware as the ghostly Braun passed through with them.

It was another room, just as bland as everything else they'd seen. Only this time, they were in a very large space. Lots of people, mostly under forty years old were scattered around, sitting or standing in quite spacious glass-domed containers. The odd one held two workers, but mostly had only one. Each person had a small desk to the side of them within their container. They weren't sizable enough to store much, but they didn't need a great deal. Just a couple of very compact electronic devices and a drink or food item took up the limited space.

The workers all wore the same outfit. Trousers, thin, roll-neck jumpers, socks, and gym pumps. All jet black and tightly fitted.

Sofia and Karl stood next to a water cooler in a small kitchen area a few metres left of the door. They chatted away as she pointed around the room, giving him an oversight of practices that meant nothing to Braun. He tuned out from what they were saying briefly and gathered his thoughts. *Just what the fuck is going on here and why should I care?*

Yet he had become somewhat engrossed, and although desperate to return home, he wanted to see what this was all about.

His movement was freer still in this room, and taking a walk around, he saw the first thing in this vision that pleased him. He noticed many people of different ethnicities, shapes, sizes, and two disabled members of staff in wheelchairs all working together. They each had their own cubicle, but he could see so many of them shouting over to each other as they collaborated and shared thoughts.

"Well, ain't that something, we're all getting along. Never thought I'd see that day. Not that I should be seeing the fucking day." He cupped his hands around his mouth, looked up to the ceiling, and said loudly, "'Cause this sure ain't my day. And I don't know for shit what they're doing in those stupid little rooms. But hey, they all seem to be working together and that is real swell."

He clapped his hands. "Okay. Queer, creepy fucking place, but it seems like in the future we're all friends. I like it. Didn't think we'd ever get there, but it looks like we do. I'm truly humbled, and I'll remember this. Now can I go home, please?"

He closed his eyes for a few seconds, hoping somehow that he could return to his own time, but it didn't work. He repeated this a few times but to no avail, as he remained in this strange time and place.

With nothing else to do, he walked around a little more and took a closer look at the glass-domed dwellers.

He was disturbed to see that they all had the same-coloured eyes – a fiery orangey brown that didn't look natural.

The situation was made even stranger when he edged closer to a woman of Samoan descent. He put his hands on the door of her glass chamber and looked closely. He could just about detect a pupil, not much bigger than a pin prick. The eyes were freaky, and he became even more unsettled over the next twenty minutes while he listened to several conversations being shared, as people opened their cubicles and threw around ideas. He heard a lot of recurring chatter, the same words being used with similar tone and pitch in their voices.

He understood that, as bizarre as it looked to him, they were somehow working on something. They seemed so enthused by what they were doing, not in a passionate sense but with an eagerness that whiffed of desperation to Braun. He focused on them and tried to see inside, but it was difficult for him. He wasn't surprised by this, because he wasn't sure how his presence was there, plus the black clothing could have distorted his view. He persisted and concentrated hard, trying to summon something up. Within a minute, he was able to shut out the chatter.

The people who weren't discussing ideas stood on circular pads within their cubicles. They had nothing in front of them but a glass screen that they gestured towards with their hands in very animated ways. Braun watched one man, who stood out due to the sheer size of him. He had a powerful build – that of someone who clearly regularly lifted very heavy things. Braun was fascinated by his neck, or lack of it, as he saw a head with two muscular slopes either side that appeared to bypass the idea of a neck, and seemed to merge straight into a pair of boulder-like shoulders. He was tall, all muscle, and the black roll neck jumper was so tight it looked as if the man would need a team of firefighters to break him out of it. His movements seemed a little more aggressive than the others, and his heavily waxed, blond mohawk showed signs of losing its hold. Sure enough it did a couple of times, as the strands of hair splattered across the top of his head like spiders' legs as he became over-animated.

Braun watched him for a while as Sofia and Karl continued chatting away in the kitchen area. He remembered reading a couple of short paragraphs about Tai Chi and briefly wondered if they could be doing that, but he doubted it. This didn't look ancient or elegant; it looked mechanical and emphatic.

He carried on staring at the mohawked man until his patience wore off. And like a magic eye effect, something unravelled as he finally saw through the black jumper and into the man's spark – or in this case, the lack of it. The smoky balls of varying textures and colours that he'd been used to seeing back home were nowhere to be seen, as this man's essence was small, beige, flaky, and lifeless. It didn't pulsate like so many he'd seen, nor did it look appetising to him.

Braun thought, *I wouldn't feed on him even if I could. He looks like he's been devoured.*

He couldn't understand it, the man looked so healthy on the outside. His skin was pale and unblemished with all those muscles, and his teeth dazzlingly white.

Braun wrote him off as a bad egg and looked around to others. He glanced over to another man of similar age, mid-twenties, healthy looking, not as built as the other guy but still in great shape. It was the same story with him, though, as Braun saw another sorry, dull, brownish pathetic orb. This one was also flaking, and reams of it swayed a little from side to side like dead coral reef.

He scanned the room, the multifarious mixture of person that made up the space, and it was the same story with all of them. As confused as he was by what they were doing, they looked happy, and to see such a cross spectrum of human beings all working and pulling together had lifted his spirits at first glance. But now he felt alarmed.

His anxiety levels on the rise, he said, "They all look different on the outside. But on the inside, they're all the fucking same."

He felt strange saying this, and a sudden depression hit him. The sameness didn't properly represent a unification of cultures. They all looked great on the surface, but something was lacking underneath.

Braun shook his head. He was in the centre of the room and he wanted to walk back to the kitchen, but yet again, the invisible wall pressed against his back. He moved from side to side, watching and listening but not hearing anything of interest.

Sofia and Karl walked towards Braun and an empty cubicle – the last nearest the wall in a row of seven. She pointed to it. "This will be your home after you've finished your training, which will be provided by…" She turned quickly with an overly dramatic spin. "… this guy right here."

She pointed to a big-nosed, skinny Hispanic man, barely out of his teens. "This is Jose—"

He interrupted, "Jorge."

"Sorry, I was nearly there! I'll start again. This is Jorge."

Karl answered with a little wave. "Hi, I'm Karl."

"What's up, Karl!" answered Jorge.

Sofia smiled. "Jorge will be showing you the ropes over the next few weeks."

"Cool. I can't wait to get going."

"We've got plenty of outfits in the closet next to the kitchen. Just take a few home with you tonight. They're available in coal black, treacle black, and crow black."

"I take it all the chalkboard blacks have gone then?" answered Karl.

"Afraid so."

"That sucks! It'll have to be the coal then."

The three laughed. Braun shook his head disapprovingly at the unfunny banter.

Sofia was eager to get on and ushered Karl nearer to the cubicle. He moved to the edge, and Sofia reached into the inside breast pocket of her suit. She pulled out two small zip-sealed plastic pouches, and two pairs of very thin, black Lycra-style gloves. She handed one of the pouches and a pair of gloves to Karl.

"Go ahead and open it."

He slipped the gloves on and pulled out two orange contact lenses, as she did the same.

"Say hello to your new eyes," she said.

"I've not done this before. I've always been a little squeamish when it comes to my eyes."

Jorge reassured him. "Just relax, Karl. It's not irrational to be squeamish when it comes to your eyes. I hated it at first but honestly, man, you'll soon get used to it. It's just like putting a pair of socks on for me now."

Karl didn't answer and fumbled around for twenty seconds until he got them in. His eyes gushed a lot of water and he blinked a couple of times before saying, "How do I look?"

Sofia gave him a thumbs up.

Braun felt a little less agitated now he knew the eye patterns that had alarmed him so much on first glance weren't real. He watched intently as the three continued.

"Jorge, would you mind stepping out of the chamber so I can show Karl the system we use?"

"Sure." He pushed the door open, stepped out of the cubicle and walked down the two steps that led up to it. "It's all yours," he said.

Karl was hesitant. "Wait a minute." He pointed to his clothes. "I'm not kitted out for it. I don't want to mess the sensors up."

"Don't worry, we've got it set to study mode," Sofia reassured him before she momentarily cast doubt on herself. "That's right, isn't it, Jose? You've done that?"

Jorge couldn't be bothered correcting her on his name this time. "Yes, of course. I set it an hour back when we were expecting you."

"Sorry, we are running a little late. Do you want to step in, Karl? It'll be a bit of a squeeze, but I'll join you."

Karl and Sofia walked up the steps and entered the domed glass cubicle. She pushed Jorge's small, narrow desk to the back and signalled to the front of the glass screen. Through the contact lenses, they could see a holographic image of a menu protruding from the front of the screen.

She told Karl, "Look up."

He looked up and he could also see the image on the ceiling.

"Pretty neat, huh? Wherever your eyes meet in here, you'll see what you need to see," she explained.

"Cool."

Braun couldn't see any of this, but he didn't find himself envious for his own pair of contact lenses. Jorge was standing next to him, arms folded.

Sofia went on, "Let's see what Jose was working on."

Karl noticed the title of the program, and said, "The Guardian Project? I thought this section was called Auto Res?"

"Yeah, it was Auto Res for a few years, but we decided that the full title of 'The Federation of Educated Automated Response', was too much of a mouthful, so we've recently rebranded. Plus, of course, it's good to shake things up with the name changes. It's a good way to sever links, and a rebranding can be used to wipe the surface clean."

She carried out the thumb and eye checks through a holographical audit box. This granted her full access when a generic, accentless, female voice from a speaker in the corner of the cubicle said, "Good morning, Sofia. How are you today?"

"I'm fine." She stopped for a second and briefly leant out of the cubicle, whispering to Jorge, "What's your curator called?"

"I knew I'd forgotten something. She's called Anastacia."

"Thanks." She faced back up to the screen. "I'm fine today, thank you, Anastacia. How are you?"

"Thank you for asking, Sofia. I am very well and enjoying my work with Jorge today."

"Great, now can you show us what you guys have been working on?"

"Of course," said the computer-generated voice named Anastacia.

It brought up a collage of photographs of a man. They ran from the floor of the dome right up to the very top. The images enveloped and ran across three sides of the dome, capturing the man during various parts of his life. His college yearbook photo was there, along with a fishing trip with friends, his wedding day, and vacation snaps demonstrated how well travelled he was. Sombre moments were also present, as Karl noticed a picture of him in a church next to a coffin, a flower arrangement shaped into the word 'Dad' sitting on a stand. Pictures of him as a child and with children of his own were scattered throughout the display.

Sofia spread her arms out wide and slowly pulled them back together a little, from top to bottom and from side to side. This boxed the collage into a smaller presentation, and details about the man sitting behind the pictures could be seen.

"Zachary Johnstone," said Sofia. "Thirty-four!" She added with surprise. "He looks older than thirty-four."

"Yeah, I thought so, too. It must be the grey hair. It seems they started creeping in during his mid-twenties. Handsome guy, though."

"He is good looking. Just a shame that his teeth are crooked," added Sofia before she summoned help. "Anastacia?"

"How can I be of assistance, Sofia?" answered the non-descript voice.

"Please show me why Zachary has been profiled today." She turned to Jorge. "Not that I'm checking up on you, Jose."

Jorge laughed. "Hey, it's all legit. You couldn't get away with shit in here! Besides, if you want to check up on me, you're entitled to. That's why you're the boss."

Braun flipped his lid and shouted in Sofia's direction. "Were you born this ignorant, lady? His name is JORGE, goddamnit! You had no problem remembering that voiced faceless things name! But the guy standing right in front of you?"

He smiled. He enjoyed the freedom to be able to say what he wanted without any repercussions. Something inside him began to tell him that this wouldn't last too much longer, and he relaxed a little as Anastacia answered, "Zachary is a top thousand algorithmic case."

Karl watched intently as Jorge joined in. "That's right, his algorithms are off the chart. I think he hit California's top three hundred for a short period last week. And here's the thing. He's not even much of a player. Upper middle management for the last ten years."

"Where does Zachary work, Anastacia?"

Braun thought, *Just fucking ask Jorge, instead of showing off that damned toy every time.*

"He has worked for Unified Media for twelve years. Unified Media formed in 2028 following the dispansion of—"

Sofia cut her off. "That's fine, thanks, Anastasia, I know who Unified Media are." She turned to Karl. "This Zachary guy is interesting. We'll have to find out some more about him."

Karl was keen to join in and asked, "I know that much of what we do is based on algorithms and artificial intelligence, but can you explain what it is we are looking for?"

"Jose will go into this in fine detail during your training. But just to give you a brief oversight, the words and behaviours that we are looking for in our individuals are programmed into Anastasia and her facilitator friends. These do change periodically, of course, but the latest requirements are provided right from the top. The family of course."

"How often do they change?"

"It varies. It depends how successful and effective certain movements, corporate agendas, narratives and so on, prove to be. They can last for months, years, even decades for the few that are deemed to be the most globally advantageous... Or they can be pulled within days or weeks. It's kind of like the fashion industry in a sense, as we sort of work within seasons."

"Right," answered Karl.

"The constant turnover keeps things interesting. We all get excited when we hear the sound of the helicopters, because we know that means the family are arriving with something new."

Karl looked excited. "What! You mean we actually get to meet the family."

Sofia laughed. "No, of course not. They access the building through the roof, where the landing pads are. They have the top two floors, which are strictly out of bounds."

Jorge chuckled. "Yeah, don't even try and thumb your way up there!" He turned to Sofia. "Do you remember a few years back when that dumbass Dan Greenwood tried to get up there? Ha-ha. He was bounced straight out of the building, never to be seen again. He lived across the road from me. When I finished work that very same day, they were moving somebody else in! They don't waste time around here, that's for sure."

"Yes." Sofia's tone turned serious. "That was very foolish and a real shame. I thought Dan had a lot of potential."

Karl nodded. "I'll keep my butt on this floor then."

Sofia got back on track and started looking further into Zachary's profile. She thought out loud, "Married ten years, two kids, a boy and a girl. He went to Stanford University. Good social media presence, music taste 'whatever's playing on local radio'.

Jorge briefly chimed in, "Auto tune the music, auto tune the mind."

Sofia read some more. "Likes to visit nice restaurants, member of the PTA, outstanding. Good, good, good. Church every Sunday. Hmmm."

Jorge interrupted, "Yeah, I was meaning to ask you about the whole church thing. I know this has been discussed a little more recently, and I get that we don't exactly encourage it anymore, but are we still not totally discouraging it?"

Sofia shook her head. "No, we don't try and move them away from it, unless fanaticism creeps in, and that doesn't appear to be the case here. We need those guys too, but that's a whole different ball game." She turned to Karl. "Zachary embodies the qualities we use to influence the mainstream crowd."

Jorge said, "He's been going to church since he was a kid. It must give him something, but it doesn't seem to be affecting his performance."

Karl joined in. "I thought you'd want to phase this out."

Sofia mused, "Perhaps eventually, but words and meanings from various books have been twisted for thousands of years to keep them obedient. Quite something when you think about it. It was only after population rates started to spiral out of control – and the second industrial revolution, of course – that our predecessors could see the textbooks beginning to wobble a bit. And once the infinite information portal became available, the books were always going to run out of steam."

Karl said, "They lost their faith."

"No, faith is still the most important thing in our locker. What do people often say when you ask them where their faith lies?"

"I put my faith in science?" offered Karl.

Sofia got excited. "Exactly! And that's what we did. We moved a lot of the fundamentals of religion over to science. People stopped believing in an afterlife, so they will do anything to protect and sustain this life as long as possible. The doctors, tech leaders, scientists, and governments are the priests, bishops, and popes of the modern world. The body of Christ, the bread and wine you'd take at mass, have been replaced by…" She pulled a finger out for each example. "…pills, gaming, nutritiously deficient food, twenty-four seven news, celebrities, anxiety, fomo, catastrophication…" She stopped herself when she noticed Karl had blown air into his top lip as he tried to contain a grin. She laughed. "Yeah, I can see that, Karl. It's a word now, okay?"

Karl held his hands up and answered, "Catastrophication. Right. Can't see me using it but, hmmm, yeaaaah, I got it."

Sofia smirked and made an okay symbol with her hand. She carried on, "Anyway, those key things have been big controlling mechanisms for us this millennia."

Karl asked, "What about some of the other religions? Things aren't much different in other parts of the world."

Sofia loved this sort of question, and her eyes opened wide as she responded. "The loudest voice comes from the West and it carries over, but ultimately we focus on our target group. Though, going back to what I was saying, I do like to pull some of the great and effective ideas from the past and see how they can be moulded into the present, the history we are creating in terms of our lineage, what came before us, the future we are creating. It's all important to ponder. I reference history a lot during meetings and seminars. And what was done with Christianity is a great example of early corporate strategizing. The core fundamentals of the original intention, I do believe were designed to liberate, whether this be from slavery or merely to open more people up to the idea of something beyond. Whether everyone saw it that way, those who had their own beliefs and faith in other things, heck, who knows? But I would guess that those spreading the word were not always received well. I figure the point is the word quickly gathered momentum, and it was networked through a large section of people – the impressionable, the dreamers.

"Okay. We all know that without an authoritative and bureaucratic stance, things can get messy. Then, of course, the Roman empire seized control and it was moulded into groups with their own sets of rules, Catholicism, then later Protestantism, etc. This really is a great early example, within the A.D. timeline, of the classic order from chaos template. You've only got to look at some of the cathedrals across the world, the

Vatican City as well, of course, to see how much was invested in it over time."

Karl looked interested, and Sofia added, "Why do you think Christianity is mocked so much where other religions aren't?"

She didn't wait for an answer. "Obviously the numbers have dropped in recent years, but it's down to where the majority are based. It's a way to move people, and crucially the money, so it can be invested somewhere else. Don't get me wrong, though, it's good to keep it bubbling under the surface. For example, a presidential candidate only has to use that magic three letter word and he's instantly got himself millions of supporters."

Alongside Karl, she read through some more of Zachary's profile and they watched some video footage of a highlight reel as he hosted conferences, charmed guests at parties, and played with his kids.

After a few minutes she'd seen enough and said, "Thank you, Anastacia. Now please show me Zachary's graphs."

"Yes, Sofia. Would you like his current report? Or an average based across Zachary's activities over the last six months?"

"Give me the six monthly, please, Anastacia," replied Sofia.

"One moment please, Sofia," it responded.

Sofia turned to Jorge and said, "This is very good work. It's great that Karl got to see such a strong example of what we are trying to achieve here."

"He's beautiful, isn't he?" said Jorge rhetorically and added, "You know that giant ass we talk about?"

Sofia squinted and nodded once quickly. Jorge knew she was trying to remain professional in front of Karl, but he finished his sentence anyway. "Well, this guy has got his lips welded onto that thing!"

Karl laughed. Sofia sniggered a little and turned to him. "We aren't that cynical here, Karl, honest."

The three of them laughed, and Sofia checked out Zachary's graphs. "Only a 60.64 for confidence?" She chewed this over for a few seconds and said, "Move that up a little when you can, Jose."

"Sure, would you say around the seventy mark?"

"No, that's too big a jump for him for now. Take it to between sixty-seven/sixty-eight."

"Okay, anything else you want me to change?"

"No, just that for now. We really don't need to meddle too much; he's doing well as it is. I would do one other thing, though, with the special requirements section."

"Uh huh?" answered Jorge.

"Can you put in a case for promotion? Let's take him up to top tier management."

Karl intervened. "What if there isn't an opening?"

"Oh, there will be an opening. Those guys at the top level don't do anything but hold meetings and nod along to whoever's talking anyway, so they can easily create another position. He'll just be an extra chair in the conference room."

"Yeah, but how do you know he'll get the job?" he asked.

"Ha, you're so green. I love it!" said Jorge patronisingly.

Sofia took over. "If we can control Zach, we can control those above him."

Jorge volunteered an idea. "I was thinking about placing an interest drop into him. He doesn't have too much going on outside the work and family."

"Yeah, that can be problematic at times. How about... hmmm... I know! See if you can guess."

Jorge answered, "Would it be golf, by any chance?"

The three laughed, and Sofia joked, "You read my mind! You haven't got my file on there, have you?"

Anastacia spoke out. "Sofia, as an employee of the Guardian Project, please be assured that your information is protected."

"Good to know, Anastacia," humoured Sofia.

"Put a note on him to get his teeth fixed, too," she directed Jorge.

He replied. "Sure, maybe I could put him in touch with your dentist."

Braun leant into Jorge and shouted into his ear, "WHO'S DOING THE ASS KISSIN' NOW, JORGE?"

Sofia laughed. "I don't think his salary would stretch that far!"

The three laughed and Braun joined in, holding his stomach sarcastically.

Jorge suggested, "How about I push up his vanity levels a couple of notches, just so he can keep up any maintenance on himself?"

"Okay," agreed Sofia, "but only a little. We don't want to ruin what we've got here."

"Why don't you just get a significant portion of the population, move their settings, mass sweep 'em into a level playing field. Surely the cream would still rise to the top and we'd get some more open competition?" queried Karl.

Sofia and Jorge sniggered.

"So green," Jorge repeated, to Karl's annoyance.

Sofia explained, "If we applied the same settings, differences from subject to subject will always occur.

And although we can compromise cognition, the cognitive differences of each individual can vary responsiveness, and there is something within – we don't like to use this word, but for argument's sake, let's metaphorically call it a soul. Whatever it is, there is something that would still separate them. What you would do with supreme confidence, wouldn't necessarily be the same as others. Besides, in a practical sense we need a few at the top, many in the middle, and tons at the bottom, otherwise this wouldn't work.

"Zach here has been highlighted through our algorithmic charts because he has been identified as someone who is easily influenced, lacking in discernment, and guaranteed to succumb to any dogmatic ideas that the right people throw at him. He will champion and cheerlead anything, no matter how bizarre or divisive it is, and he will seamlessly switch from one thing to another as our seasonal support and outrage plans are pushed out to the media and governments, before they enter corporate terms. So, we do devote a fair bit of time on some individuals who we know will nudge whatever is conjured up here. Jose knows exactly the sort of person we are looking for, and just one guy like Zachary can operate a trickle effect that can pour into thousands, who in turn will pick up the ball he throws at them and kick it around to countless others. He's demonstrated clear leadership qualities.

"You see, we use the highly influenced and turn them into the influencers. They are the ones who don't have problems suppressing or compromising their personalities to get what they want, or even what they think they want. But in order to assimilate, they still have to gravitate. And we provide the pull."

Karl rubbed his hands together and said excitably, "To be part of this, *man!* As a big gamer all of my life, this is the dream. The ultimate game. Pulling the strings of the world." He looked at Jorge. "I can imagine it gives you an amazing sense of power, knowing and influencing so much and they... I mean our subjects, billions of them... they don't have any idea. Something real special about having that kind of power. Oh wow, this excites me."

Jorge smiled, and Sofia was encouraged by Karl's attitude and enthusiasm. She added, "We care about what we are doing, and the prosperity of the organisation is paramount to everything we do. We are all free on campus to talk about what we want. You have all been vetted to the highest degree. But one thing that people are dissuaded from, and this is important..." She breathed hard through her nostrils "...and that is empathy for our subjects. That can make you soft, and there is no room for that here. It really isn't good to think along those lines.

"The design has been produced in such a sophisticated way that they feel like the owners of their thoughts. They rarely glitch and truly consider that what they are being triggered by, ummm, what they love to get behind is all from within. It has been so hardwired into them that anyone with any sort of counter opinion is the bad guy, and we can all point at them and shout 'boooooo!'. They need the bad guys to strengthen their resolve. It's very important that we continue with that. I know that to the uninitiated, this could come across as sinister, but we have to think this way. Desensitizing is the only option. Our evolution, where we are heading with further human-tech synthesis. It all depends on what we are doing here."

Jorge laughed and tipped his head to Sophia. "Based as ever, boss. It is hard work but rewarding. As it is our organisation and the other branches that provide a great experience for the people, we keep them safe, occupied, and entertained. That's what we do, and it pisses me off when people suggest we define them for institutional convenience. They need regulating to create the sense of order that you spoke about, Sofia..." He shrugged his shoulders. "And if that involves a little tweaking and mechanising here and there, then so be it. I do believe that everything that occurs in the Universe is predetermined. I really do..."

He stroked his chin and opened up a little more. "It's funny. Years ago, people thought that the robots would take over, but what they didn't realise was that the humans would become the robots! Ha-ha. And don't get me wrong, I'm not saying that's a bad thing. It was an inevitability of our advancement and survival that we should take this approach for the people."

Sofia nodded and answered, "Very well put, Jose, but I wouldn't broadcast that 'robot' thought to anyone. It doesn't sound kind."

Jorge nodded and Sofia asked, "Tell Karl how many members you look after."

"Three hundred and seventy-five thousand."

Karl was surprised. "Woah, how is that even possible? I mean how can one person look after so many?"

"Quite easily actually," answered Sofia. "Of course, we do have our fair share of rogues, or rabble rousers as we call them, but human beings are a very obedient species, and our work is made easier by their willingness to comply."

"Rabble rousers? You mean criminals?"

"No, the law-breaking criminals don't bother us. They are imprisoned and institutionalized. It's the independents, the philosophers, the ones who don't clap along. Again, they don't pose any major kind of threat, and if they tried to, we could easily squash them."

"Yes, but if enough people start questioning their existence, what is real and what isn't, what would we do?"

"It's very strange. We have a mass setting for most that keeps the autonomy and stoic levels extremely low. But somehow there is a minority that just can't be tamed, and although they never quite get there, some of them come dangerously close to seeing what's really going on. We must keep an eye on it, but the numbers are so few that it's easy to write them off as conspiracy nuts. The media have that well covered. Why do you think people who question the system are always portrayed as weirdos in films and television shows? Although, perversely, we do kind of need some kickback. You always need a little bacterium. We just point them out as screwballs, and the masses see them as dangerous or modern-day village idiots. They are managed resistance, but most of them don't even realise it."

"I see." Karl nodded.

"Look, what we offer is too enticing. It will always overpower the naysayers. If you want that big holiday every year, the sports car, the big, detached house, then... well, what they need to do is fed into them. Some know this, and others are guided like a magnet by their cravings and desires. When the bells ring, it is they who sing the loudest who are groomed for bigger and better things."

"I hope you don't mind me asking, but have the satellites ever malfunctioned?"

Jorge pulled a mocked pained expression and said, "Oh yes, they did! Damn, that was intense. It was a few years back; it was around the time when Dan Greenwood got canned. You know, Sofia, I'm sure he was involved with that."

Sofia took it on. "A couple of years ago they did go out for forty-five minutes. It was 4:45am, our time, on a Sunday morning over the holidays. We don't know what happened but somehow the system malfunctioned." Shock came over her face briefly as she recalled the incident. "Luckily we got them back up and running."

Karl's intrigue was written all over his face. "Woah!! What happened during the forty-five minutes? Did any weird shit go down in California?"

"No, because everyone has a backup charge of..." She paused. "...I think it was only an hour at the time. So it was a close shave. But we've managed to get a six-hour charge now as a safety net."

Karl nodded. "This is fascinating, Sofia. I'm so stoked to be a part of this."

She smiled. "We're excited to have you here, Karl. Now, I've got a meeting in ten minutes. Are you okay to take over, Jose?"

Jorge nodded. "Sure, I'll take him through Zachary's adjustments."

Braun watched as Sofia walked out of the room. He'd seen enough. Although the talk was alien to him, with the modern language used, he nevertheless understood what they were saying, and it shocked him to the core. He had only seen a snapshot of a potential future occurrence, and he knew that somehow the effervescent might that plagued him was going to be a contributor to the heinous levels of control on display within this miserable building.

This thought was mixed in with questions of himself. *Was he supposed to do something? He had never been spiritual, but was he being groomed to be a holy warrior of his time?* After all, the freedom of the era he was from was becoming apparent to him, despite the hardships he had known. The grumblings he'd heard about the end of the wandering nomadic lifestyle seemed to be coming to fruition, the destruction of much untamed and wild land, beauty he'd taken for granted, that notion being the same of the human spirit. It left him cold and empty. Every time a sense of crusade would fill him up, a secondary voice would remind him of his need to take from others and leave him totally confused to what he now was. Knowing that ultimately the only way out of this was to figure out what was happening to him, he was thoroughly fed up with the conflictions presented through any attempt to theorise his situation.

As Jorge joined Karl in the glass chamber and closed the door behind him, Braun held his breath for as long as he could until he passed out and left this scenario.

Chapter Ten

"Are you nervous?" Agnes asked Braun.

"Nervous? Heck, no. Standing in front of a priest and saying a couple of words doesn't fill me with fear. We aren't playing to a crowd, and I'll damn mean everything I say. It's lying that fills me with nerves, the truth doesn't." He was briefly overcome with suspicion. "Why d'you ask? Are you feeling jittery? Am I getting this right? Is it the event? Or the marriage itself?"

She smiled, grabbed his arm, and pulled her head into his shoulder.

Braun reached over with his free arm and rubbed her neck. The affectionate warmth he felt from her provided the answer he needed.

The stagecoach encountered a bumpy patch of land. They passed over a few mounds unscathed until a particularly high one bounced Agnes' head up hard and fast, striking Braun's chin with force.

Agnes shouted, "Ow!"

The stagecoach driver apologised. "Sorry, ma'am. There are so many darn gophers out here. Damn nuisances. I should have spread my pathway over a little more to the right, but I know time is short, so just be aware that it's gonna be a little choppy for the next mile or so. Hold onto your hats and whatever is in your stomachs, hahaha."

Braun shook his head as Agnes rubbed the top of her head. "I think I'm lucky to be conscious. You've got one hard noggin, missus."

She laughed and snuggled back into him.

He liked it but still protested. "What are you doing? The driver told us—"

Before he could finish his sentence, they struck another bump, and her head bashed him again – this time on the cheek. He was annoyed now. "Do you want to get married or beat the crap out of me?" He touched his cheek. "Guaranteed bruise."

Agnes thought back to the magical disappearing bite wound on their day out by the lake. She understood why he tried to present an air of normality, but it still annoyed her when he did.

They arrived at St Joseph's Chapel an hour later. It was out of the way, and they passed several other places of worship before they got there. Braun had described the chapel during one of their marriage discussions, and Agnes was convinced she knew the place.

As they arrived, she could see it was a lovely Greystone Chapel, but not the one she'd had in her mind. She was happily surprised, as this was just as charming, if not more so.

Braun had written to the priest a few weeks back. And although reluctant at first, due to Agnes' previous marriage, he'd agreed to meet them at a saloon halfway, to discuss the possibility. After an hour in their company and seeing just how deeply in love they were, he waived principals that the church leaders had tried to instil into him.

This was an act that deeply touched Braun, and it was a much-needed break from the nihilistic thoughts that followed the many dejecting views of the future. But with his love for Agnes, he had a saving grace and it prevented him from descending into full-on misanthropy.

The priest recognised the importance of their love, and although he sensed a peculiarity with Braun, he instinctively knew, and gathered from their conversation, that Agnes was the foundation that kept him from falling apart. He cared about people and didn't feel entitled to deny them the happiness that marriage would clearly bring them.

The stagecoach reached the chapel ten minutes earlier than scheduled, and Braun and Agnes stepped out.

Braun said to the driver, "Hey Frank, you're more than welcome to come inside and see me bawl like a baby."

Frank laughed. "Will that be tears of joy or despair?"

Agnes joined in. "Oh, they will most certainly be little droplets of happiness, won't they, Braun?"

Braun teased, "Yes, I'm sure the despairing tears will roll down my cheeks later on."

Agnes smiled and shook her head as Frank looked her up and down admiringly.

"Well, you sure look like a peach, Mrs McCleary."

"Thank you, Frank. You're a little premature with my new name. I may get cold feet at the altar next to this buffoon and make a run for it."

Frank laughed. "I guess I better wait outside then. I don't want you to take off in my stagecoach and leave us stranded."

Braun was getting impatient. "Come on, Agnes, let's get inside." He turned to the driver. "You staying here then, Frank?"

"Yes, if it's all the same with you. I'm not one for formal occasions and..." He looked down at his dusty trousers and faded grey shirt, as he pulled on his scraggly, greasy, brown beard. "...I'm not exactly dressed for the occasion. You said the priest has a witness for you, right?"

Braun nodded. "We shouldn't be too long."

He patted Frank's shoulder, and in the blink of an eye, the pores in his chest opened to pull some of Frank's self into his own.

Agnes quietly sighed as she noticed Frank's whole-body judder for a split second. Braun's power would often entice her when he channelled it the right way. The strength of his love for her was immense, but she would never be able to accept his need to take from others to feed his might. She could only hope that over time they would be able to work on something that would keep him going without the necessity to feast from the unbeknown.

Frank looked slightly dazed for a second or two as he waved his thumb in the air and stuttered, "Gggood luck."

Braun smiled. He had made purgative advancements through accepting his fate and remaining in the moment, but he was only too aware that his future would most likely be blighted with stronger episodes of darkness as the little control he'd had over the phenomena slipped a little further by the day.

As he drank from Frank, he no longer knew whether such motions were voluntary or involuntary, and that scared him. But for today and the next few weeks at least, his focus was on marrying Agnes and setting plans in motion for a future together. They were a little long in the tooth, but they hadn't ruled out the possibility of children, although again, he was torn as he fretted over what kind of offspring he would spawn.

The soon-to-be-newlyweds crossed through the picket-fenced barrier and into the church grounds, as Frank wished them all the best again.

Braun's moleskin trousers were tight, and he complained sarcastically, "Well, Timothy really surpassed himself with these trousers. Extra tight and sweaty. I don't know what he was thinking when he measured me up for these. My balls are being pushed into my stomach."

Agnes tutted as she pulled down her white veil. "Do you have to be so crude today of all days? You look very handsome. Just don't be fidgeting with your crotch when we're stood in front of the altar." She smiled and added, "You'll be out of that suit in a few hours' time."

Braun laughed. "Is that a promise?"

Agnes nudged him with her elbow. "I suppose we can have a little fun when we get back. It is our wedding night, after all."

Braun rubbed his hands together and said, "I'll go easy on the whiskey then!"

He looked at her and smiled. In the short time he'd known her, she'd never looked more beautiful and radiant. The purple dress she wore was very angular in the shoulders and chest area, and it matched her sharp cheekbones and long triangular nose. Her lace veil was short and snug against her face, draping over each peak and valley of her bone structure. Braun hated not being able to see her face properly, but he couldn't wait to pull up the veil and plant a big kiss on her.

They reached the door, and as Braun pulled it open for her, his grey top hat fell to the dusty ground. He wiped it down and they walked inside.

Salvador, the priest, waited for them by the altar. He greeted them both. "Welcome to St Joseph's Chapel, and may I say how wonderful you both look."

Braun laughed. "Yes, I scrub up pretty well, don't I, Father?" He winked at the priest. "She ain't looking too bad either."

Salvador laughed. "Well, my compliment was mostly aimed at Agnes, if I'm being honest, but you are looking very smart, Braun."

They reached the altar and Salvador said, "Are you ready?"

Agnes joked, "Actually, can I have a little longer to think about it?"

Braun chuckled. "She's just kidding, Father." A momentary cloud of doubt hung over his head as he sought assurance. "You are kidding, right, Agnes?"

She dug him with her elbow again and said, "Of course I'm playing."

He breathed a sigh of relief, but a pang of anxiety hit him as he thought. *Why are you feeling so insecure? She is ready to commit herself to you. Just knock it off, you clown, and enjoy the damn occasion.*

He grinned and kissed her on the top of the head.

The priest laughed. "Save the kisses for now, Braun. We've got to get through the words first." Salvador turned around. "But before we do that, I'll call our witness."

He shouted, "Christen, we are ready for you."

The tall, young blond man emerged from a corridor behind the altar, looking incredibly thin and haunted as the chief's curse ate away at him. Imaginary or not, the words and the threat had filled him with such unease that his health, appetite, and spirit had only deteriorated since.

He was dressed smartly but awkwardly. Black trousers hovered just above his ankles, and his white shirt was tucked in as much as it would allow to avoid looking too puffed out. Without any clothes of his own, and reluctant to spend what little money he had, he'd been borrowing from Salvador's wardrobe. And the vast differences in their body types prevented any kind of good fit.

Agnes was too busy fixing her veil to notice at first as Braun greeted the boy.

"Glad to meet you, young man. We sure do appreciate you giving up your time for us."

Christen responded. "Well, there isn't much to do around here."

Braun laughed, unsure if the boy was joking or not.

Agnes knew the voice, and she froze in horror as she recognised the face behind it, although it was far gaunter than the last time she'd encountered him. She was stunned, saddened, and crushed by the coincidence. Her immediate thought screamed at God, *You really are cruel.*

Christen had not recognised Agnes underneath her thick veil. Consumed by shock, she decided to bide her time for a minute or so, as Father Salvador started the ceremony.

"You ready to get started?"

Braun said, "Yes, Father."

Agnes couldn't find her voice through her distress, so she nodded.

Christen walked across the altar, as an icy spike of nervous energy ran through Agnes. He passed them before sitting down a few metres behind in the closest left-sided pew.

Further thoughts aimed at God rattled through her head. *You have placed the demon responsible for the end of my first marriage to preside over this, my next marriage! That thing and his dog friends killed my Patrick, a man who never hurt anyone. Why do this to me? Haven't I been through enough? Is this meant to be poetic somehow? A test? Whatever it is you want from me, you twisted bully, I don't care to figure it out!*

Salvador began, "The marriage banns were made to my parishioners before mass last Sunday, and thank the Lord, no reasons were given why this ceremony shouldn't take place here today."

Braun laughed. "Good job they don't know me!"

Salvador continued, "You are both aware that marriage is unification under God, and it should be entered into with full commitment."

"Yes," answered Braun.

Again, the best Agnes could manage was a nod.

She looked up to the row of paintings on the right wall, of many shapes and sizes, some beautiful, others looking like the works of a child with a modicum of artistic ability. The frames were the same, many cobbled together from dirty, semi-rotted wood. Other woods looked pristine and held a natural varnished look. Life encapsulated, as always, through the ugly and beautiful.

She was momentarily captivated by a particularly crude oil-painted depiction of Jesus on his knees while a Roman soldier lashed him with a tipped whip as the crowd looked on. Each member of the crowd was lazily painted with the same look of horror – a ghoulish expression permeated throughout the women, children, and men. Jesus' eyes were merely downward brown slits, with his beard hair and mouth the same colour. Yet, through the basic representation, the sheer pain of the man emanated through the canvas.

Agnes welled up as she pondered his plight. She hated herself in this moment as she struggled to find comfort in his suffering. She had lived through the most immense emotional pain, and today should have been a large step towards retribution for her. But here it was, sullied, as her tormentor watched over what should have been her resurrection.

This confirmed to her what she'd always fought against, that the whole thing was one big cruel joke. She now only cared about one thing. She needed to kill the boy.

Unbeknownst to Braun, Agnes had kept a pocket pistol with her every day since the attack and the slaying of her husband. It was tucked under her pillow, and she'd come close to using it once, when a customer started to get a little rough. Her friend Heather had heard her screams as the man instigated unconsented asphyxiation designs, grabbing Agnes gently but firmly around the throat. Heather kicked the door open, and between the two of them they managed to beat the crap out of him. But if Heather had arrived five seconds later, Agnes would have put a few holes in the man.

She had tested the gun out on several occasions to make sure it worked. The bullets wouldn't fly much further than ten yards or so, but close up she was confident that the tiny pistol could get the job done. She just needed to pick her moment, and an unexpected dilemma now faced her. *Should she marry Braun first, before taking the shot? Or should she seize the opportunity and take the boy out before he recognised her?* Either way it was going to mean a life on the run, or a life behind bars for her. She wouldn't take out the priest as well, as much as she knew that could give them a better chance to make a run for it. She wanted to murder the young man, but she wasn't a killer. And executing a priest was out of the question.

What she knew for certain was that a few minutes were needed to gather her thoughts. She shuffled about, trying to still her mind from the commotion streaming through it.

Salvador cleared his throat and sensed her agitation. He said, "Are you feeling okay, Agnes?"

Just an unconvincing silent nod was used to falsely confirm this.

Braun was concerned. "You're starting to worry me, my dear."

Agnes turned to Braun, and with a little inward facing wave, she ushered him to get closer.

He nodded, but before he edged closer, he said, "Sorry about this, Father."

Salvador assured him, "Not at all, Braun. Take your time, if you need a moment."

Braun responded, "Thank you, Father. If you could just give us a couple of minutes or so."

Salvador looked over to Christen and said, "Come on, young man, let's leave them to it. My throat is very dry. We'll have a glass of water."

Christen huffed and stood up. As he quickly passed Agnes, the draught from his movement again chilled her to the bone.

They walked around to the corridor behind the altar, leaving Braun to ask Agnes gently as he took her hand softly, "Hey, listen, if this doesn't feel right today,

I could reschedule with Salvador. Hell…" He put his hand over his mouth and with his free hand, he signed himself with the cross. "…Sorry, God, poor choice of words. I mean heck, it doesn't look like he's all kinds of busy right here in nowhere land." He sighed. "Did I push this too hard?"

Agnes wanted to put Braun's mind to rest, but she was so preoccupied by the immense shock of seeing Christen that she could only think of getting to him. She took a deep breath and said, "How far does your love and commitment to me reach?"

"I love you with every part of me, Agnes. The priest was just about to ask that kind of question. But you need to hear it from me first?"

"No, I don't want to seem needy, Braun, because that forms no part of me, and please don't read too much into this, but I, um… I just need a moment to myself."

"Damn, Agnes, how can that not hurt my head! Minutes from committing yourself to me, you…" He impersonated her with an exaggerated, high-pitched voice. "—need a moment."

This lack of taking her seriously, through such an insulting and dismissive impersonation, infuriated her. But before she snapped at him, she stopped, as insecurity and hurt was suddenly written all over his face. His agony was extra apparent, not through his line- and blemish-free face. The heartache was in his eyes.

"I do want to marry you, Braun. Just let me straighten out a bit."

He puffed. "Why don't you go and sit with the priest and the kid back there for a few minutes? Give yourself a little break from me."

Agnes was pissed off again, and didn't respond. She walked to the back of the church and sat down in the middle of the first bench. Braun left her to it and took a seat on the farthest bench from her, facing the altar. She closed her eyes and again pondered how she intended for the next ten minutes to play out.

Did she want to complete the vows before taking the shot? Or would prolonging it be too risky and merely give the boy more opportunity to recognise her?

She opened her small handbag and checked out the pocket pistol. She knew it was fully loaded with five bullets, but she still wanted to see them. Pulling the barrel out confirmed what she already knew. All the bullets were nestled into their chambers and ready to embark on their journey into flesh.

It didn't take her too long to reach a decision. She was going to press on through the vows. Her thoughts and motivations had been cleared up. And now, faced with the question, she knew that the vengeance for her murdered husband and her own assault was more important than her love for Braun, as real as that was. Any consequences that followed what she wanted to do, did not matter. And like so many others who had reacted only with impulse, she was led only by the notion that she had to do this.

She owed so much to Braun, and if Christen hadn't been at the church, she would not have had any second thoughts of spending the rest of her days with him. But she had been presented with this juncture, and she had to take it. She knew she might not get the chance again. Once the veil was lifted and Christen recognised her, he would either make a run for it, or perhaps he would try and come for her. But fear of what he may or may not do was not her motivation for killing him.

She closed her handbag and walked over to Braun. He heard her footsteps but remained facing the altar. She kissed the back of his head gently and quietly spoke to him.

"Thank you, Braun. I'm sorry to have worried you. That quiet time was just what I needed, so please don't think I was considering walking out on you. I just wanted to say a prayer and speak to Patrick."

Braun turned to Agnes and rubbed his head against her arm. "Of course. I hope he knows that I will look after you as much as he did."

Agnes smiled nervously. She didn't feel ready but knew that she never could be prepared for what she was about to do. She kissed Braun on the cheek and said, "Go and get the priest."

Braun walked towards the back, and Agnes anxiously reached into her bag to make sure the pistol was positioned well enough to grab it quickly. She moved it to the top and placed it over a makeup powder case and a silver-handled, porcupine-quilled hairbrush – one of the few nice things she'd retained from her former days.

Braun came back through as the priest and the moody boy followed. As Christen passed, Agnes turned her head. He glanced at her, but her veil-covered face was turned as far away as her neck would allow.

Salvador took his position, centre on the second step down from the altar. Clasping his hands together, he took a deep breath and said, "So, my friends. Are we ready to proceed?"

Braun turned to his fiancée. "Agnes?"

She lowered her head and whispered, "Yes, Father."

Salvador wasn't convinced, but not wanting to interfere, he maintained an upbeat stance. "Let us begin."

Braun turned around and stretched an arm out to summon Agnes. She shuffled over to him and grabbed his hand. He gave her a gentle squeeze, and she positioned herself next to him.

The priest started, "Entering into this is not only important for you, but it is important to God. You are both gifts from God, and now our Lord is inviting you to share your lives with each other. You both understand that?"

Agnes nodded her head as Braun answered proudly, "We do."

The priest laboured his point as he added, "This is a serious commitment, not to be entered into lightly." He smiled, and the couple smiled back. It was time for him to get into the vows. "Will you have each other in sickness and health, forsaking all other, as long as you shall live?"

Braun answered quickly, "I will."

Salvador prompted Agnes. "Miss?"

She responded quietly, "I will."

She could hear Christen fidgeting behind them. He cracked his knuckles and yawned loudly, not even attempting to stifle the sound as it rose above Braun's vow.

This pleased her, she wanted him to be obnoxious and give her the fodder to fire herself up. As much as she wanted to avenge Patrick and her violation, she still couldn't shake off the awful feeling of guilt that preceded point-blank shooting somebody, probably unarmed, in a house of God. *But why had God brought her to this place now? Was this supposed to be how fate unfolded?* She knew that no parabolist would have deemed her story with Christen as suitable for a Bible entry. But years of living by the Bible hadn't exactly served her well. She'd lost count of the number of times she'd read the book front to back, and all the years spent writing inspiring verses down with her best fountain pen. She would pin them to the wall in a collage, and every day she would take one off and put it in her purse, whatever felt most relevant. She'd stopped doing this after her fateful day, and although she knew 'thou shalt not kill' was one of the most important guidelines of the book, she also didn't recall seeing the words 'ye shalt not be raped in front of murdered husband'. Her loyalty to the book had vanished.

Salvador handed the reins over to Braun. "Do you have the ring?"

Braun fumbled awkwardly in his pocket for a few seconds, briefly considering trying to lighten the mood by pretending he couldn't find it, but he quickly reconsidered that Agnes might have acted with relief for some temporary respite. He knew he wouldn't be able to take that, so he went ahead and pulled out the ring. It was a chunky, well-cut diamond, protruding from an atypical band, with two well carved crevices running through the mid-section. He'd spent a fair portion of his cash on this, and he was hopeful that Agnes would like it.

She looked down and her lips curled up a little on each side, managing a slight smile. She loved the ring, although it did look a little wide for her thin fourth finger. This proved to be the case as Braun took her hand and slid it on.

He whispered, "I'll get it resized."

She looked at him. "I love it, Braun."

He was overjoyed to hear this and said, "With this ring, I thee wed, Agnes Roberts."

Agnes smiled. She felt a great deal of love for Braun in that moment, and it came close to the love she'd held for Patrick. But still, seconds later, sadness washed over her before dwelling on it. She could have abandoned her plan and lived a happy life with Braun, but crucially the need to avenge Patrick ran stronger.

Salvador finished. "I now pronounce you man and wife. You may kiss the bride."

Braun lifted Agnes' veil and kissed her soft lips tenderly.

She closed her eyes and whispered, "Thank you."

She pulled the veil down, and again she had no way of knowing whether Christen had seen her or not, but she still hoped to surprise him as she bent over and reached into her bag.

"Excuse me," Braun laughed. "You don't need to touch up your make up, Agnes. We're married now."

She was mildly annoyed by his assurances that now she was his wife she didn't have to trouble herself with looking her best. But she knew he meant well.

Suddenly she pulled the gun out and turned around in a flash, firing two shots at the boy. But he was quick and jumped out of the way the second he saw her.

Salvador could only shout, "OH NO, NO, NO, NO!"

One of the bullets struck Christen on the shoulder while the other wedged into the wooden headboard of the bench behind him.

He dropped to the floor and tried to roll under to pass through to the next bench, but the space was too narrow, and he couldn't slip under. Agnes walked a little closer to him as Braun watched in shock. He knew he had to act quickly before she got ever closer to the boy and more accurate with her next shot. She remained silent and focused. Salvador felt helpless and could only hold his head, covering his eyes with the palms of his hands.

She made her way around to the side of the bench.

Christen squealed, "Please, please, lady. I've changed. God lives inside me now. I cannot change what I have done... D-d-don't do this... Please.... Putting me six feet under will not resurrect your husband..." He tried to resist the urge to yield a scornful remark, but the pause and reflection couldn't stop it as he sniped, "... Although, seemingly, you have moved forward rather hastily."

She stared at him, her lips pursed, totally unmoved by what came out of his mouth.

He sensed he wasn't getting anywhere but carried on in his determination. "I'm sorry, that is none of my business. I'm trying so hard to be a good person now. My friend Salvador is a loyal servant of God, and he can see that I am not completely weak and awful." He raised his voice and shouted towards Salvador, "TELL HER THIS IS SO, FATHER."

Salvador was riddled with shock, the bizarreness of the situation was overwhelming, but he managed to mutter, "I don't know how Christen has wronged you. He has not confessed all his past mistakes, but I do know he's done some terrible things and I'm incredibly sorry for what he's left you with." He choked up momentarily and bit down hard on his thumb. He talked through this and tried to offer further assurances. "I will make him better, I promise you. With the Lord's help, I have driven some of the demons away. He is young and he can reform. This is the best place for him to repent for his sins... where God watches him..."

He stretched his arms out and finished, "Could you please put the gun down and we can talk about it?"

Not a word from Salvador resonated with Agnes as she watched Christen cowering with his arms over his head, his face peripherally focused on her as he glanced slightly from what he could see through his arms.

Through the determination on her face, he could see that his appeals had fallen on deaf ears, and Agnes lined up another shot with the gun pointed at his head. She had surprised herself with the complete ruthlessness that was driving her, a characteristic that must have been harboured somewhere deep within but always pushed away, until this very moment when she needed it. She even toyed with smiling at Christen, just as he had while his friends raped her.

She had entered the kill zone and was only focused on completing the process. Christen was helpless and she raised her gun hand. But just as she was about to pull the trigger, she was halted. Something struck her hard in the back and jolted her forward.

Braun had remained quiet after his early plea. He had been busying himself, trying to summon one of his power geysers, and just before Agnes could pull the trigger, he unleashed it. An invisible beam popped out of his chest and flew across the five metres that separated him from Agnes.

It gripped onto her back, right between the shoulder blades, locking her body into a mostly paralytic and rigid state. Her eyes were one of the few things that stayed active, and she was just able to swivel them in Braun's direction. The horror in her eyes instantly struck Braun, and he badly wanted to release her, but he couldn't allow her to kill the boy and ruin the rest of her life.

Salvador was unable to see what Braun was doing and assumed she was having some kind of upright seizure, as her body convulsed mildly but noticeably. It didn't take long for her to drop the gun, and Braun released the hold.

She turned to him and screamed, "I TRIED TO CONVINCE MYSELF, BUT I NOW KNOW I WAS WRONG. YOU ARE NOT HUMAN. YOU ARE A MONSTROSITY."

She turned to pick up the gun again, but it was too late. Agnes had blindsided Braun, and Christen had moved very quickly. He was crouched in a low squat and he had hold of the weapon. She sighed in resignation and Christen pulled the trigger. A point-blank shot to the heart took her out instantly. She was dead before she hit the ground.

Braun screamed in anguish, and Christen leapt onto the bench behind him. Befitting the mismatched nature of the chapel, this was a different type of bench, with its feet raising it further from the floor. Unlike Salvador, Christen knew that Braun had done something to incapacitate Agnes. There was something in the malevolence that he recognised, and he was fully aware that Braun was incredibly dangerous.

He had enough room to drop to the floor and roll under the bench as Braun began firing power surges out at a rate and force that he had never managed before. He was crying for Agnes, and his grief, boiled with anger, made him extremely potent.

Salvador sat down on a ridge of the altar completely crestfallen; there was nothing he could do. He no longer felt compelled to defend Christen, and he caught glimpses of Braun's might as some of his misfires began to knock over chairs, sending loosely scattered Bibles everywhere.

The priest closed his eyes to pray, using one of his adapted and most cherished comfort blanket psalms. "Whoever dwells in the shelter of the most high will rest in the shadow of The Almighty. The Lord is my refuge and my fortress. My God, in whom I trust, will cover you with his feathers, and under his wings you will find refuge; his faithfulness will be your shield."

Christen was able to move on his stomach, like a snake, weaving in and out of the benches all the way to the back of the church, making it difficult for Braun to get a straight target.

He made it to the back, knowing his next move would be to get outside. From there, he knew his chances were slim, with nowhere to hide in the vast desert landscape. Without time to think of a plan, he just had to move the best way he could for avoidance. Once outside with Braun following him, he would turn around and fire a shot. He figured that he probably had two bullets to work with, so he needed to make them count. He wouldn't be afforded with such an easy shot as Agnes had found herself victim to, but it was the only chance he had.

Braun's energy was fresh after the reluctant feed from his now deceased wife, and he could lash out with ease. It was just unfortunate that his aim was off, with each misfire only adding fuel to his fury. Benches continued to be toppled over and pictures were sent from the wall, rendering the holy environment into an unholy mess.

Amazingly, Christen managed to reach the front, where he remained on the floor. The large door was made from thin, light wood, so he was able to push it from his position, swinging it open enough for him to squat and dive out onto the spot where Salvador had found him injured months before. Here he was again trying to evade another broken-hearted person of someone he'd wronged. He considered this for a second, and with his chances so lacking anyway, he contemplated for a moment that maybe it was time for him to call it a day. But just as he'd done when his brother was killed, he soon rubbed out the thought of giving up. He'd never once quit in his short life, and he wasn't going to go out like that.

Mercifully, Braun had given him a brief period of respite – not out of any goodwill, but because he toyed with him, readying himself for a grand finale.

This gave Christen a few seconds to reflect as he ran towards the end of the fenced area in front of the chapel. *I knew it. Salvador would not accept this, but the chief was right. This entity has been sent for me.* His confused thoughts papered over the pain of his shoulder as slews of blood chugged out of it.

Braun slowly walked out of the church as Salvador snapped out of his prayerful introspections. He kept his distance for fear of Braun harming him but walked a few feet from the altar. "My son, my son..."

That was all he could briefly muster, not thinking it was strange to call someone clearly older than him 'son'. Braun carried on walking slowly, not turning around.

Salvador attempted to plead more successfully. "You are being compelled to do this by something else. Your soul... it is trying to protect you. You're still there, Braun, grappling and facing down whatever the creature is. It will use everything it has to control you. But we can banish it and send it back to wherever it came from. I know I can help. Please, just turn around and we will tend to your wife."

Braun turned his head as his body urged forward. "No, I have lost control of that force in the past, but this time..." He hammered his chest four times with a clenched fist and shouted almost demonically, "...IT IS ANSWERING TO ME!"

The tone of Braun's voice scared Salvador, and he didn't respond. Instead, he slowly shuffled behind as Braun kicked the doors open and walked outside. The noise of the doors alerted Christen as he passed through the gate at the end of the church land.

Braun had him in his sights but he wasn't in a rush to unleash the weapon. He hadn't launched it so far before, but he was confident that he could catch up with the boy. He felt the torch bubbling away inside as it reached boiling point.

Christen made the most of his head start and ran as fast he could through the lonely scope of the desert. His movements impulsively stepped into a protective zig-zagged pattern, and it wasn't long before his feet (tucked inside cheap penny loafers) noticed the impact of the harsh bare earth underneath the lightly dusted sand. His fear and the pain in his bullet wounded shoulder neutralised much of the discomfort as he ran for his life, with his right hand clasped tightly around the pistol. It was now more of a symbol of what had given him hope before he knew the extent of what Braun was capable of. He realised that he had no chance of realistically striking Braun from any great distance with the basic weapon. Still, he was better having it than not, and he kept waving it futilely around as though it still held serious threat.

Braun was surprised at how quickly Christen had pulled away from him. He thought the injury would have slowed the boy down, but it seemed to have had the opposite effect; the terror had clearly put a rocket up his ass. Still, Braun knew with his surge in full flow, he could out-run, out-jump, and out-strength anyone.

He'd not really put a lot of this into practice, apart from some experimental exercises when no-one was around. He'd once uprooted a seven-foot high and thick cactus with ease and tossed it across twenty metres, without putting much effort into it. He had not been able to run since he was a child with his poor alcohol-ruined body, so just being able to stay in a consistent jog would have been something for him, but his daily early morning sprints had left him feeling superhuman.

It was time for him to start up before Christen became less than a dot on the horizon.

Salvador had joined him outside. "Let the boy go, the Lord should decide his fate."

Braun turned back. Grief and stress contorted his mouth into a snarl as he said, "Look, Father, can you forget about the damn collar for one minute and just be..." He paused for a few seconds to jog his memory before the priest intervened.

"Salvador."

Braun closed his eyes and continued. "Of course. Salvador."

He took a deep breath. "Tell me something, Salvador. Have you ever felt the big love? And I mean the true, deep love. I ain't talking about what you had for your parents or Jesus Christ, nor your God. I'm talking about love for another person unconnected. That feeling like your guts are all twisted up. You know I've got some strange juices flowing inside me, my fucking brain has lightning sizzling through it, and my blood is molten lava. I've felt things that even the smartest sonofabitch in the world couldn't describe, but all of it combined was nothing... absolutely nothing compared to the love I had for Agnes. It took me forty years, but I had it." He choked up. "And for that I am grateful."

Salvador carried on trying to speak for Christen. "He was defending himself."

"No, Father, she was defending herself. That boy ruined her life. She fought back and not only survived something that would have broken many others, but she saved my life as well. He will die for what he has done, and you might want to look at your own judgement before you judge me for what I am about to do. I don't know what kind of monster I am, but I know what kind he is. And you, Father, you welcomed that darkness into your home and cared for it."

Salvador shook his head. "He is not a monster. He has done some terrible things, but he is young and his life has been very hard. I saw good in him. With God by my side, I truly did." He paused for a second and added, "If we lead by love and take shelter under it, we can all make it through this."

Braun respected what Salvador said, but he knew what he had to do. "I know you're a good man, Salvador, but…" He welled up and his voice croaked again. "…the only reason I had any remnants of soul left was because of Agnes." Braun pointed into the distance. "He has ripped it to shreds, and I will do the same to him. And as for your God, I ask, where is He? He hasn't been there for me. He promises an end to torment and suffering in the afterlife but isn't that just waiving any responsibility for our fucking time here? We have no other choice but to take on the faith, just to be able to wade through this all this shit before we can get there. I read something in a book recently: 'The greatest trick the Devil ever pulled was convincing the world he didn't exist.' Got me thinking that I must not be part of that writer's world, 'cause I've been well aware of that son of a bitch all of my life. Maybe his real best trick was convincing us that God exists." He didn't wait for Salvador to answer as he turned around and started to run.

His initial warm-up jog quickly transcended into a full-on sprint, and within ten seconds his visual perception of Christen had gone from a tiny dot weaving in and out like a fly through invisible obstacles, to a larger shape. He surmised that Christen was heading towards the small village that the church represented. It was the boy's best chance of hiding, but even at his youthful pace it would take him at least an hour to get there. Braun knew this and he would be able to play a cat and mouse game for as much of that time as he wanted. He was tempted to carry it on and torment the boy, because he knew that once he'd put the hammer down on him, he would have to shift his focus onto the suffering of losing Agnes. But after briefly stopping to ponder this, he recognised the futility of delaying the inevitable.

Picking up the pace further, he edged closer to the boy, running through speeds that would have easily held unsurpassable Olympic records.

Once within twenty yards of Christen, he stopped and flung out his first assault. It hit the boy on the back and froze him to the spot. The lack of feeling surprised Braun, and he momentarily shut off the energy surge.

The invisible whip knocked the stuffing out of Christen, and he hit the ground, barely managing to shout as he wheezed, "I'LL SHOOT YOU."

Braun ignored the comment and walked a few metres towards him.

Christen was only too aware that his next attempt to dissuade Braun was not a last roll of the dice, but merely his plea would be a prelude to his death croak. "I MEAN IT. DON'T COME ANY CLOSER."

Braun stepped ever nearer and was at a distance where Christen felt ready to take a shot. He tried to get to his feet, but as he did, Braun zapped him again. And from his crouch, his legs lost their strength and put him out on his back.

Now ten metres from his target, Braun folded his arms together. Unsmiling, he slowly tipped his brow to Christen as if to say, *Go ahead, son, try and get back on your feet*.

Christen considered using the last bullet. He was a crack shot, and his tormentor was within damage-potential range. But with Braun's prompt, Christen decided to call his bluff and attempted to stand up.

He placed his hands on the ground and pushed himself up, but as his strength reliance shifted into his legs, he didn't get very far. The two hits had taken their toll. His legs were as useful as a paper umbrella, and they buckled like baby Bambi taking her first steps.

Christen knew he had to take the shot, but before he did, he turned to the sun which was in peak desert-view shimmer. Incredibly, he didn't need to squint, as though his eyes had become newly equipped with a filter. He was able to look at the golden dome sitting low on the horizon in a way that he had never dared or been able to before. He wanted to feel incredibly small at this moment, and the almighty sight succoured and eased him through his pointless endeavoured attempts to defeat Braun.

The shot was fired, another beautiful hit, striking Braun through the breastbone. This ripped open his flesh quite considerably and created a sizeable hole in his scrawny chest. The bullet embedded in the aorta section of his heart, and a little blood trickled out.

The initial pain stopped Braun in his tracks.

Christen found inspiration in this and managed to find some leg strength, as he took off a little further to leave Braun dealing with what was no more than a minor issue for him but would have resulted in certain death for most others.

Braun was happy to let Christen to go on ahead for a short while, as he pinched his thumb and index finger, plunging them into the fleshy gap in his chest. He tinkered around for a bit, reaching through his shattered breastbone until he found the folded shrapnel lodged into his heart. He pulled it out and dropped it to the floor, groaning as he felt a few seconds of the real pain he should have been enduring. Moments later, the wound weaved the broken bones and flesh back together again, and he was near full strength.

Christen was uselessly maintaining a criss-crossed running technique. His weakened sea legs gave the illusion of a dance, similar to a drunken episode that Braun was all too familiar with. Still he persevered, as the blood chugged out from the main artery in his shoulder.

Braun jogged a little closer. It was time for him to take Christen. He fired out an imperceptible lasso over the twenty metres that separated them, which caught the boy and rooted him to the spot.

Braun was disappointed that he'd clenched onto Christen from the back. He'd like to have seen the look on the boy's face as he shook him about, but he sensed that his production was running a little dry, so he kept the hold. Christen's arms flapped around like a rag doll in a very strong wind as the pull began. The putrid taste that Braun was expecting did not come. Instead, he didn't detect anything. He had felt nastiness from others in the past. Borderline evil at times. But this time, the boy didn't give him any flavour – just purity like water. It pumped him up, but the apathetic feed again surprised him and slowed the extraction down. He mused briefly about the boy, *What led him down this path? Could things have been different for him in another time or another place?*

Still, this curiosity wasn't enough for him to let Christen off the hook. He had taken Agnes, and Braun knew that any hope of his life getting better was now gone. The life he'd always fantasised about was over, and he would remove the boy before he removed himself.

He pushed and pulled harder; pushing to retain the clench, and pulling for extraction. The pump effect was in such a flow that Christen's feet left the ground, and within seconds he was ten foot high in the air.

Braun leant back, lifting him further still, until he reached thirty-five feet. He was a minute into the process, and he could feel that he was already reaching the dregs of Christen. It was time to exercise a final pull, and just as he was about to heave it through, he noticed three crows flying in strange patterns around Christen. One bird – the smallest of the three – flapped its wings frenetically as it hovered above the boy's head. The other two cawed as they weaved in and out between his legs.

This placed Braun's final act on hold. He didn't want to harm the birds, and he could see that whatever was radiating in the air from Christen was altering their patterns of movement. He had to pull him to the side and out of the crows' path to prevent them from being caught up in what would be a messy encounter.

He manoeuvred the boy to the left. He hung limply, his eyes had rolled into the back of his head, and Braun had no idea whether he was still alive.

One last push followed by a pull. Boom! Christen exploded into a mass of red and black dust which flowered and expanded like a firework, surprisingly visible in the brilliant blue sky.

Braun didn't go back for Agnes. Instead, he walked on as a rain of dust fell from above and covered him from head to toe.

Chapter Eleven

Braun's legs could carry him no further. Close to twenty-four hours in peak desert conditions, day and night, had taken him to the brink. No water, no humans to feed on, and only brief rests in the pitch black had all taken its toll.

He sat beside a bone-dry bush, one of the few pieces of plantation he'd come across on his journey.

Drained of energy, he'd reached the longest period that he'd gone without feeding since his transformation. Minor acts of movement had become an uphill task. Reaching up to flick flies off his face exhausted him. The decline had been rapid, and he sensed the end was near. But despite the discomfort, he was calm and mostly free of thoughts and distress.

Although brief by pilgrimage standards, this quiet period of solitude and reflection was exactly where he wanted to be. It dawned on him that he'd wasted so much of his time self-loathing and making such a mess of his life.

Sitting beside a grey and twisted, wispy bush, looking up at a perfect blue sky, just like Christen had the previous day, Braun would catch half second glimpses of the eye-watering, shimmering sun. He sensed a spiritual presence watching over and cradling him. If he'd worked on achieving this as a younger man, things could have been so much different.

He was slowing down rapidly; the deep contemplation he'd generated had been powered through love. He couldn't move out of this and did not want to. He knew that if he tried to break out of it, the pain and sadness of losing Agnes would sully his exit from the world.

An hour later, his cross-legged sitting position proved to be too much for such a weakened body, and he slumped over to his left side. His jaw was slack, mouth slightly ajar, enough for a sand lizard to scuttle in and consider it as a temporary shelter from the sun. It tapped a few of Braun's teeth with its claws and decided better of it, just before Braun bit down. What little saliva festered in his mouth now tasted of sand, with unfamiliar notes of lizard slime.

He closed his eyes and fell asleep for a short while before being awoken by the nudge of a stick into his ribs.

He opened his eyes to see a very old Native American standing a metre away from him. Immediately Braun felt a buzz in his chest, and he whispered as loudly as he could manage, "Get away from me."

It was too late. The surge flicked out of his chest and reached out for the man.

The native dropped to the floor at a speed belying his great age, and he ducked the attempt. Undiscouraged, the force went for him again on the rebound, and the man rolled to the ground, avoiding it masterfully. He pulled up to a hunched position and jumped in the air as it tried to get him a third time.

The man dropped to his rear and rolled backwards to pull himself five metres away from Braun. The extractor gave up, and like an overly stretched elastic band, it snapped back into place, striking Braun hard in the chest. This forced spout of energy was something that Braun had even less control of at this stage of his decline, but the range and prowess of the energy had lessened with its host's weakened state.

Braun was stunned and managed to slur his way through a croaky sentence, "You..." He coughed a few times, the dryness hurting his chest, but he carried on. "You... see it?"

The man named Howahkan continued to lie down but turned himself around to face Braun. He just about figured out what was said, and he answered in broken English, "Yes, before, many years ago I see this. Man who tell his people to take our land. They kill my people..." He beat his chest. "...Most, but not all."

Braun closed his eyes, feeling a confusing mixture of hope and despair. Despair through what had happened to the man and his tribe. But needing to have some optimism in his last moments, he turned to the glimmer of hope. He could barely move his voice to another octave as he whispered to himself, "If people can see it, it can be defeated. He tells me it is in others. I knew it. I felt it. But it picked the wrong house to haunt. It makes mistakes. This is good..." He groaned as his throat hurt, before repeating to himself croakily. "This is good."

Howahkan kept his distance. He could see that Braun would die if he didn't help him, but he didn't want to get too close and have part of his soul and spirit eaten by the monstrous entity desperate for a bite.

Braun's energy was fading fast, but with what little he had left, through what felt like an involuntary movement, he positioned himself into a foetal position. For the first time in hours, he felt comfortable as Mother Earth carried him before what he hoped would be his rebirth somewhere without pain, without judgement, somewhere that he could truly find himself.

Howahkan shouted over, "What happened to you?"

Braun could no longer speak without a coughing fit preceding it, stripping his mouth of the last few drops of saliva.

He wheezed back, not knowing whether his new friend could hear him, "I spent too much of my time trying to fit in with people. I wasn't like them, as much as I tried to be."

He stopped for a few seconds and Howahkhan listened. A life of desert dwelling had well accustomed him to the heat, but the burn of the sun on this day would have left even those with the most hardened skin uncomfortable. He had with him a full drawstringed water container made from buffalo bladder and a walking cane that doubled as a flute. He took the cane and pitched it into the sand before removing a loin cloth from his mid-section. Naked apart from buckskin sandals, his bare backside faced the sun, as he draped the loin cloth over the top of the stick, sitting underneath it to keep his head shaded from the sun.

Having some company had pushed a button in Braun and he whispered his way through. "They ridicule those who are different, as you will be well aware, my friend, not just because of what we look like on the outside but for what they can't see. I thought it could be different when I discovered this power. It was there for me to take, and I gave it a home. I felt strong with it, the world suddenly leapt out to me; it was mine for the taking if I wanted it. I knew that..." He paused briefly to catch his breath. After some shallow wheezes he pushed on, "But I quickly realised that I would have to hurt many people, the animals, and the land, to achieve that."

Braun stopped again, and this time Howahkhan spoke. "You speak to yourself, but it is Wetiko that has taken you." He drummed both sets of fingers over his chest.

Braun managed a little smile. He had no idea what or who Wetiko was, but it was clear that Howahkhan was referring to the darkness inside of him. It struck a nerve, and he was right. In all the time Braun had been plagued by this entity, he had rarely addressed it directly. Knowing this minor renaissance couldn't last much longer, he decided to do something he had barely done throughout his invasion. He spoke directly to the beast within. He turned a wheezy cough into a snigger as he realised that he had been following its every desire, engaging with it, no matter how uncomfortable it made him feel.

He was a different proposition to such a tempter. Many others would have loved the power granted to them, and they would have served it wholeheartedly.

Braun's towering thought presented him with the notion that although good couldn't exist without evil, and after his experiences seeing and feeling first-hand how power can corrupt, the fight to lessen evil as much as possible, to create more good, would allow the souls of the righteous to blossom and dance together in beautiful patterns. Evil needed a host to project its force, and he was no longer prepared to be that. Only wickedness could commandeer such an unfair distribution of the quality of life that a place of birth or lineage afforded. If the ego and the selfishness of the few could be curtailed, then maybe most wouldn't be hobbled before the race began. Perhaps Braun would have had more opportunities, access to better food, the chance to expand his mind.

Questions rattled through him, as Howakhan watched over him respectfully but ominously.

Braun grappled with the question: *Could those with innate dark desires resist them?* No, this was too much to ponder, but he was certain that the core lights had been extinguished for many of those with great power, and replaced by the kind of external nefarious forces that had tried so hard to puppeteer him since his meeting with the evil substance.

He had never actually said a firm no, and it was time to look the Motherfucker in the face. "You've lost. Your time is up now. It's over with me. I'm finished." He laughed. "And the funny thing is, I still didn't become what I wanted – the accepted figure. I was chasing the wrong thing, and it didn't work. Contentment comes from within, not from being part of a damn posse. The people still knew I wasn't like them; somewhere in their minds, they knew they were rabbits and I was a wolf. I could have taken a lot more than I did..." He gritted his teeth and managed to shake his head a little. "I could have crushed 'em. Pulled everything they had into me. But everyone has their own mind, their own heart and soul, small miracles one and all." He sighed. "This is beaten out of them. Our lives belong to us."

Howakhan didn't hear or wasn't able to understand much of what Braun said, but he felt it and said, "Our first teacher is our heart."

A great discomfort suddenly hit Braun. He shifted from the foetal position onto his ass as he felt a rumbling in his stomach and a thumping in his chest. Adrenaline surged through him, and before he could offer any sort of quizzical response, blue liquid poured from his eyes, ears, mouth, and nose. The adrenaline spike left him with enough strength to move quickly from his position.

Not wanting any of the blue liquid to drop onto any part of him, he kicked his legs out and tumbled face-down to the ground. He buried his face onto the sand to release it all.

Half a pint came out of him, and he rubbed his head in the sand to try and rid himself of what was left. The stuff was sticky, and through his peripheral vision he could see parts of his face covered in blue. It bubbled, fizzed, and increased in temperature by the second. Braun knew that if it was still active, it would form, solidify, and re-enter him. Whether it was still as potent as it had been, or rebirthed and extra potent, he didn't care to find out.

He noticed Howakhan's flask, and he croaked, "Water."

Howakhan slightly loosened the drawstring for the weak Braun and threw the water carrier over.

Braun poured it over his face to remove the electric blue mask. The fizz and vibrancy of the substance was extinguished as the purity of the water drowned it. He instantly became acutely aware of the sort of pain, aches and emotions that had eluded him for so long. He took a sip of water. The human instinct had returned. Howakhan smiled at him and for the first time since his childhood Braun felt truly alive.

Epilogue

Not a soul passed through this part of the desert for three-and-a-half days, until a salesman of Hamlin's Wizard Oil found himself in a sandstorm and veered off his path. He was running a little low on water and was just starting to feel the effects of rationing it between himself and his horse. Having not seen anything apart from small gatherings of cacti here and there, he found himself interested when he spotted the bush. He didn't know whether his eyes were playing tricks on him, but something appeared to be moving in it – a flicker of light.

In his distraction, the young salesman didn't notice the awkwardly levelled patch of sand beneath him, and a box containing twelve bottles of the alleged healing concoction fell from inside his stage, smashing to the ground. He had hundreds of them and intended to collect more the further east he went, but the thought of losing money needled him a lot more than the loss of the magic 'curing potion'.

He moved the horse out of harm's way before climbing down to see if he could rescue any bottles from the damaged box. Salvaging what he could, he'd forgotten what had side-tracked him in the first place. He placed the loose bottles carefully into the carriage and put his hat back on, before putting his foot into the stirrup ready to climb back onto his horse.

Just before he swung his leg around, he noticed something in the corner of his eye. A tiny blue glint of light was nestled in the bush. He stepped off the horse.

www.ingramcontent.com/pod-product-compliance
Lightning Source LLC
Chambersburg PA
CBHW020440270626
47155CB00022B/784